M000288211

It's a Ball!

It's a Ball!

J. Morgan McGrady

Copyright © 2014 by J Morgan McGrady
All rights reserved. No part of this publication may be reproduced,
stored in or introduced into a retrieval system, or transmitted in
any form, or by any means (electronic, mechanical, photocopying,
recording, or otherwise), without the prior written permission of
both the copyright owner and the publisher of this book.

ISBN 978-0-615-99730-8

Manufactured in the United States of America
NetPublications, Inc.

Contents

Legal Disclaimer

Most legal disclaimers are at the end of television commercials or at the back of instruction manuals for blenders, lawnmowers, or vibrators. However, due to the contentious nature of the subject matter enclosed, attorneys have advised me to include a legal disclaimer, a kind of a "Buyer Beware" notice. After all, you really should know what you're getting yourself into here.

So instead of an introduction, here are a few cautions for individuals who are easily offended or insulted:

First, these stories are based on exaggerations of real women, but they are fictionalized. No guarantee is made that anything you read is strictly true, correct, or precise. Except for the parts that are. Also, I'm not dumb enough to use real names. All names have been changed to spare people the potential humiliation of everyone reading about their unsavory actions, activities, or statements. For those individuals who believe I'm making slanderous personal reference to their character in the stories or comments enclosed, I am NOT…but then again, you never know.

Second, my momma said that women who use profanities are uncouth and uneducated, and that Southern ladies do NOT cuss or use foul language. Of course, she also said that true ladies don't sweat, they perspire. So, if you believe I have employed lewd vocabulary and/or blasphemous terminology, consider it verbal sweltering.

Third, as with male virility pills, the reader should be aware that this book may carry some potential side effects.

Symptoms may include acid indigestion, Irritable Bowel Syndrome, nightmares, hemorrhoids, hair loss, bubble-gut, and/or vomiting. Mental images in this book may be graphic and in rare cases may cause strong emotional reactions. In such cases, laughter is the recommended treatment.

Fourth, if you are a narcissistic and self-absorbed crybaby contemplating legal action against me for any alleged libelous assertions made against your personal character in the enclosed stories, don't even think about it. Like I said, this is fiction, honey. I am not directly condemning anyone, regardless of their bad behavior or lack of social civility. Oh, and if you steal any of the stories and/or literary material within the pages of this book and proclaim them as your own original work, I will hire a few gals from the Honky-Tonk Heartbreakers roller derby team to "work you over."

Last, don't be an idiot and attempt any of the outrageous physical stunts described in this book.

This book is sold "as is" with no implied warranties, however if you would like to know more about the humorous consequences caused by reading this novel please visit my website: www.JMorganMcGrady.com.

1

Queen of the Court

A strange transformation occurs when middle-aged women begin playing competitive team tennis. Happy homemakers, dutiful wives, and maternal moms morph into highly aggressive zealots. Imagine Beaver's mother, June Cleaver, in a very short, vividly colored Spandex dress and a matching baseball cap…with a raging crystal meth addiction. That is what a typical tennis mother looks like. For these perimenopausal women, it's the competitive adrenaline rush that is so addicting. Hormonally jacked-up with a stark-raving mad desire to score a game at any cost, these intensely ferocious gals would not hesitate to kick your kitty cage while demurely clutching their pearls. With the exception of a double orgasm, there is nothing more satisfying than winning a spirited tennis match. Winning is a gateway drug which leads to a more serious compulsion: the uncontrollable urge to become Queen of the Court. Victory grants a woman the right to claim her throne and title. And as everyone knows, Southern women cotton to the notion of royalty.

A Queen of the Court doesn't actually don a tiara or preside over anything like a small country or regional agriculture. Unlike Miss Butter Bean of DeRidder, Louisiana, Princess Pecan of Victoria, Texas, or even Miss Grapefruit, the

1

reigning Citrus Queen of the Rio Grande Valley, being a Queen of the Court is a metaphysical state. Tennis Queens have no actual imperial domain. They have only bragging rights and a certain authority over a slab of green-colored cement. Once a woman discovers her inner tennis czarina, however, she will do anything to become sovereign. Different from beauty pageant queens, homecoming queens, or an *actual* sovereign, a Queen of the Court can lose her throne at any time. Tennis Queens are crowned and dethroned every day on community and private tennis courts south of the Mason-Dixon Line.[1]

I first made my queenly ascension five seasons ago in the middle of a doubles match against two reigning monarchs, women I preferred to call the "Royal Bitches" or "Royal Pains in the Ass!" In this memorable game I was playing the worst tennis of my life—hitting the ball outside the boundary lines, double faulting, failing to volley—a complete meltdown. In frustration and anger, I boomeranged my racquet across the court. Everyone ducked as it whirled through the air and smashed into a net post, crumpling into a gnarly mess of metal and string. It wasn't just unladylike, it was bad sportsmanship. I felt horrible. I was letting down my partner, Bernice, the Queen Mother of the Court and the number one ranked National Collegiate champion in both singles and doubles when wooden racquets and catgut string were in fashion. During the change-over, Bernice grabbed the waistband of my tennis skirt and yanked me

◇◇◇◇◇◇◇◇◇◇◇◇◇◇◇

1 If this cliché Queenly crap is all too much for you, not to worry. Although the worn out theme of Southern Queens has been preheated, overcooked, and burnt-to-a-crisp in the publishing industry, this chapter is NOT the same old literary casserole, regardless of the title. Admittedly, in the minds and hearts of all Tennis Queens, they are royalty all unto themselves and do not share the same lineage with those other lesser queens—make no bones about it.

over to the water cooler for a private consult. Now, tennis skirts all have a built-in shorts liner. And Bernice tugged my skirt so hard it gave me a camel toe$^{\text{♛}}$ and caused a stinging sensation I can still feel today.

With a spray of spittle in my ear, Bernice sternly whispered, "If you want to be successful at this game, you better take command of the court." Those words of wisdom penetrated my heart like that bunched-up skirt had barged through my pink saloon doors.$^{\text{♛}}$ At that very moment, a sense of royal empowerment descended over my consciousness, and I became a Queen of the Court. Bernice and I ended up winning the game. The final score was 1-6, 7-6, 6-0.

Some would think tennis is a mannerly, civilized sport. This is not the case. Novice players quickly learn that this is a hoax perpetrated by veteran players, mostly the losing ones. It was once said, "Tennis is not a gentle game. Psychologically, it is vicious." Believe me, there is nothing civilized about getting a Chuck Norris ass kickin' from some skinny, 5'2", tan, perfectly coiffured blonde chick with flawless air-brushed makeup who hands your busted buttocks back to you with a snarky little "Well, that was fun!"

There is no other place in the United States more competitive and passionate about women's team tennis than Texas. About eight years ago, I became a member of Cedarway, a tennis club located in Austin, Texas. The country club was established in 1972 and during Cedarway's heyday, the giants of the tennis world—Jimmy Connors, Chris Evert, and Rod Laver, for example—graced the same courts where I would later run my fat, cottage cheese ass with considerably less elegance.

Tennis season in Austin commences in September, but team practice begins months earlier, during the hottest days in the Texas Hill Country. With temperatures reaching above 100 degrees, heat waves ripple across the courts and players use potholders to hold their racquets. It can get so intensely hot that I've seen a woman actually roast a brisket between her thighs.

Competitive play starts on the first day of school, when elementary-aged children find themselves shoved unceremoniously out of Mom's Range Rover, Suburban, or SUV and abandoned at the curb. Women who play tennis do *not* drive minivans. Apologies to those who own one, but in the occult world of tennis, those outdated "mom mobiles" are banned for clashing with our cute little skirts. If you ever begin to play country club tennis competitively, I strongly recommend trading it for something more practical, like a Hummer or a Peterbilt truck or some other V-12 diesel-type vehicle. Something you can use to *accidentally* crush your opponent's car in the parking lot if you should lose a hard match.

Tennis is an expensive sport. Instead of finding commercial sponsors like the professionals, Queens of the Court rely on rich husbands or copious monthly alimony payments to subsidize their addiction. It's just not the cost of the balls, racquets, or sweat bands. By the time an average woman steps onto the court for her inaugural match, she will have spent more than the overall GDP of a small European country. Countless pairs of shoes, numerous private lessons with the pro, and matching seasonal team uniforms are the bulk of the fiscal outflow. And, of course, after the matches are the obligatory three-martini lunches. After all, the best part of tennis is sharing moments after each match, and taking the opportunity to laugh at the hysterical incidents that occurred on the court.

What is it about competitive tennis that diminishes women's inhibitions? Between the grunting and cussing and menopausal bitching, women's team tennis can sometimes reach the high hormone levels of a Nordstrom's 75%-Off One-Day Shoe Sale. Consider that professional Queen of the Court, Serena Williams, who once threatened to cram a tennis ball down a line judge's throat (accompanied with a few expletives). Of course, most people disapproved. Serena's verbal tantrum was the first time a professional female player had ever made threatening remarks to an official or dropped numerous f-bombs on prime time television. But the way I see it, the primary appeal of tennis for a lot of women is the opportunity to release physical aggression without being arrested for a felony assault.

Some may play for the exercise and socialization with other women. Others—let's be honest—play to get away from the crises at home. Then there are those rare, twisted women who work out pent-up rage by slamming overhead shots targeting an opponent's "Gucci." And I'm not talking about her designer purse.

Queens of the Court have a unique perspective on the female body, and employ discreet code words for various parts of the human anatomy for the sake of keeping our *somewhat* polite, ladylike status. "Gucci," for example, is the term our team has coined for a woman's private recreational area. After all, like a Gucci bag, it is expensive and uniquely designed, as well as ergonomically convenient. Of course, not everyone shares our level of verbal comfort…just last season, I was placed on a two week probation for inappropriate language. I was rallying my teammates, crying across the court for them to "Kick vagina!" The opposing team apparently did not appreciate my witty cheer. I thought it was more accurate than the commonly used "Kick butt" since our opponents were women and I presumed most of them *had* vaginas.[2]

Back to the story: I have seen some players take it to a whole new level. Last year, our Cedarway team faced the number one ranking team for six consecutive tennis seasons, the Hot Flashes. They had a roster of eight 70-something-year-old women who can beat the crap out of any opponent (6-0, 6-0) and never run a single step on the tennis court. They are infamously willing to do anything to win. Their strategy last year was carefully conceived. Upon arriving at the clubhouse, the overpowering aroma of Ben-Gay and Preparation-H lulled our gullible team into a false sense of confidence. Even more sinister and conniving was the pro shop, a beautifully appointed tennis store with cunning displays of a vast array of knee braces, osteoarthritis ankle stabilizers, wrist and elbow wraps, walkers, and even portable poop pans for convenient usage during the middle of a match. Any unsuspecting competitor would have logically thought an "easy win" awaited them. This was not the case. It was all part of the mental game the post-menopausal grannies had devised to tranquilize their opponents.[3]

◇◇◇◇◇◇◇◇◇◇◇◇◇◇◇◇

2 I didn't get it. Why do most women (and men) cringe at V-A-G-I-N-A? They seem to think it's a four letter word. For crying out loud, just get over it! After all, the same prudish folks don't seem to find the womanly organ offensive when it is put to good use (wink, wink)!

3 Now I'm not slamming old people. After all, I'll have my AARP card in my pocketbook soon enough.

Not only did the old biddies use "off court" trickery to ensure victory, they used "on court" strategies even more sinister and nefarious. Their weapon of choice was distraction, and they employed a three-pronged tactic.

First, these bladder-defunct me-maws shuffled onto the courts wearing matching white, sheer Danskin shirts and oversized shorts to accommodate their Depends. The synchronized *whishing* sounds of eight adult diapers rubbing against polyester tennis shorts announced the Hot Flashes' arrival.

Second, when we all met center court for the formal introductory handshake, my teammates and I noticed something odd: the beam of erect nipples protruding from large, baloney-shaped mammary glands silhouetted through the Hot Flashes' white shirts. Those hood ornaments were located near their waist lines, not at the normal chest level, but it was still clear—those grey-haired grandmothers were playing tennis braless!

Dumbfounded, I asked, "Why are y'all playing tennis without brassieres?"

Their team captain stepped forward and pointed up toward the clubhouse. "You see those good-lookin' men up there watching us?" she asked. In concert, sixteen women turned obediently and gazed up towards a large window. There, looking down, stood a group of male country club members. Every one of those old coots was wearing Bermuda shorts, a Mexican Guayabera shirt, black knee-high socks, and white Oxford shoes. (Why don't old men know that combining clothes from different countries is a fashion, as well as a cultural, *faux pas*?) Those horny grandpas stood gawking through binoculars at the pre-game parade.

The Hot Flashes waved modestly at the ogling old buzzards, with half-cocked smiles. The team captain continued her explanation for her teammates' lack of lingerie, "Well, we want that youthful tight skin like the younger women. So we go bra-less and let gravity pull all the wrinkles from our faces." Our team's mouths dropped open like a school of catfish. No one had the heart to tell them that those geezers were not looking at their faces. Little did we know…

The pruny grandmas looked more like contestants at a geriatric wet T-shirt contest than tennis players. During the matches when one of them would hit a backhand shot, her boobs would sling over on the other side of her body as she repositioned to hit a forehand shot. It was like a "head fake," but done with tits—a "tit fake," if you will. Between all the distractions—emergency incontinence breaks, lecherous old men, and swinging mammary glands—our team lost the final match. Because of that, we came in second place for the overall season.

Maybe you're wondering: *For all the grueling hours playing tennis under the blistering Texas sun, the financial expenses, and combat, what is the grand prize?* The answer is: A round, four-inch-diameter plastic disk for your racquet bag. That is the Austin Women's Tennis League's grand champion prize. It is amazing to what lengths a woman will go to win a plastic bag tag. But the boundless amounts of blood, sweat, and swearing isn't just to win a stupid circular synthetic petrochemical polymer (which ironically can also be used as an emergency IUD). That disk symbolizes a diamond-encrusted crown for a Tennis Queen. Envy and jealousy swell inside every competitor when they hear the *cling, cling, cling* of those plastic bag tags melodiously chiming against a racquet bag. That is the sound of several years of championship titles.

So are you asking, "Why is recreational women's tennis so addictive? Why the obsessive striving to ascend from mediocrity and become a reigning Queen of the Court?" I have two answers. First, you learn a lot about yourself playing tennis. Bernice's brief pep-talk at the start of my journey was the best counsel I have ever received; it is sage advice I use both on and off the tennis court. She taught me not to allow other people to dictate my actions. Think about it. If you let someone dictate your response, then you are allowing that person to be in control. If you instead take command of your actions, then you remove their power over you. A true Queen of the Court is always in control.

The second answer is the more important. After all, I have found that tennis is just an appetizer for more competitive and aggressive female suburban sports, like:

- "Red Tag Sale" Boxing at Steinmart,
- Grocery Cart Jousting at HEB, or
- School Carnival Mud Wrestling.

(Actually, I've never been to a public school carnival where mothers mud wrestle, but it would be a fantastic fundraiser positioned next to the MILF Kissing Booth.)

I really think the *most* addictive trait of women's recreational tennis is simply the opportunity to socialize with wonderful (and at times not so wonderful) women. Queens of the Court love having fun, just like we did in our college days as sorority sisters. Those days have long since passed, but every cellulite dimple, every birthing stretch mark, and all the road-ridden wisdom we've gained tells the story of our sisterhood.

A Queen of the Court's standard sporting equipment

2

Snot Slingin' Martinis and the Wishing Wand

The French concept of *joie de vivre*—the enjoyment of all things that make life worth living—was the inspiration behind forming a new Cedarway women's tennis team; kicking ass on the tennis court was a secondary motivation! I admit, I also wanted to administer a righteous smack-down to those Royal Pains in the Ass. I abhor snobby women, and one of the things I enjoy most in life—my personal *joie de vivre*—is in bitch slapping these conceited madams on the tennis courts. I'm not really sadistic; I wouldn't *literally* want to slap the crap out of them. I just want to demoralize them with a stinging defeat (6-0, 6-0) and make them admit my superiority. I feel it is part of my cosmic duty, a way to help achieve a more harmonious balance in the universe. So, my best friend, Mavolyn, and I decided to organize a new tennis team around the *joie de vivre* of pounding high-falutin' players with fun-loving friends.

According to the rules and regulations of the Austin, Texas Tennis League, each tennis team consists of four doubles teams (eight women, for the math-impaired). Mavolyn and I made one team, so we needed to draft six more ladies. We later learned that recruiting six top-ranked players for a new team was a more ambitious undertaking than we anticipated. They call it "catching lightning in a bottle," but for Mavolyn and me it was more like trying to capture a belch in a ziplock baggy.

I inaugurated myself as captain, since I liked the idea of being head honcho. Mavolyn would be assistant captain, because every regent needs a sidekick. Believe me, underneath her sweet veneer lies a woman who knows exactly how to grab a bull by the horns (or any type of appendage on a bull that requires manhandling). Mavolyn is a "get it done" kind of gal with a placid demeanor similar to that of Lady Bird Johnson, but when she gets agitated on the court, she is meaner than a javelina in heat.

Recruiting season starts at the beginning of the summer. Drafting tennis players is like football scouting for Texas universities, except without the scholarships, prostitutes, or financial perks (yeah, they say they don't, but give me a frickin' break! How many college football players from Waxahachie drive brand new Mercedes Benz 550SLs?). As co-captain and captain, Mavolyn and I couldn't offer luxurious, expensive gifts to sway potential players, unlike our nemesis: Capitol City Country Club (CCCC). Those rich sluts gave away massage coupons and free private lessons with young muscle-bound tennis pros to sway prospective players—it was just unfair. We didn't have a large financial war chest, so we made do with vouchers for twelve-piece chicken liver dinners at Chicken Express and bottles of Fix-A-Flat purchased at Costco to entice women to our team. Even so, we had over fifty potential candidates. Our interviewing procedure was similar to, but more ruthless than, sorority rush. Tennis skills aside, we felt the most important element in each prospective teammate was character. If the would-be colleague was a cheater, mean-spirited, crass, or a lazy PTA mom, we didn't want her on our Cedarway team. Let the CCCC have her.

To ensure quality and disposition, we ran a thorough four-point diagnostic review on each nominee:

(1) Personal interview

(2) A written exam on USTA rules and regulations

(3) Physical and tennis skills evaluation

(4) The "Snot-Slingin' Martini" drinking test

Of these, #4 was the most important. This is a simple, unobtrusive exam to appraise a woman's ability to be classy and dignified while artfully coaxing her into telling scandalous stories about fellow players and naughty neighbors.

You can tell a lot about a woman when she is drunk. Her innermost feelings are usually revealed in slurred, unvarnished words that would never be uttered in a sober state of mind. The CIA and FBI have their covert and secretive recruitment procedures—electronic lie detector machines and injections of psychoactive truth serums—to evaluate likely candidates. Mavolyn and I had vodka. We needed to know if we were recruiting the right women, but since we did not have access to sodium pentothal, booze was the next best option. I know it may sound a bit excessive, but these were desperate times. We needed real women for a real job.

As for the vodka concoction we call the "Snot-Slingin' Martini," it is a combustible mix of pickled jalapeno juice, Red Bull, and Tito's vodka. This drink produces a tantalizing feeling of mind-numbing relaxation with a hint of wild abandon. In addition, it doubles as a colon cleanser.

After "round robin," elimination-type tennis matches, the potential candidates met at Cedarway Country Club... which I have dubbed "The Litter Box." This middle class bar & grill is a Serengeti watering hole for country club cougars. Female felines of every scientific species, genus, and phylum socialize at The Litter Box, drinking their little catnip-cosmos while prowling for cute young caddies and stalking unsuspecting businessmen. Picture, if you will, a large, handsomely decorated dining room bordered by a long mesquite wooden bar, with a panoramic view of live oak trees and lush green manicured grass dotted with men playing with their putters and little white dimpled balls. It is the perfect backdrop for the proverbial *martini lunch.* There is no better place to witness safari-type manhunts and watch potential cat fights ensue between golf goddesses, soccer moms, church ladies, and bridge-playing old biddies. Occasionally the pernicious trollops from CCCC slither in from their uptown multimillion dollar dens for a little territorial leg-lifting...that is when the fur really flies!

One must be prepared, as the conversation at a martini lunch may suddenly turn shocking and weird. We have talked about everything from: "What was the biggest lie you ever told?" to "What body part do you wash first?" to "What is the strangest talent you have?" and "Is the saying, 'panty waist' or 'panty waste'?" Last week's confabulation was "Who, where, and when did you lose you virginity?" Most of the women on our team cashed-in their V-card at the usual ages, between 16-24, but several gals had their first ground-breaking event in rather unconventional places: a thirty-foot high diving board at a public swimming pool, behind the Catholic Church after catechism class, and in a cattle trailer while transporting cows to the Houston Livestock and Rodeo.

For a few of us, the *who* was more of a *what.* I lost my virginity at the winsome age of 14 in the back woods of a vacant subdivision lot just across from NASA (Johnson Space Center-Houston), an encounter that happened while racing my Schwinn five-speed bicycle. It was modified with a purple banana seat, sissy bar, and a neon orange rectangular sign on a flexible pole that read, "Caution leper" on one side, and on the other, the biblical citation Leviticus 13:45-46. The 100-yard caliche track was considered by the community of our school bus to be the Indy 500 Speedway of push-pedal cycles. High-gear contests against other neighborhood kids were staged every weekend and every day in the summer.

Pedaling fast and furiously, a brisk breeze blew through my pixie-cut hair while the bike and I headed for victory at the finish line; however, as I hit the last stretch, a three-foot earthen ramp catapulted me into the air. After the ensuing descent from what felt like atmospheric heights, the girthy, long purple plastic seat pierced my yellow pair of Bermuda shorts and cotton panties, then penetrated 14 inches into my unsullied womanhood. I fell off the bike onto the ground, grasping my crotch and screaming like a Howler monkey. Instantly, a circle of children surrounded me, hands masking astonished and disgusted expressions on their otherwise innocent faces. As a prepubescent girl, I remember the pain was excruciating, but surprisingly accompanied by a euphoric tingle that took over my body... an experience I had never felt before and quite honestly, I have never felt since. With the passing years of numerous impassioned dalliances, I have occasionally reflected back on that incident with wistful yearning. Shhh! Don't tell my husband.

Even so, I have considered a class action lawsuit against the Schwinn bicycle company for the manufacturing of a seat guilty of the violation of countless young girls. I'm sure there were other adolescents like me who shamefully endured a banana seat invasion. During my encounter, I gave no consent; it just made a thrusting ingress with not even a "Howdy do?" After all, how do you tell a bicycle equipped with hi-rise handlebars and frilly plastic handgrips that "no means no"? Of course, no one could come close to the story of my deflowering by the Johnny Homes of bicycle benches.

Meanwhile back at the martini lunch: Mavolyn and I were busy administrating the first phase of the "Snot Slingin' Martini" test at a private room in the back of the clubhouse. Mind you, we didn't consume any of our own gut-rot hooch. Maintaining our sobriety and staying clearheaded while babysitting fifty inebriated candidates was a huge chore in itself. As odd as it may seem, I am a teetotaler and Mavolyn never drinks in public, given her husband's political position as a highly respected Texas state judge. Socially conscientious and mindful of public perception, Mavolyn is fastidious about protecting her husband's reputation, never putting herself or her children in potentially embarrassing situations which could cause any unforeseeable scandals and jeopardize his reelection. Okay, technically Mavolyn does drink in public, she just hides her "giggle water" in a twenty ounce plastic Rudy's Barbecue cup. Yep, you could say Mavolyn is a closet drinker; however, I don't drink for other reasons. During my college years, I guzzled down my fair share of alcoholic beverages—beer bongs, oyster tequila shots, anus-burning trashcan punches—subsequently destroying part of my frontal lobe, resulting in involuntary drooling when my blood pressure becomes elevated. Without a doubt, *this* is the very reason why I do not drink, but as the days of tennis season lapsed, the stress as captain of the team tested my sobriety.

On the flip side, most all tennis women and members of country clubs are big drinkers. After four rounds of "Snot Slingin' Martinis," the ladies were jacked-up and hoofing around the country club like an unruly herd of Brahman cows. Jalapeño juice and Red Bull, combined with a stiff shot of vodka is like jet fuel for suburban moms. Normally these busy women are dog tired, embracing the traditional female role of a housewife and managing the usual motherly chores. They are typically sleep deprived with their worn-out asses dragging in the dirt. But our special cocktail had them hootin' and hollerin' and carryin' on. Voices loudly broadcasting scandalous rumors and riotous laughter caused by punch lines from dirty jokes reverberated off the walls.

I stared curiously at the collection of women. They were all ages, different personalities, ranging in distinctive sizes, shapes, and color of hair. I could only choose six. It was a hard decision. As I looked down at my clipboard appraising the names, a little thrill ran through me, half excitement and half nerves. It was a weird feeling, a sort of premonition. Somehow I intuitively knew that the chosen six would soon be great new friends. And with those new friends would come shared new adventures—the special kind that make a mark on your mind like indelible ink… or like a big period stain on your favorite white pants.

Right off the bat, ten of the applicants were eliminated due to their over-indulgence and an inability to "hold their liquor." It is an unspoken Southern rule: ladies do not get commode-hugging drunk. Mavolyn and I summarily checked these gals off the list of prospective teammates. As respectful hostesses we called cabs and husbands to arrange rides home for the sloshed participants. However, three slipped by us and staggered out of the club. Hooked arm-in-arm, singing at the tops of their lungs, they attempted to walk home. Let's just say that they didn't get too far. Later that afternoon we saw them in front of the clubhouse passed out, face-planted in a flowerbed next to a lighted Cedarway granite monument. The three were spread-eagled, panties down at their ankles, white naked asses up in the air shining like beacons. You never know what drunk people are thinking. Alcohol has a funny way of shutting off the part of the brain that provides simple logic and reasoning along with good judgment and manners. Apparently the wasted women were rummaging around the bushes attempting to discreetly pee, but fell into unconsciousness. A closer look at the comatose gals lying there in the mulch revealed that our butt-fire brew had kicked in, and they were dealing with a problem that was coming out at both ends. We checked for pulses—still alive. I know it may sound cruel, but Mavolyn and I left them lying there in the flowerbed, twigs and leaves stuck in their disheveled hair and vomit caked on the sides of their faces. I know there are those of you who think it was pathetic leaving them flailed out in public like that. I know it's horrible and I should be ashamed. But I'm not. Those hammered hoochie mommas were fine and needed to sleep it off. Besides, recreational women's tennis league ain't for pussies. So if you can't play with the big girls, you obviously can't drink with them either.

Back at the luncheon, the remaining gals were adequately sauced up after the fifth round of martinis. They were pumped and primed, ready for us to begin the last phase of the evaluation. The final assessment was more a preschool child's game than an ordinary interview, a sort of "musical chairs," if you will, but without music.

Mavolyn issued a long, high pitched whistle to grab the attention of the schnockered ladies. Her rich, throaty voice rang through the room and commanded the group to shut up. It was like magic; the women immediately sat in the chairs facing each other.

Walking in the middle of the round-up with a flair of showmanship, I undraped a shrouded object and presented… "the wishing wand." Actually, it was a decorated, battery-operated cattle prod I grabbed from the barn at my ranch. Adorned with purple crepe paper, glitter, and silver buttons dangling from dental floss, the bovine butt baton was a sight to behold. Astounded *oohs* and *aahs* rushed across the room. Of course, it doesn't take much to impress a bunch of wasted women.

The guidelines to the game were simple. The "wishing wand" was passed around the corral with the instruction for each to stand up and loudly announce a truthful yet racy wish. Mind you, NO common wishes were allowed. Spankings from spouses or aspirations for more money were unacceptable. After the personal wish was revealed, it was openly discussed and voted on by the assembly. If the wish was deemed to be either not honest or not imaginatively spicy enough, the holder of the "wishing wand" would be eliminated with a painful 9,000 volt shock on the tush from the festooned cattle prod and summarily booted out of the game. It was the perfect democratic method to bump off candidates from the roster and qualify the ones who would meet our high standards.

The underlying intention of the game was to discover hidden kinds of cravings—the subversive personal secrets otherwise considered off limits. There is a fine line between humorously naughty and downright sexually twisted. Skanky women were not the teammates we wanted. It was important to cut them from our list of potential players. Pain and humiliation are very motivating. And the "wishing wand" provided both, pushing the gate wide open to some really wild-ass crap.

The first round took out about twenty ladies in fifteen minutes who were swiftly voted off the hacienda. Among the more sexually perverse desires I recall rejected in the second and third qualifying rounds: "I wish I could have sex with Phyllis Diller." Yuck! What was that gal thinking? And "I had an orgasm *with* a jet ski riding on Lake Travis and I wish I could do it again." I'm still trying to figure that one out. I suppose I'm not very mechanically minded.

As the game progressed, the participants were actually getting into it, truly thinking the "wishing wand" had some type of mystical wish granting powers. I just chalked it up to drunkenness. It was the booze that had magical qualities. Even more deviant aspirations were exposed: "I wish I could hire a septic tank truck to dump excremental byproduct inside my ex-husband's car," and "I wish I could cram a Dr. Pepper bottle up my neighbor's butt hole." Those wishes seemed a bit too harsh for the group.

Today it is weird to bump into some of those women. Sometimes I see them hiding behind the produce stand at

HEB or quickly ducking behind the bleachers at school football games. They know Mavolyn and I have knowledge of confessions that could potentially incriminate and cause them embarrassment. But here's the thing: I love it! I feel a gangsta' sense of empowerment knowing that those chicks are silently cursing me and they can't do a thing about it but be ashamed. I'm talking HARD-CORE blackmail. You just gotta love that. Because the way I see it, I've got lots of extortion payments coming to me.

One of the more intriguing wishes seemed rather innocent at first, but strangely perverse after a longwinded explanation. "I wish I could go to Disney World again and ride the Pinocchio amusement attraction," declaimed a buzzed candidate, rubbing the "wishing wand" a little too vigorously between her thighs.

The gal explained that at the tender age of 13 she had a sexual encounter at Disney World riding on the Pinocchio ride. In the middle of Fantasyland, the themed amusement ride featured all the characters from the animated film— Pinocchio, Jiminy Cricket, Geppeto, the Blue Fairy, Figaro, Cleo, and Monstro the whale. She then explained that as a youngster she never had any desirous feelings for the movie or the little puppet boy, but when she crawled into the plastic head of Pinocchio and the ride began to spin around, a sexual sense of uninhibitedness took over her loins. She straddled Pinocchio's nose, and while the ride was swinging and gyrating, she forcefully screamed what sounded like "Lie to me! Lie to me!" Her earsplitting yelps and high-pitched howls caused a huge commotion. Mothers and fathers watched below; jaws dropped in sheer astonishment. She almost reached "Pleasure Island" when her parents snatched her off Pinocchio's face. With utter embarrassment, the family immediately walked out of the park, never to return again. Breathlessly the woman repeated, "I wish I could go to Disney World. I wish I could go to Disney World," all the while stroking the cattle prod. The remaining group decided it was a little too creepy, so her ass got zapped to Never Neverland.

As the afternoon came to a close, strewn empty vodka bottles, discarded jalapeño jars, and vacant chairs were scattered around the clubhouse's back room. All that remained were six women, catatonic and blurry-eyed, sitting in the last chairs. At last, our new teammates.

As unorthodox as it may seem, the "Snot Slingin' Martini" test (although snot was actually never slung) and the decorated moo-mover played a big part in rustling up a tennis team of six extraordinary women, new friends with good moral character and strong stomachs: women I now lovingly call my "Racq Pacq" sisters. More importantly, they were women who could win the Austin Texas Tennis League Grand Championship.

3

Band of Sisters[1]

News of our recently developed team spread like wildfire throughout Cedarway Country Club. Mavolyn and I bestowed six invitations, akin to sorority bids, but without the stupid rush party skits and pledge pins. Within minutes of poking a thumbtack through the announcement onto the bulletin board, the whole club knew. Although we were considered the underdogs of the League, our enthusiasm was not dampened. We just saw it as motivation to work harder: there's nothing like proving people wrong.

To celebrate the auspicious occasion, I decided to hold a small meet & greet cocktail party, "Margaritas and Manicures"[2] for our new teammates at a nearby Korean nail boutique. The salon is located in the front of Cedarway along with the neighborhood grocer and other stores.

◊◊◊◊◊◊◊◊◊◊◊◊◊◊◊◊

1 My cousin, 3M, thought of several clever titles for this chapter including: Toe-pocalypse, Das Foot, The Thin Pink Line and Full Metal Va-jay-jay. Thank you, 3M.

2 Although I do not partake in the consumption of alcohol, all…and I mean ALL tennis get-togethers and parties have themes and plenty of booze. In spring we have "Magnolias and Mimosas," quarterly PTA meetings are "Donuts and Daiquiris," and during Christmas we rejoice with our annual "Hot Toddies and Santa's Hot Naughties." The "Hottie Party," as we like to call it, is when we dress up like CCCC members in skimpy red elf outfits and exchange X-rated "White Elephant" gifts while drinking steaming hot libations.

Locals call outdoor shopping malls "strip sinners"; I never saw anything corrupt or illegal about shopping…until that afternoon. I should have known better. The nail salon advertises as giving "the best hand jobs in town." At the time, I thought it was the perfect setting to have everyone get acquainted. I envisioned us relaxing with a few drinks, bonding over foot care: having cuticles and callouses removed, ingrown toe nails clipped, gremlin cheese dug, sock poop extracted, and fungal smegma eradicated. Afterwards, we would emerge with brightly colored toes, ready to kick some major *asphalt* this tennis season.

Booming through the front door, our eight boisterous girls sent a half-dozen tiny Asians scrambling to prepare massage chairs with heated water basins.

(You will have to excuse me, I really don't know why I call myself a "girl." I think I must have trouble accepting my age. My friends and I haven't been girls for at least twenty… okay, forty years! Maybe I'm too immature to embrace my own womanhood. Honestly, I would rather embrace something more interesting in the manhood category.)

Although many of the ladies already knew one another from previous tournaments, school, and community functions, my goal was to have a female bonding experience. NOT one of those weird mind/body/soul empowerment discussion groups assembled in a big circle talking to gym sock hand puppets that look like pink pusswiggles. It's not that I have a problem talking about my vagina (as you already know); I just don't want to talk to other women's makeshift sock puppet twats.

So, with margaritas sloshing around in one hand and bottles of brightly colored nail polish in the other, the girls sat giggling in vibrating massage chairs.

"I hate getting my nails done at public places," said Della, staring down at the swirling blue water with disdain. "I swear, I see brown toe jam floating around this bacteria-infested tub." Della is the Johnny Cash of the team, a rebel. She is known statewide as the biggest bad ass of the Texas league. Della can knock the yellow fuzz off a tennis ball, a technique she mastered while knocking the hair off four ex-husbands' testicles during divorce proceedings. No one wants to piss off this 5'1," brown-haired medusa. She is one woman you don't want to meet alone in an alley. Especially the alley on a tennis court.

Slamming back the last sip of her third margarita, Starr Noel suggested, "Just splash a few jiggers of tequila in the tub with your feet. That'll kill all those gross germs," with a high-pitched laugh. Starr Noel is a Rubenesque beauty who tends to chuckle after every comment she makes, especially when referencing her gazongas. Although it may sound anatomically implausible, Starr Noel's breasts are approximately three times the size of her head. I have never had an actual face-to-face conversation with her because my eyes can't seem to get beyond those high-beamed boob-rays. They look like googly eyes. It is so strangely mesmerizing! Due to the proportions of Starr Noel's "love bubbles"—that is what she calls her tits—she is notorious for popping out of her tightly trussed outfits, especially during mixed doubles tennis or poker tournaments. "Those ornery Winnebagos always cause a commotion," she says. I think she actually figures that exposing them will give her at least a point or two on the tennis courts, and a double-or-nothing bluff on the green felt.

Norma slurred across the salon, "Yeah. Then you would have a mixed drink with toe-quila! Get it? Toe-quila. Tequila!" One would never guess that the blonde bombshell grew up in a sanitarium in the small town of Blessing, Texas. At the age of nine months, her biological folks dropped her off at the hospital, where the nurses gave her a room recently vacated by a deceased "abnormal" patient. Norma said that the Blessing hospital didn't have much community funding, so the medical staff used the same nameplate from the previous occupant and just scraped off the letters A, B and L – (AB)NORMA(L), á la Mel Brooks in *Young Frankenstein*. Weird as that may seem, personnel at the Blessing infirmary swore it was true. Although Norma never knew her biological parents, I feel quite confident she was conceived from the mental loins of Jerry Lewis and birthed from the cerebral uterus of Lucille Ball: a unique combination of unintentional slapstick comedy and pure nonsense.

Inari, who is from Japan, watched all the commotion with utter astonishment. "I have never had a pedicure," she announced. Having lived in the United States for only five years, Inari was still struggling with the language and with Texas culture. She's very courteous, but last year, she got kicked off the court for profanity. She was shouting at her partner to "focus, focus" but due to her thick accent, her offended opponents thought she was yelling at them, "F-ck us! F-ck us!" Apparently, the other team found the idea of requesting sex in the middle of a tennis match too much. Maybe after, but certainly not *during* a match!

"You have never had a pedicure or manicure, Inari?" asked Beulah Rose, a leggy, drop-dead gorgeous woman. By definition she is the classic beauty: long rust-colored hair and apple-green eyes with an awesome figure that houses 10,000 kilowatts of boundless energy. It is Beulah Rose's obsession with fame and money that generates her unlimited vigor. She is an entrepreneur of sorts and peddles everything from bedazzled animal skulls to smoked deer jerky at a roadside stand. Ask anyone in her social circle what she "does" for a living and a confused pause will ensue. It is hard to pin down to one job title: in addition to being a capitalist wiz, mother of three children and wife, she is an inventor and is always developing new gadgets and creative apparatuses. Currently, she has a patent pending for a new iPhone app called "Rumor Has It!" (which you can find at Rumor-Has-It.net). It alerts subscribers to everything from sales at Neiman Marcus to local clandestine marital infidelities. She claims, "It's not gossiping, it's networking." Mass marketing begins next autumn, and you can be sure Beulah Rose will be in the middle of vending her wares!

"Noooooo," Inari's voice trailed off as the chair vibrated. The jiggling caused her round tortoise-shell eyeglasses bounce down her nose. She explained, "In Japan we have places that have pedicures and manicures, but no one can understand the people who work there, so we do not go. They are usually foreigners."

Leaning over, Beulah Rose whispered, "It must be a universal thing, because we can't understand the manicurists either! I assumed that nail spas would be on every street corner in Asian countries, just like Starbuck's is on every street corner here in North America."

"Oh, coffee! I could go for a Grande iced, half-caff, triple caramel macchiato," Sonia exclaimed. This devout

Catholic wears her Bible belt cinched up tighter than any churchgoing woman I have ever met. She is of Mexican descent, with long, jet-black hair and bewitching almond-shaped eyes, a real Hispanic hottie.

Sonia claims the only unfortunate thing about her heritage is the facial hair on her chin. If she doesn't shave in the morning she can easily be mistaken for a member of ZZ Top. Why she doesn't use electrolysis to remove her Frida Kahlo-esque mustache God only knows.

Neatly tucked into a side pocket of her tennis bag are a mirror and a battery operated tweezer that looks more like a Weed Eater. During set breaks, Sonia pulls out her grooming equipment and plucks her coarse, dark facial hairs while her opponents look on in disgust and amazement. It must really psyche them out, because the Mexican-American Saint wins 99% of her matches.

"How about a Venti, sugar free vanilla, half pump mocha, cinnamon dolce, caramel Frappuccino with whip?"

"You have got to be kiddin'!" shouted Starr Noel. "Forget the obnoxious coffee drinks. How about another round of margaritas?" and she sloshed green liquid over her ta-tas.

In one synchronized affirmation, the team howled like hyenas for another round. By this point our manicurists were seriously pissed off. Earlier we had played a team-building ring toss game I ingeniously constructed with plywood, four plastic speculums, and a red glowing dildo. After a few rounds of ring-a-ding, we played Flip Cup, a relay race with plastic Solo cups. Tequila, salt, and limes were splatted over the entire floor. We thought it was hilarious and fun as HELL, but the manicurists didn't see the humor, so they

Homemade XXX Ring-a-Ding
(aka "team-building")

responded with exasperated sighs, in unison.

Listening to the spa workers' chitter-chattering, I overheard the kwanjang (i.e., the grandmaster or manager of the nail salon) speak in Korean to her jokyos (i.e., assistant manicurists). From her impassioned tone, I could tell it was something like, "Oh, crap! We have to deal with these shit-housed chicks for another hour!"

Della stretched over her massage chair to Inari and asked, "What did those gals just say?" pointing to the two manicurists. Thanks to her job as a purchasing agent for a big computer company, Inari speaks three and a half languages: her native Japanese, Mandarin Chinese, Korean, and half-mastered English in the Texas vernacular.

Embarrassed, Inari shyly said, "She said that our feet stink like shit, and it is making her house smell like a chicken coop."

Della stood straight up in her water basin and bellowed, "What the hell?!" Everyone in the salon stopped to stare at her in drop-jawed confusion. Slinging back the remaining margarita in one gulp, Della wiped her mouth with the back of her hand and flashed her teeth like a five-foot alligator gar. She pointed to the manicurists and announced, "She just called us stinky Lincoln Logs. I for one am not going to take this verbal abuse. Offending my tennis team is a huge no-no on this playground." Without hesitation, Della grabbed a margarita-soaked lime from her cup and threw it across the spa into the kwanjang's baffled face.

With disbelief and anger, seven jokyos stood up from their stools and let out a bloodcurdling battle cry of such rage, I thought the acoustic ceiling tiles would crumble above our heads. This was clearly not their first combat. Armed with toenail clippers, nail files, and bottles of nail polish, the manicurists strategically took a command post at the far side of the shop. They initiated their first assault by chunking vials of colored lacquer at us!

Mavolyn, Beulah Rose, and I leapt from our vibrating chairs and took cover as small bombs of Princess Pink and Royal Red forcefully smashed against the rampart, dragging our bottles of tequila, sleeve of plastic cups, and the salt, for fear they might be plundered as spoils of war.

"I'm going to call the police!" Mavolyn screamed, only to bring upon us a second, more forceful barrage of colorful nail polish bombs. In my mind, it was clarification that these Koreans were illegal aliens and didn't want us leave the salon with their secret. (This explains why we didn't call the police…we were too busy defending ourselves.)

Starr Noel grabbed Inari and bolted behind the reception desk, escaping with about six partly frozen twelve-ounce containers of concentrated lime juice. The makeshift barricade was a good stronghold, deflecting an aerial blitz of small cuticle scissors and artificial nail tips.

This left Sonia and Della on the front line, their feet still in the water basins. Fortunately, they had an ice cooler full of ammo, about fifty lime slices, positioned between their chairs. A platoon of petite warriors approached, screaming while wheeling serrated nail files over their heads like Samurais. Quickly, Sonia and Della torpedoed green fruit grenades, defending themselves against the ambush.

And like any good story, there's a soundtrack. Patriotically belting out military battle hymns, Norma hid under a circular, nail dryer table. Why, you ask? There is no rhyme or reason to Norma's silly behavior. I think her peculiarities have something to do with consuming too many mushrooms picked in a goat pasture outside Llano during her experimental college years. But there Norma was…hunkered down under her wheeled fortress, crooning for the troops like she was part of an overseas USO tour.

A rapid fire of nail polish rockets bombarded and smacked Sonia on the left eye. "Oh, sweet baby Jesus!" she yelled, covering her wounded brow. "!Te voy a tope de este lado de la tienda en la que el otro!"

Looking over while still vigorously hurling limes, Della proclaimed, "Oh, now you done made Momma mad. Have y'all ever seen a Mexican woman get angry? Watch out!"

"Okay, you little kimchee eaters! Take this!" Sonia grimaced, revenge in her voice. Dumping the remaining ammo from the cooler, Sonia flung the plastic box at the hostile brigade and let out a blood-curdling scream. Frigid water and cubes of ice pelted the startled jokyos. For a moment they stood still as terra cotta soldiers. I used the advantage to begin heaving plastic cups of tequila shots, a weapon I dubbed the Margarita Missile (basically like a Molotov cocktail, but with firewater instead of gasoline). While Mavolyn, Beulah Rose, and I were engaged in our alcoholic air strikes, Starr Noel and Inari began tossing half-frozen containers of lime juice as hand grenades.

Pulling the tin lids off with their teeth to maximize the explosion upon impact, they besieged the spa workers. The wily Asian women ducked and launched a counter attack by lobbing toenail clippers at our heads. We took refuge behind our respective fortifications.

Green goo splatting against the walls, lime bombs and tequila napalm hurled overhead, we were gaining air superiority, and the manicurists began to withdraw. It was time to get out. The battle theater looked like the Black Mamba versus the Crazy 88 fight scene from *Kill Bill*, only with aestheticians instead of ninjas and red nail polish and melted margarita mix instead of spewing blood.

Our final pincer maneuver came as Norma, still cowering under the nail drying table and singing her grand finale, "Battle Hymn of the Republic," pushed her rolling DMZ (Demilitarized Zone) across the spa as a diversion. Della and Sonia managed to scuttle through the battlefield to the wheeled fortress. Collectively, the girls made their way to the reception desk where Starr Noel and Inari were hunkered down. Flying tweezers struck the table top, narrowly missing them. Meanwhile, Mavolyn, Beulah Rose, and I trench-crawled across the sticky floor. We met at the rendezvous point near the exit. Like the soldiers hoisting the Stars and Stripes at Iwo Jima, we jointly pushed down the door and ran for the parking lot, the manicurists cursing at us in Korean, narrowly escaping POW camp in their dank waxing room. We were grateful that we had no casualties. Sonia, our presumptive army chaplain, led us in a prayer to express our gratitude to be alive.

Before heading to our respective vehicles, I considered giving my girls a motivational speech: words to stir the inner athletic soul, like Lou Gehrig or Vince Lombardi would say. But I saw from the faces of these eccentric and incredible women, words were not needed. We intuitively shared a battle-worn determination to win the league's season and beat Capitol City Country Club!

4

Name Calling
and Tattle Tales

In Shakespeare's famous play Juliet elegantly tells Romeo, "What is in a name? That which we call a rose, by any other name would smell as sweet." I guess he meant that it matters more what something IS than what it is called... and I suppose he's right, because no matter what it's called, a rose is still a flower. And I'm here to tell you, when that once sweet smelling rose wilts, it gets thrown into the trash with all the other garbage. However, when a group of women congregate to decide on a name for a tennis team, what you're called matters a lot.

So why is choosing a team name so important? To our team's way of thinking, a name is just not a name. A name defines the character and personality of the team. It can influence the expectations of others about the team and announce your status as a Queen of the Court. It can also be a self-fulfilling prophecy. If your name sounds forceful, mean, and nasty, you and your teammates are more than likely going to act those things. Take, for example, a few names of last year's teams: Ace Kickers, Serves You Right, Love Hurts, Simply Smashing, It's Not My Fault, Point

Taken, and It's A Racket. Those are some pretty aggressive names for ladies who just want to socialize and casually exercise. The magnitude of choosing the proper name for our team was as great as naming a first-born child. And in our case it was as torturous and tedious as field dressing a deer with a butter knife.

To discuss this weighty issue, we convened for lunch at a local dance hall and restaurant, The Broken Spoke. It's an Austin icon, a honky tonk with a history that dates back to Bob Wills and The Texas Playboys. The saloon is a faded, rundown red metal building, with two flashing neon signs shaped like wagon wheels. Near the front door a dilapidated vintage tour bus is parked, and you can barely read the name "Texas Top Hands" underneath the rust and wear. The place is literally a time machine to the early 1960's when Conway Twitty, Merle Haggard, and Patsy Cline ruled the radio waves. Plus it serves a cardiac-inducing chicken fried steak and the coldest beers in town.

Amid a thicket of professional businessmen, political wonks, and an assortment of working class stiffs, I spotted my friends around a table, their faces illuminated by a brightly lit Corona sign as they enjoyed each other's company. It absolutely warmed my heart, like a scene from *Little Women*, only with a Texas twang and a lot more swearing.

It was a Friday afternoon. I love Fridays. Most people do. I'm sure the sentiment comes from our school years, patiently waiting…waiting…waiting for the last three o'clock bell to ring, then flinging open the classroom doors, bounding out of the schoolyard for two days of no responsibilities. Somehow, Fridays bring out that inner child in adults, at least for me. The old club was jam packed with folks celebrating the end of a work week. A cacophonic mixture of loud conversations and country western music resonated against the walls. The smell of stale beer hung in the air—that unforgettable aroma that reminds me of a frat house. It was a rowdy sensory scene. Those familiar sounds, smells, and high-spirited bustling set the mood for FUN.

I could hear the Racq Pacq's babbling and ripples of laughter drifting across the room, rising and falling, and then swelling again to a crest of hilarity. Hearing their hoopla I felt gratitude welling up inside. I am really lucky to know such wonderful ladies. Not only are they funny and charming, they are extremely intelligent. They have college degrees ranging from chemo-pharmacology (the science of mixing wine and pharmaceuticals) to animal husbandry (the practice of breeding with husbands that act like animals). Blue-blooded Eastern socialites and West Coast glitterati may assume Southern women have dirt daubers in their heads and don't know Jack Shit. Their mistake. My teammates, as well as most women west of the Mississippi River, are highly educated…and very well acquainted with the Shit family, considering most of them live in Texas.

Mavolyn, Norma, and Starr Noel graduated from University of Texas. Mavolyn is one smart cookie and double majored with a political science and a finance degree from the highly respected School of Business; Norma's diploma is in aerospace engineering, and Starr graduated with a degree in quantum mathematics. Beulah Rose attended Texas Tech University. Not only did she receive her diploma, but during football games she rode the school's black stallion mascot (as well as most of the football players). Della's graduation walk at Texas Christian University was made possible by a ~~bribe~~ generous donation from her father for the construction of the new science department building. Sonia attended Rice University and earned her master's degree at NYU. Inari graduated from the prestigious Hiroshima Institute of Technology.

I graduated from Sam Houston State University in Huntsville, Texas, home of the state's largest penal system. Back in the early 1940's, Sam Houston was a school strictly for future teachers. In those years, it was called Sam Houston Institute of Teachers. When the 1950's rolled around, attendance grew, and an athletic department was added to the curriculum, as well as a new football team. It was during the first football game against Northwestern State University that Sam Houston Institute of Teachers made a crucial name change. Spectators overflowed the bleachers for the inaugural game.

Cheerleaders, waving their pom-poms, began the chant, "Give me an S!"

The crowd obediently yelled "S."

"Give me an H!" The cheerleaders hollered through megaphones.

Again, the supporters chanted "H!"

"Give me an I!"

"I!"

"Give me a T!"

"T!"

The cheerleaders screamed, "What's that spell?"

Obediently the crowd responded, "Shit!" A burst of laughter engulfed the stands, while dozens of administrative jaws dropped. Needless to the say, the attending professors, deans, and other staff members were appalled. The following day an emergency board of directors meeting was called, and a unanimous vote re-named the school: Sam Houston State University.

What is in a name, indeed? A rose may smell the same no matter what, but some things end up smelling like manure. Names convey meanings; like my alma mater, an inappropriate name gives people the wrong idea.

Back at The Broken Spoke, a cantankerous waitress with a nauseatingly stained apron slung seven frosty, lime-crowned bottles of Negra Modelo beer around our table of cackling women. Mavolyn discreetly poured her beer in a Styrofoam cup with a straw. I ordered a root beer, appointing myself as the designated driver. Chicken-fried steaks plopped down, dripping with globs of white gravy, as Johnny Cash's song, "Ring of Fire" played on the old juke box.

"Oh, God. I hope I don't get a 'Ring of Fire' after I eat this meal. Fried foods always makes me gassy," Starr Noel snorted, laughing around a mouthful of rubbery beef. With a cast iron stomach and a rubber tailpipe, Starr Noel is notorious for producing more methane than a petroleum factory. I simply don't understand it. Despite her zaftig figure, she will eat anything that wouldn't eat her first. In fact, I've never seen a woman who can consume as much food or guzzle down more brewskies than her. She refers to beer as sunshine in a bottle. "It makes me hoppy!" she says, a goofy pun accompanied with her signature high pitched, donkey laugh.

""Aye, yai, yai! Blessed be the patron saint of everything immoral and disgusting."" Sonia rolled her eyes. "Are we going to start in with the potty talk? If I wanted to hear gross stuff at lunch, I would have invited my sons' soccer teams." She has developed the strongest backhand swing I have ever seen from years of swatting her three unruly boys upside the head like piñatas.

"You have got to be kidding me?" Della said bombastically. "There is actually a patron saint for debauchery and filth?"

"Saint Malo," Sonia retorted without hesitation. "Patron saint of pig keepers."

Della shook her head in disbelief.

Carefully dabbing gravy from her mouth with the corner of her napkin, Mavolyn said in her genteel, confident voice, "OK. Let's get down to business." Her organizational skills were well-suited for her job as team assistant captain. Looking down at her clipboard of copious notes taken at the last Austin Tennis Association meeting, she said, "According to the tennis league's rules, we have to decide on the team's name by the end of the week, so I think we should vote on a name today. I know a few of y'all have some ideas, but may I make a suggestion?" This was clearly a rhetorical question. "I think our team's name should be clever and ladylike, yet it ought to be intimidating, evoking terror in the other teams."

At the time, the idea of choosing a name that was both ladylike and intimidating didn't seem odd. Looking back, the notion of something being mannerly and at the same time frightening is absolutely moronic. I'm telling you, a person can lose themselves in the drama of recreational tennis.

"Oh, hell. I'm all for that," Della said, gulping her last swig of beer and slamming the empty bottle on the table. "I love terror!" Della is the quintessential tomboy, full of swagger and smack-talk. Fortunately, she can back up the braggadocio. Coupled with audacity, Della has a sense of humor drier than the Chihuahua Desert. We're used to hearing acerbic comments like "I don't suffer from insanity. I enjoy every minute." Despite the crusty demeanor and deadpan expressions, a loving woman with compassion and kindness lives inside her—just behind her left kidney, below her pancreas.

Like a female Arnold Horshack, Norma waved her hand frantically, "A few names I have come up with are 'High Strung' and 'Strung Out.'" She giggled at her own wit. Norma is happy-go-lucky, an "empty nester"—with no children at home and a husband who travelled two weeks out of the month, who wouldn't be happy all the time? But she often felt lonesome and abandoned. She had hoped that signing up on a new tennis team might fill some of those lonely daytime hours.

"What the heck!? 'High Strung' and 'Strung Out.' What kind of names are those?" Sonia objected. "Sounds like a team of druggies, like those gals from the 'High Ball' last season." Sonia prides herself on clean living and wholesome values. And for that reason, we love teasing her, especially Della, who baits Sonia with bawdy comments. Sonia always retorts with a corresponding Bible verse or an old Spanish proverb. Taunting each other is their part time occupation.

"Yep. The last time we played tennis with the High Ball team those women were so wasted they couldn't keep score," Mavolyn said, rolling her eyes in amazement. "Sonia is correct. We can't use those names. Besides, most of us still have impressionable children. And personally, I can't be associated with anything risqué or off-colored…the Judge would absolutely kill me." Mavolyn always addressed her husband as "the Judge." To people that didn't know her well, the title seemed like an adoring nickname, but I knew it was an indicator of a burden.

"As the marketing slogan says, 'Keep Austin Weird,'" interjected Beulah Rose, who prides herself on ingenious marketing ideas and newfangled contraptions. Not only has she launched the new iPhone app, she recently franchised a profitable mobile dog grooming business called "Doggy Style." Last autumn she harnessed her husband's passion for hunting and set him up with a roadside roach coach♚ retailing smoked deer jerky off of Highway 71. The company's name? "Jerk Off." The motto is "You Can't Beat Our Meat."

Born into a dirt-poor cotton farming family in Uvalde, Texas, Beulah Rose pulled herself out of poverty by her bootstraps, even though she couldn't afford the straps or the boots. We always call her by her initials, "BR."[1] After all, who would want to be called "Beulah Rose? She was named after her daddy's favorite milk cow, Rose, and Aunt

---

1 I don't understand why Southern folks still give double names to their children. In the ol' days the tradition prevented confusion due to all the cousin pokin'. Nowadays we just do like veterinarians and use microchips to distinguish between offspring.

Beulah, an eccentric dwarf who lived alone with a herd of pigmy goats on her ranch outside Buffalo Gap. The goats were potty-trained and lived inside the house, where the well-behaved little cud chewers sat in La-z-boy chairs and watched television. Aunt Beulah said their favorite was *Bewitched.*

"What are you talking about? Those aren't druggie names!" responded Norma, pushing back a palomino-colored tendril that had fallen from under her cap.

BR replied, "I beg your pardon, honey! Those names would imply we were either 'Strung Out' on some kind of Prozac or 'High Strung' on Ecstasy. Like I said, it's all about marketing. Our name should state who we are. And evoke an image of strength and superiority."

Starr Noel interrupted with a high-pitched giggle, "I choose the Ecstasy, so I vote for High Strung."

Mavolyn had had enough. "Inari, what do you think? Have you thought of a name for our tennis team?"

Peering from behind a fortress of empty beer bottles, Inari shook her head, "I don't know. I have never tried Prozac or Ecstasy. So I am not a good judge of that." Bewilderment in her eyes was magnified by her glasses, framed by a short pageboy haircut. She couldn't quite make sense of the conversation. Inari is a little gun-shy about speaking up on unfamiliar topics. The week prior she was listening to a heated political exchange at the Cedarway clubhouse (Texas politics can get people hotter than a Serrano pepper). The debate was regarding laissez-faire and governmental interference with regards to petroleum lubricants. Inari thought that laissez-faire was a word to define a lesbian affair and couldn't understand why these women shouldn't be allowed to use KY jelly.

It's hard enough to assimilate into a foreign country. Learning English with all the added Texas colloquialisms can be downright demoralizing. Inari came to the United States with one suitcase and a laptop computer, not knowing a single person. Yet she has swiftly moved up the corporate ladder. I always feel the need to hug Inari for her bravery. Courage in a small package. No one would ever expect that a demure Japanese lady could own such a strong will.

Pounding her third beer on the table, Della gruffly stated, "Well, I like the names 'Get A Grip' and 'Kiss My Ace.'"

"We can't use those names. They're taken by other teams," Norma replied, sucking the lime atop beer #4.

"I know. I know. What about the "'Sweet Spots'?" asked BR, pointing down to her cooter and grinning conspiratorially. "Do you get it? How's that for a cute play on words?"

"Nope. That name has been taken too!" said Mavolyn. "And I just found out from the captains' pre-season meeting that the CCCC cougars have renamed themselves 'The Alley Cats.' Their captain told me that the team changed the name because "Chicks with Sticks" sounded too much like they were all wearing strap-on dildos. So they changed it."[2]

"Well, they ARE an ungodly group. And they DO run around country clubs with strap-ons!" Sonia sneered. "Mercy be,

◇◇◇◇◇◇◇◇◇◇◇◇◇◇◇◇

2 It didn't matter what the Alley Cats called themselves. We referred to Capitol City Country Club as "C4" – plastic explosive. Those women have TNT tempers in Rubbermaid bodies. Undeniably, most of the hotheaded country club members had their plastic surgeons on speed dial. Silicone implants, lip injections, rhinoplasty, and booty transplants are like leisure activities there.

that's just common knowledge. Everyone in Austin knows their bad reputation." Preacher-like, she bellowed, "And HE breaketh down the houses of the Sodomites…"

Della cried with exasperation, "OH, hell. Here she goes again, standing on her papal pedestal quoting Scripture," and rolled her eyes.

Ignoring the brouhaha at the other end of the table, Norma pouted, "Dang! All the good names have been taken. I just hope we don't get stuck with some crappy name."

"I still like Sweet Spots," BR said, disappointed.

Frustrated that no one listened to her religious diatribe, the church lady sighed, "Why does our team name have to relate to sex? There is too much sex on the TV. Too much sex on the internet. Everything is sex, sex, sex. From my perspective, this whole world is over-sexed. Our team should not bow down to those sexual idols."

"Who said our team has to bow down to have sex?" quipped Della. "Sonia, I know you are a member of the 'holier than thou' vestal sisterhood, but you gotta lighten up a little before you pop a gasket or something."

"Listen, I've got three active boys. You know, once you have kids your sex life will never be the same. In fact, your entire life won't ever be, either. I was just hoping we could take the high moral ground and chose a name like the Crusaders or the Illuminatus," Sonia replied.

"What?" Mavolyn lifted her left eyebrow with complete astonishment. "Those names aren't ladylike. We can't name ourselves either of those! If my historical facts are correct, both the Crusaders and the Illuminatus did a bunch of killing, destroying, and annihilating. And I'm pretty sure there was a lot of sex, sex, and SEX!"

Disillusioned, Sonia looked deep into the sudsy bottom of her beer bottle, crooked a finger at the waitress, and ordered another round for herself.

"Oh, just admit it, Sonia!" Della said flippantly. "Underneath that veneer of Christian purity lies a sexually suppressed siren, longing for an opportunity to rip off those Suzy Homemaker apron strings, bind them around her husband's wrists and ankles, and spank his butta cake."

"You are disgusting! The Bible says, 'If we confess our sins, He will forgive us and cleanse us from all unrighteousness.' You, Della, need your mouth cleaned out with a righteous bar of spiritual soap!" Sonia countered. "I don't know what butta cake is, but it sounds like it has a lot of calories."

Inari raised her hand. "I have a name."

Everyone leaned forward to hear Inari's thought.

"You know how everyone swings the racquets, forehand and backhand? What about the name 'Swingers'?"

With perfect synchronization beer spurted from the mouths of BR, Norma, and Starr Noel (plus Della's nose). Foam spewed at Inari from all angles, like at a carwash. Her naïveté was just too much for the girls to contain themselves.

Inari sat dumbfounded, beer dripping from her face and glasses, her once-smooth hair now blown back by the force of the spray. It looked like a perverted beer baptismal. She knew she had missed something.

Timidly, Inari said, "I guess you didn't like the name."

We all roared with laughter, including Inari. Starr Noel's hyena-like howl rose about twenty decibels above the rest of us and finally caught the attention of the manager.

"Can I hep[3] y'all?" the gruff old manager directed his question towards Starr Noel.

"Oh, no," Mavolyn said, trying to placate the man. She didn't want the team to get thrown out for disorderly conduct. If the Judge found out that we had been escorted off the premises, he would have been madder than a kicked mound full of red ants. Trying to humor him, Mavolyn said, "You'll have to excuse her," pointing at Starr Noel, who was still hysterically laughing. "Her momma birthed her at Gilley's Night Club. Plus growing up in Pasadena, Texas next to all those petroleum and chemical plants, she has some serious issues. I truly apologize."

Confused, he asked, "She was born at Mickey Gilley's honky tonk?" while looking over at Starr Noel, still snorting and laughing uncontrollably.

Della took over. "Yep. Her momma was a bit of a rabble-rouser and bar fly. At seven months pregnant, she decided to ride the mechanical bull, thinking that it might jar the baby out of her belly. In the middle of all the kickin' and buckin', Starr Noel shot out like a 12 gauge over-and-under shotgun across the dance floor and landed on her head on top of a case of Lone Star Beer. And that is how she got her name."

Cocking his head, he leaned forward to examine her more closely, "She got her name by hitting her head on a case of

◇◇◇◇◇◇◇◇◇◇◇◇◇◇◇◇
3 Hep – facilitate, assist, to give or provide what is necessary to accomplish a task or satisfy a need.

Lone Star?"

BR chimed in. "Even though it was the middle of summer, Starr Noel's momma thought it was a sign from God that the baby landed on that case of Lone Star Beer. And as all Texans know, the Lone Star is synonymous with the nativity star. Therefore the baby girl was named Noel Lone Starr. Double R in Starr. We just call her Starr."

"Plus, her great grandmomma, Belle Starr, was a wild West 'Bandit Queen' in the mid 1800's, no joke!" put in Mavolyn. She loves historical accuracy. "Belle Starr ran with a band of Oklahoma outlaws until 1889, when she was killed by a shotgun shell to the back of her head. And Belle Starr's daughter, Pearl Starr, was the infamous Texas brothel owner. Pearl Starr's scandalous past is currently being displayed at the Bob Bullock Museum. An unconfirmed anecdote has it that the German brewmaster J.B. Ackerman named his beer company Pearl after taking a shine to Pearl Starr. It has been said he was a regular customer of her bordello, the biggest poke palace in San Antonio."

The manger stared at Starr. She looked up at him with a huge smile, Negra Modelo dripping from her chin onto her bodacious Cadillac bumper bullets. He eyed her for a moment, then said, "I think you gals need another round of beer." The manager walked off, scratching his head.

As preposterous as it sounds, Starr was actually named after beer. Can you image if she had popped out and fallen on a case of Mad Dog 20/20, Blue Moon, or Anheuser-Busch? In Texas, the brand is more like a question than a name: "And how's yer bush?" I don't know about you, but I wouldn't want a name inquiring after my lady garden.

Everyone has one—a name, that is. But few people give names much thought. Not our tennis team. All of us—seven intoxicated women and me, sober as a judge—sat through six rounds, laughing, until it hit us on the head like a case of beer. Together, our fun-loving team was having a ball! The final vote was unanimous: "It's a Ball."

5

Haute Couture Mommas

The next decision—team uniforms. Marilyn Monroe once said, "Give a girl the right shoes, and she can conquer the world." Can you imagine what Marilyn could have conquered if she wore the right tennis outfit? A fashionable get-up that would take over the WTA® world. That is what we wanted, but nothing ordinary or "over the counter" like Nike, Bolle, or Adidas. Arriving at the first match of the season only to find that the opposing team had the same uniform was equivalent to traipsing into The Crystal Ball wearing the same dress as someone else. How bourgeois?! Everybody in Austin has those polyester/elasthane blend things, and they all run around the grocery stores in them as if to say, *Look at me! I've been playing tennis. I have an excuse to wear short, short skirts in public. Don't I look sexy?* Most refuse to see the hard reality: outside the confines of the cyclone fence, their skimpy costumes just scream, *I'm a middle-aged mother with Saggy Knee Syndrome® and lunch lady arms® trying to recapture my youth by wearing this sassy little dress.* All teasing aside, tennis outfits *are* rather comfortable; the material is stretchy and feels good, so we all understand why some women wear them everywhere.

There was no question. We would design our team uniforms

from scratch. However, the idea of creating our own outfits seemed daunting: like "Project Runway" meets "Deadliest Catch." The Racq Pacq wanted an edgy yet classic design to knock those tennis fashionistas flat on their asses. An ensemble that would scream, "Game on, bitches!" at the trendy and rich Alley Cats. We had to acknowledge that C4's go-to designers—Tom Ford, Vera Wang, or Donna Karan—were beyond our reach. But we believed we could create an economical uniform that would complement our team's quirky and unique personality. The common thread of agreement: beat the feline freaks both on the court with our physical prowess and off the court with our *haute couture* athletic dresses. So we ironed out a new fashion concept in anticipation of a championship meow down♛ with the pompous cougars.

I'm not really "into" fashion. In fact, I just found out last week that Jimmy Choo's isn't a chain of Chinese food restaurants. This is not the case for the rest of my team, and every gal has their own personal style and particular tastes. The difficulty of choosing one outfit for the whole group could only be diminished by one catalyst: booze.

After practice, the team usually congregates at a local alcoholery♛ for a little "wine down," some female bonding and a few good laughs. Walking into any restaurant, we tend to make as much commotion as a flock of mockingbirds (Texas's notable state bird)—chirping, teasing, poking fun. We cause more than one head to turn, and quite a few shocked expressions.[1]

◇◇◇◇◇◇◇◇◇◇◇◇◇◇◇◇

1 Mockingbirds are notoriously mean as hell and will peck your eyes out when defending their nests, reminiscent of the Alfred Hitchcock film *The Birds*. A word to the wise: Don't mess with Texas mockingbirds or Texas Mommas!

This particular afternoon we met at a neighborhood wine bar called The Bottleneck. It aims to resemble an old world *caves á vin*, but the interior is more "Texas Tuscan" meets Liberace. (I've never understood how gullible people are with respect to interior design. "Texas Tuscan," are you kidding me? Who mixes Renaissance motifs with rough, ranch-style decorations? That's like decorating the Pitti Palace in Florence with cowhide rugs, antler chandeliers, and pool tables in the dining room. What's next, "Pennsylvania Persian"?) The popular tavern serves only wine, no cocktails and no fare…well, that and t-shirts that feature their logo on the front and the following slogan on the back: **LIQUOR? We don't even know HER!**

The Bottleneck is a kind of reverse BYOB: you bring your own food, making it a BYOF bar. Therefore, Mavolyn volunteered to prepare lunches for the team. That day, our brown bags were packed with individually wrapped smoked duck and fig dumplings; Parmesan-crusted beef tenderloin sandwiches; arugula, citrus, and fennel salads; and lastly, creamy lemon curd and sweet basil *budinos* for dessert. We had the whole bar sniffing over our shoulders. Not only is Mavolyn our designated executive chef—picnics and making all restaurant reservations—she is the team's "snack lady." Food is a big deal for our group of gals. Most Southern mothers have a genetic marker, yet to been discovered in the DNA spirals, which causes them to fixate on food. During tennis season, it is customary for the hosting teams to provide snacks and drinks for all participants after the matches. As "snack lady" for home games, Mavolyn always presented our guest players a banquet fit for Julia Child or pre-weight loss Paula Deen. Most teams just throw out a couple of six packs of RC cola and stale pimiento cheese sandwiches or some type of cheap sacrelicious♛ casserole made with communion wafers and copious amounts of cayenne pepper. (My grandmother always pronounced it "canine" pepper because they both have a bite!) Indicative of their lusty behavior, the Alley Cats always serve Pop-Tarts and wiener wraps.

A young waitress handed out menus the size of Moses's tablets and chirped, "May I take your order?"

Her wrist bending at a dangerous angle, Della rhetorically uttered, "You serve any wine in this canteen?"

Apparently she didn't speak sarcasm, because the waitress went on, "Indeed. We have a wide variety of wines from all regions of the world, ranging from Chardonnays to Beaujolais, Merlots to Bordeauxs, Malbecs to Brunellos and everything in between. Perhaps a recommendation to complement your lunch?"

Hefting the tombstone-like menu, Norma inquired, "What vintage is your Harlan *cuvee*?"

Our server nodded. "Oh, yes. Harlan, one of Napa Valley's finest vintners. The cases we currently have in our cellars are 1992, 1998, and 2000."

"That is a shame," Norma murmured, nonchalantly pressing an index finger against her chin. "The 1997 was the vineyard's best year." She sighed with a bit of discontent, her eyes still on the list.

The table went silent. We all know Norma's no dumb blonde, but she sure could play one on TV. She often gives the impression of being a "wheels are still turnin' but the hamster is dead" type thinker. How did she know about Harlan, a label that retails for roughly $1,500 per bottle?

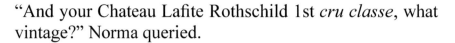

"And your Chateau Lafite Rothschild 1st *cru classe*, what vintage?" Norma queried.

"1980, 1997, and 1991," the waitress confirmed.

"A pity," Norma shook her head with disappointment. "Of course you know, the 1961 and 1982 are the best years for Lafite. And the 2000 has been noted to be a legendary vintage for the Chateau. Your 1997 is a good price, but there's not enough time to decant it. It takes at least two hours for the wine to reach its maximum potential."

By now, we were all staring at Norma in amazement, wondering how a common-folk gal from Blessing, Texas obtained this expertise.

"Okay, then I'll settle for a glass of your house Châteauneuf-du-Pape," Norma said, casually closing the menu with a contented thump. "You know, Châteauneuf-du-Pape is sorta like our team, a special blend of different varieties of fruit, beautifully merged to construct a magnificent symphony of flavor." Clearly proud of the analogy, Norma looked around for affirmation, but we were too stunned to smile or nod.

"Very good," the waitress agreed, and turn to address the rest of the table, "And what can I pour for you ladies?"

There was an awkward silence as we struggled to activate our tongues, then Norma interjected, "I think they would like the '97 Opus One. It should pair nicely with the duck and the tenderloin. I think the girls will enjoy the wine's austere character and seductive vanilla notes. It offers terrific aromatic perfume, with black tea and singed mesquite wafting through the bouquet. The wine is earthy, however, it grips the taste buds with refined black currant, cassis, and boysenberry that glides along gently, peaks with scorched iron and juniper, yet stays well-supported through the finish."

"Very good," the waitress acknowledged.

"Oh, and make that four bottles," Norma concluded. Straining under the weight of the menus, our waitress departed for the cellar.

BR was the first to find her voice: "What the hell is happening here? Between Mavolyn's fancy-ass, gourmet meal and Norma acting like Robert Parker, this feels more like something out of *Wine Spectator* or *Food & Wine* magazine than my team."

Everyone else just stared at Norma.

She finally shrugged, "What?" Removing her tennis cap, she nonchalantly pulled her long hair up into a ponytail. "Oh, are y'all talkin' about the wine deal? It's really not very interesting."

Here we felt conflicted, knowing that all Norma's stories tend toward the long and obtuse. But we had to find out.

"Well, as y'all already know, I was abandoned as a baby at the Blessing hospital. I was there for thirteen years, until I was sent off to live with a foster family in Denison, Texas." Going off on one of her anecdotal tangents, Norma calls them "side stories." "As everyone knows, in 1880 the vineyards of France were on the verge of destruction from the phylloxera root louse. The grapevine plague spread throughout France and in particular the Cognac region. The whole winemakers' economy was at risk of failure, so the French government selected a scientist to find a cure for the plague. His research lead him to Denison, Texas, which has similar soil properties. He surmised that the Texas rootstock would be resistant to the phylloxera louse, and he was correct. Subsequently, he bundled up thousands of Texas rootstocks and shipped them to France to be grafted with the French vines. The experiment was a success, and it saved the vineyards from total devastation. This same grafting procedure continues to this day. Isn't that neat-o? There is a little bit of Texas in every bottle of French wine!"

"Interesting history lesson...but how do you know so much about wine?" Sonia doesn't have much tolerance for blabber infections. She wanted Norma to stop the wordy dissertation and get to the point of her story.

"Well, the citizens of Cognac and the surrounding wine region are still grateful for Denison's efforts to help their vineyards, so they have a foreign exchange student program between the corresponding towns. As a result, I lived in the town of Cognac, France during my high school years. I learned a lot about oenology, which is the science of vinification, as well as consuming a variety of wines. And that is my story. *Voila! Parlez-vous français?*" Norma concluded with perfect French inflection.

"Whatever!" Della grunted with disappointment, "You can just put a cork in it. Who cares about your BS degree in grape-ology, Albert Wine-stain. Tell us about playing tongue hockey with a handsome, rich Frenchman and bumping uglies at his chateau on the banks of the Rhone River. Something with some love triangles and chocolate."

Astonished, Norma exclaimed, "Oh, no! Nothing like that ever happened! But I *do* have a story about chocolate and a little doohickey I purchased on Avenue de Champs-

Elysees." Norma gave a wily grin and bit her lip.

Everyone's eyes lit with interest, but Mavolyn called us back to order. "Girls, please. Let's get our minds out of the gouttière and talk about these uniforms." The crucial need to choose a uniform was the only thing that could have gotten us off of the suddenly-intriguing topic. Mavoyln always kept us focused on the task at hand.

A fresh, Vogue-style outfit from a custom tailor would have been ideal, but our budget didn't allow it. So Beulah Rose declared herself head seamstress for the team. BR learned to sew as a child, explaining, "I was a string bean growing up and poor as dirt, so my momma and I sewed all my clothes." She insisted that with a few stitches and a little bit of super glue we could craft an outfit that Coco Chanel would be proud to wear.

Sizing would be an obvious challenge, as the team was a fruit salad of physiques: watermelons, bananas, honeydews, mandarin oranges, Granny Smith apples, and marshmallows.[2] Sizes ranged from 2 to 12, A to triple-D cup, from 4'5" to 6'1."

How were we going balance the need to enhance everyone's best physical features with comfort in the overbearing Texas heat? Not only is Austin the state capital, it is the antiperspirant capital of the South. The fact is, sweat is a fashion statement here in the River City. Hiding unbecoming pit puddles was a serious consideration for potential fabric choices. But we also needed to address a more important concern than overactive apocrine glands. We needed a magical material similar to a mildew resistant trampoline

◇◇◇◇◇◇◇◇◇◇◇◇◇◇◇◇
2 Yes, marshmallows are considered a white berry in Southern fruit salads.

vinyl that taunted gravity. This magic fabric must hide unseemly FUPA🏵 and also shape the hind-end ham hocks, the terrain of the female geography most difficult to hide.

The delicious lunch and fabulous wine eased the transition to the team's individual fashion pitches. Ideas ranged from a Dr. Seuss theme with psychedelic colors to a 1950's motif with traditional sheer pink blouses, built-in retro "bullet bras," and cigarette pants like Mary Tyler Moore used to wear on the *Dick Van Dyke Show*. Someone suggested Catholic school uniforms with short, plaid jumper-dresses; another idea was a romantic *Phantom of the Opera* theme with amethyst-hued silk skirts and black lace bustiers.

"I just won't wear anything from the 1980's. I hate those linebacker shoulder pads," Sonia announced.

"And I absolutely abhor flowers on tennis outfits. I don't want to look like a damn rose garden. Only frumpy old ladies wear blossoming plants on their clothes," Della countered, holding her upturned nose as if smelling a strongly floral perfume.

"Remember last year, the gals from Net Results and their hideous uniform? They wore matching red tops and sheer flowing skirts with red brocade flowers. They looked like big, walking blood clots!" BR said. "I'm for no buds, too!"

"Oh, but those would be great to wear during our menstrual cycles," Norma argued.

"Who in the hell still has their periods besides Inari, J. Morgan, and BR? Most of us are in our early 50's!" moaned Starr. "Ablations, hysterectomies, and tube tying have stopped those red letter days."

"Holy Virgin and all the saints!" Sonia interrupted, shaking her head in disgust, "Why do we always talk about gross stuff? Can we please get the conversation back on track?"

Mavolyn stepped in with a soothing, sorghum-sweet tone: "Okay, we need to be considerate of everyone's personal sensibilities. Sorry, Sonia." Pausing for a moment to give the table a "behave yourselves" look, Mavolyn mutated into her alter ego, the methodical and organized dictator we like to call *The Hausfrau*. "Let's make some fashion decisions here, we don't have much time."

"If we don't agree on something soon, we are going to be in a big peccadillo," Inari piped in.

"Don't you mean *pickle*?" Mavolyn asked.

"Peccadillo! I haven't heard that word in a long time," Starr said with a smile of distant reminiscence. Starting to giggle, she explained, "In my child's mind, I assumed that peccadillos were jarred picked armadillos. And sold at the Piggly Wiggly grocery store on the same shelves as the sweet pickles and the dill pickle relish." Her laughter got more hysterical and pig-like.

"Please, I beg you. Let's take her to the doctor's office and smash her tongue in a mammogram machine. Even better, let's stick her lips in a Sub Zero freezer and slam it shut!" Della pled; she cringes every time Starr starts in with the snorting. She chugged the remaining wine in her glass and waved for the waitress to bring another bottle. "More snake bite medicine, *por favor*!"

"What?" Inari asked. "Armadillo?" Ever since moving to Texas, she has been enamored with the shelled rodents. Once after a match, Inari had us stop the carpool on the side of I-35 so she could examine a roadkill armadillo up close. Blood and guts all smooshed in the gravel with just the animal's snout-like nose sticking up out of the displaced organs. She collected the remains in a discarded potato chip bag and took it home with her. I know it's weird, but hey, everyone has got their thing. And for Inari, it is armadillos.

Calming herself a little, Starr went on to brag about her ancestor. She was proud of her roots. "Well, my great grandmomma, Belle Starr, dressed rather outlandishly during her time; they call it 'taking a fashion risk' nowadays. Her favorite outfit was a full-length black velvet dress complemented with a man's Stetson cowboy hat ornamented with ostrich feathers. Around her waist hung a pair of shiny, polished revolvers."

"What in blue blazes are you talkin' about?" Della's voice dripped sarcasm. "Your ornery grandmomma wasn't afraid of taking a fashion risk. Think about it. No one was gonna tell a woman brandishing handguns that her pre-Johnny Cash black getup looked like crap. They'd get their faces blown off!"

"Sophia Loren once said, 'A woman's dress should be like a barbed-wire fence: serving its purpose without obstructing the view.' Now that would be a new stylized and trend-setting uniform," BR proclaimed. "Which reminds me, do y'all recall that fun game we played at the Bunco party two weeks ago, 'Blab-Or-Bare'?"

Everyone giggled, nodding at the recollection of a somewhat provocative question and answer game we played at a recent Girl's Night Potluck Dinner hosted by Mavolyn.

"Remember that question about female infatuation? 'What

girl crush would you sleep with?'" BR asked.

Eyes rolled and wine-stained teeth were flashed. Everyone recalled that night.

"Well, I figured out my answer!" BR announced, as if it were an epiphany. "I would choose Sophia Loren."

"Blab or Bare" is usually for events like a bachelorette party. Basically, it is a simplistic version of truth-or-dare played with about 100 two-sided cards. One side of the card features a "Blab" question concerning a dark hidden secret; the other features a dare or "Bare" assignment, usually an act of danger, indecency, or some type of disgusting deed. We decided to ignore the "Bare" side of the cards because most of us are mothers and members of sororities. We already performed and/or were bystanders of absolutely everything daring, audacious, and hazardous years ago. After things like childbirth, teaching 16-year-old boys to drive, cleaning the toxic remains of an exploded diaper off a shopping cart at Target, volunteering as "Room Mothers" for kindergarten classes, and performing clandestine blowjobs in the utility room while the kids watched TV, the "Bare" stuff had no appeal. So we used the "Blab" side for a tribal powwow where every team member had to answer the same hypothetical question.

One question got everyone in a dither: "What 'girl crush' would you take to bed?" Now girl crushes are absolutely no big deal; most are based on feelings of deep admiration and affection. But the thought of having sex with said girl crush put a new, bidirectional (so to speak) twist on the question. Most of the gals picked movie stars like Sandra Bullock, Jessica Lange, and Jane Seymour. Others shared awkward anecdotes about near-miss kisses with next-door neighbors and best friends. Della said that she would do it with BR, her tennis partner. Inari said that she would have "in-her course" with her college roommate, Kusai Sakana. Sonia insisted that because of her religious upbringing she "could not and would not have sex with any woman or any type of mechanical object." Basically everyone's answers were boring, not nearly as provocative as the question seemed to suggest. However, BR was utterly stumped. She quietly pondered the question all evening long ...as if she would actually ask a woman on a potential sexcursion.

We finally skipped BR, so I was the last person to reply. I stood in the center and answered, "Condoleezza Rice." A sudden burst of raucous laughter consumed the room. *What is wrong with having an affair with Condi Rice?* I thought. *Why is that so funny?* The wild surge of amusement carried on for a long time, and I felt my face turning red as a polished apple; I just couldn't understand why a finger fishing trip with Condoleezza was so funny.

"You can't have sex with the ex-Secretary of State," Della told me, grinning so that the deep dimple on her left cheek showed, an absurd feature on such a feisty face. But there it was, a puckish contradiction.

I felt like I was sitting in the middle of that annoying "Song of the South" ride at Disney World.[3] Condescending laughter, the singing and high-pitched tittering of the animatronic animals at Brer Fox's Laughing Place, echoed in my ear. I was both agitated and perplexed, *Well, that's the whole point of dry humping Condi,* I quietly contemplated. *She*

◇◇◇◇◇◇◇◇◇◇◇◇◇◇◇◇◇◇
3 This is on the side of the park opposite from Fantasyland and the infamous Pinocchio ride that was the site of the climactic nose job for one of our team candidates.

was the Secretary of State, the most influential and powerful woman in the WORLD. I re-stated my position, "You bet. I like Condoleezza Rice. She would be the 'girl crush' I would take on a magical imaginary Splash Mountain romp. Anyway, it's a pretend question." Honestly, I'm not interested in Ms. Rice physically. I just want to have sweet pillow talk with Condi, divulging all those international secrets that only she and Dick Cheney know about.

So, if you happen to attend a potluck and face the question, "What girl crush would you take to bed?" while playing Blab or Bare, prepare to be teased if you select anyone with intellectual acuity. Give a second thought before choosing the likes of Texas Senator Barbara Jordan, Supreme Court Justice Ruth Bader Ginsburg, or Secretary of Homeland Security Janet Napolitano. You will be taunted!

Meanwhile, back at the wine bar, BR slammed her wine glass on the table like a judge's gavel and proclaimed, "Yep, I would have sex with Sophia Loren." It only took her two weeks to think of an answer.

"Oh, precious Mother of God!" Exasperated with the whole discussion about sex, Sonia threw up her arms in frustration. Her strict Christian ethics prevent Sonia from even bantering on the sinful subject of sexual intercourse. "Why does everything have to be about coitus? It is completely disgusting! Y'all need to get your minds out of the septic tank OR I swear on a stack of holy Bibles, I will cram a suppository in each every one of y'alls' mouths if you can't keep the subject matter to at least a PG-13 rating."

"Well, that particular question *was* more interesting than the ones like 'Have you ever masturbated?'" Della quantified. "Oops! We are not allowed to say that word in front of

Sonia." Theatrically placing her hand over her mouth, she loudly whispered, "Masturbate."

Muted giggles erupted. We all knew that Sonia didn't like talking about sex, and the subject of masturbation was absolutely off limits. Della delights in making people, especially Sonia, feel uncomfortable, albeit in good humor. This topic was Sonia's "sacred cow," never to be touched or discussed and certainly never to be verbally barbequed and eaten; Della was about to light the charcoals on Sonia's fire pit.

"How about substituting that...word...for 'teasing the weasel' or 'applying the hand brake'? Would those be age-appropriate terms?" she asked, devilishly shaking her curly, brown head.

Inari interjected, "At the Bunco party Sonia said that she has never masturbated. Remember, she said it's nasty, and it goes against her religious beliefs. Also, you will go to HELL if you masturbate." Honesty radiated from her soft-as-a kitten's-ear face. "HELL, Sonia said. Hell is a very bad place. In Indonesia, the penalty for masturbation is decapitation." Inari had no idea she had just opened up a can of hot, shaken-up beer.

By that time, we had eaten most of our gourmet lunch and the waitress had poured the contents of the fifth bottle of wine into six crystal glasses around the table. Covertly, Mavolyn grabbed the bottle and poured the remaining wine under the table into her usual nondescript, plastic roadie cup. I, of course was the abstemious chauffeur and drank Diet Dr. Pepper. Della raised her stemmed glass in a toast, "Cheers! And here's to seeing Sonia in HELL!"

A collective resounding, "CHEERS!" rattled the room, as well as the numerous bottles in The Bottleneck's cellar.

"Jesus, Mary and Joseph! That does it!" Sonia shrilled.

"Now, don't bring the whole family into our conversation!" wryly taunted Della.

"That does it!" Sonia shrilled. "I'm going to treat y'all just like my three boys and cram a roll of toilet paper in those potty mouths." We watched the small, upright figure rise in sanctimonious indignation and storm off to the bathroom. Dynamite under a short tennis dress—that is Sonia. There's a hidden charge, and when ignited, everyone better take cover. I was rather nervous about Sonia's return. I could absolutely see her returning with an armful of toilet paper, soap, or a couple cans of disinfectant spray for a thorough moral cleansing of the team.

I thought it might be best to get back to the topic of fashion. Clothes have a non-verbal language that can either whisper the stylish elegance and grace of a woman's soul or scream, *I buy everything at TG&Y*.[4] I asked Inari what language her inner fashion was speaking, and she meekly suggested a neon outfit with vibrant oranges, yellows, and pinks.

"Oh, Inari. We can't possibly wear vivid colors on the courts. We would be human targets, sorta like clay pigeons at a skeet shooting range," Mavolyn countered. "Do you recall Point Taken? Last year they wore electric blue uniforms; one of their opponents hit a powerful cross-court forehand shot and pounded the Point Taken team member smack in her Gucci. The ball hit her so hard, it knocked out

◇◇◇◇◇◇◇◇◇◇◇◇◇◇◇◇◇◇
4. T.G.& Y was the predecessor to today's discount stores, Dollar General and Dollar Tree. Due to inflation these old timey dime stores are now dollar stores.

one of her ovaries right there on the court."

"Yeah, I remember that match. That gal laid in a fetal position, hands grasping her crotch, with spit bubbles frothing out of her mouth. That was a strange deal," Della confirmed.

Mavolyn continued with *sotto voce* affirmation, "No, Inari, we have to wear something that blends into the landscape of the court."

With a twinkle of sudden mischief, Inari peered over her round spectacles and suggested, "Well, if you want uniforms that blend into the green tennis courts, why not those camouflaged coveralls that people use to go hunting?"

A drunken, thoughtful silence descended over the table. The possibility had a sudden, profound brilliance.

BR broke the silence and slapped her knee with mirth, "Honey, I think that is a great idea!" She lifted her half empty glass to Inari.

Everyone boisterously lifted their glasses with approval. Inari beamed with delight.

"Cheers!" We were excited. We might be very different individuals, but we seemingly were cut from the same camouflage cloth, ready to strut on the catwalk.

"Dang! I'm feeling a little gassy. I shouldn't have eaten those fig dumplings," Starr said, accompanied with a small burp. "Or maybe it was the leftover fried gizzards I ate for breakfast this morning." Lifting her right cheek slightly, she shot a small mud duck® from her badonkadonk.

"Dadburnit, Starr," BR gasped. "That smells like a

petroleum factory in Beaumont."

Sitting cattywampus on her chair, Starr earnestly rebutted, "It just comes out without permission. I don't do it on purpose."

Returning from the bathroom (thankfully without an armload full of cleaning products), Sonia caught a whiff of Starr's Texas Oil Boom. " What in Christ's name?! I leave for two seconds and chemical warfare has erupted."

Pointing back at the bathroom, Mavolyn ordered, "You need to go to the porcelain timeout chair. NOW!"

Our team decided to call the new clothing line "the Hunt Collection." This would be a trend-setting new look, a hillbilly hunting safari motif to reduce the appearance of our lunch lady arms, slenderize our Howdy Dowdies, and obscure our wrinkly knee caps. True utilitarian *panache* captured the appeal of sportsmanship, and the fabric didn't make us "sweat bullets." This was the game-changing style the whole team wanted to achieve.

BR sewed everything with help from Inari, who was terrific with a hot glue gun and glitter. They stitched and pasted camouflage Spandex mini-skirts, with sewed-in safety orange-colored shorts. Apparently humans can see this bright color, but wild animals can't. So we figured it would be a perfect disguise from the floozy felines. Norma helped with knitting thin piping for the edges of the skirts in the same orange. Camo short-sleeved shirts were tailored into tank tops to fit every bust size on our team. Modified lightweight shooting vests with shotgun shell pockets were redesigned for storing tennis balls. Rubber-soled Justin Roper boots completed the ensemble. The uniform combined functional style with a bulletproof feel and redneck *savoir faire.*

For accessories, Starr and Mavolyn created gorgeously strung shotgun shell necklaces with matching earrings. *Bijoux* brooches were handcrafted from deer antlers found at my ranch, exuding a gamey flair with a dash of ladylike nuance. Iris Apfel, one of the in-house designers at YSL, once said, "The only thing that separates us from the animals is our ability to accessorize." Well, if that is the case, then our team's accessories were "killer," so to speak.

It's a Ball team uniform

"As accessories go, a rifle says so much about a woman," Della deadpanned.

"Are you kidding me?" retorted Mavolyn, surprised that Della would even consider garnishing our outfits with gunnery. "According to USTA rules, firearms are prohibited on the tennis courts."

"I was just teasing. Don't get your ovaries in an uproar." Della laughed until the tiny lines around her eyes crinkled into little fans. "I wouldn't dare think about wasting a bullet on one of those Alley Cats."

The only thing left to decide was hats. Baseball caps are

the tennis queen's tiara. Around town this is the secret Masonic sign. Nine times out of ten, if a woman is sporting a baseball cap, she is a tennis player.

"I know a place in Marble Falls that sells hunter orange caps," Norma suggested. "I saw them at Kowboy Kountry Konvenience & Gas. They had a deer head with big antlers on the front and the caption, 'Nice Rack!'"

Kowboy Kountry Konvenience is located on the outskirts of Marble Falls off Highway 71. You can buy beer and bullets at the same place—I don't know of any place in Texas where a person can buy ammo and alcoholic beverages at the same time. That seems like a bad combination to me. The shop is next to what used to be known as Cathy's Custom Cuts & Nail, a women's hair salon and nail boutique. Last year the city council made Cathy change the name. Every Friday night after the high school games, the local teens always changed the letters on her plastic signage. On Saturday mornings the whole town would wake up to an ad for a very different establishment: "Cathy's Custom Cunts."

These hats would be the *piece de resistance*, the crown jewel on our heads. "Yes!" we brayed in raucous unison.

From an outsider's perspective the uniforms may seem homespun and unsophisticated, a bit like Scarlett O'Hara's "drapes" dress in *Gone With the Wind*. What many folks don't realize is that the famous curtain frock was in fact 16 yards of lush Italian cotton velveteen with gold silk tassels. It was an expensive gown! And even though Scarlett may have been a downright conniving bitch, her makeshift dress seduced Rhett Butler, resulting in her third marriage and rescuing the Tara plantation from financial ruin.[5]

Not long after our uniforms were finished, Mavolyn called an emergency meeting. She had heard through the grapevine what the C4 women would be wearing this season. Sitting around her kitchen table, we felt like guitar strings, strung up tight, as if the lightest touch might make a horrible sound. We were fearful that those hoity-toity tiger moms would once again steal the spotlight from the floor show.

"Well, they have a tailored, black pinstriped uniform inspired by a man's business suit. It was designed by Ralph Lauren," Mavolyn said this quickly, hoping that speed could diminish the pain of the news, like ripping off a Band Aid. But still the wound was exposed and the scabby truth hurt, nevertheless. The Alley Cats hired Ralph Lauren because one of the gals on the C4 team is his niece. Occasionally, he and Andy Roddick play tennis at Capitol City Country Club for charity functions, along with other famous luminaries. Members have these stars sign their tennis bags and brag that they are actually friends. It is total crap!

A huge, deflated sigh gusted around the table.

Mavolyn continued, "It's no surprise that the outfits are extremely provocative. The dresses exaggerate their tiny wasp waists, accentuate their long, shapely gams, and display more cleavage than legally permissible. They have red silk Salvatore Ferragamo power ties, matching sweat

◇◇◇◇◇◇◇◇◇◇◇◇◇◇◇◇

5 Why is Scarlett O'Hara a romantic heroine? Although I appreciate her scrappy ingenuity, I still think she was a self-absorbed, slutty bitch, a drama queen, and a gold-digger obsessed with social status…much like our archenemies, the Alley Cats. The mere fact that so many people admire Scarlett as a woman of refinement and poise, elevating her to goddess status despite her flaws, is a little creepy to me. Quite honestly, I can't stand her guts!

bands, caps, panties, and lipstick. Supposedly they look like the Robert Palmer girls from that 1980's 'Addicted to Love' music video." Mavolyn paused for a moment and then exhaled in defeat. "I bet the Alley Cats look awesome."

"Those COCK SUCKERS!" screamed Della, slamming her fist on the table in complete frustration. "Why do they always have to outdo us? I am sick and tired of always playing second fiddle to them. It just doesn't seem fair."

Our excitement seemed to have evaporated. It's easy to get sucked into a vortex of disappointment, and everyone was crestfallen. We knew the Alley Cats' uniforms would be talked about in Austin for weeks, and probably featured in *Texas Monthly* and *Tribeza* magazines.

"Girls, girls!" I said, trying to restore order, "Come on, y'all. We can't let this thing get us down. Let's not waller in self-pity. If we do, then those bitches at C4 have already won the season. Clothes may say a lot about a woman, but our uniforms certainly can't determine the outcome of a match. The ONLY factor to winning is how well we hit that tennis ball. And I'm sure the ball doesn't care who is dressed in the most fashionable *or* the most expensive uniform." I paused for dramatic effect. Then I really let them have it. "PULL YOUR HEADS OUT OF YOUR VAGINAS! It doesn't matter what we wear on the court." Sometimes you just have to put things into perspective.

The team bowed their heads, embarrassed that they had let the uniform situation psych them out. Perhaps clothes communicate something important, but the girls all agreed that what matters is the person inside the clothes—both on and off the court. That alteration in attitude was the real game changer. We were now ready to start the season!

6

Road Blocks, Rivals, and Revenge

Standing in a parking lot inhaling the hot, early morning air blended with faint wafts of coffee, I felt like Marlon Brando in *Apocalypse Now*. The only difference is that to me, Brewed Awakenings coffee (instead of napalm) smells like victory. This was our team's checkpoint to carpool for "across town" tennis matches. It was in close proximity to the elementary school for those insane teammates who hadn't closed up the baby-making shop until recent years. This was also the ideal spot to mix our traditional pregame Café Latte Vodka Mocha for the gals who needed a little extra kick before competitive play. (Vodka is the preferred alcoholic beverage for most tennis bitches…along with tequila, gin, and of course we mustn't forget wine.)

"I don't think I could live without coffee," Sonia said, holding her grande, double espresso close to her heart, savoring the aroma. "I drink about ten to twelve cups of bean juice every day." Indeed, Sonia did consume a vast amount of coffee. She needed it to keep up with those wild-ass boys. Quite honestly, I think Brewed Awakenings owns the mortgage on her house.

"Hell, yeah. You do drink a lot of coffee," Della confirmed. "Why do you think Juan Valdez named his donkey after you?"

"You know, I am in my happy place and I will ignore your sarcasm." Sonia clutched the warm paper cup with both hands and gazed into it, almost hypnotized by the brew.

Patiently waiting for BR, Mavolyn opened the back hatch of her enormous, dual-wheeled Ford Expedition; everyone unceremoniously threw racquet bags in the back, plopping them on top of each other like sofa pillows. Seven passengers piled in the seats, including Velveeta, Della's yellow cat, who is part tabby, part ocelot. The cat confidently bounded into the SUV as Della stowed her portable litter box in the back. Velveeta goes everywhere with Della, so it almost became normal to have her accompany us to all of our matches. By end of the season, we had accepted Velveeta as our team's mascot. Without instruction Velveeta instinctively followed Della to the courts. She would sit near the net posts like a wide-eyed umpire at the US Open. Quite remarkable! It was amusing to have her with us, except when she made use of that litter box, which would cause a pungent vapor, similar to a bag of fried pork skins, that enveloped the vehicle. In those moments, emergency evacuation was necessary; on two occasions the team had to leave the contaminated car on the side of road and walk to the match.

My Aunt Idalee and Uncle Roscoe had a cat as attentive and smart as Velveeta. Her name was Miss Trixie, a black Burmese. They absolutely adored that cat and treated it like a child. Adorned daily with colorful bonnets, she also had a red patent leather chest harness and matching leash. She was potty trained and did her "business" on daily walks, never needing a litter box.

Miss Trixie often traveled across the United States with Aunt Idalee and Uncle Roscoe. On one summer road trip to Yosemite National Park, Uncle Roscoe stopped at a gas station to fill up their brand new 1974 Chevy Impala. Aunt Idalee got out of the car to purchase banana moon pies and Big Reds, leaving the windows down and Miss Trixie unattended in the back seat on her special crocheted pillow. Within ten minutes they were back on the road, driving to their campsite. As they motored down the interstate, a steady *thump, thump, thump* began to sound.

"Idalee, what's that hullabaloo outside?" Uncle Roscoe asked. *Thump, thump, thump.* "I think I will roll up the windows. Maybe that racket is the wind."

"I have no idea. I hope it's not the engine," said Aunt Idalee, head cocked, listening to the noise. "Did you get that extended warranty? I'd hate to be stuck out here in BF Egypt and have to pay for an expensive repair." Turning to the back seat, she suddenly noticed that no cat sat upon the pillow! "Miss Trixie. Miss Trixie. Where are you, little snuggle kitty?" she called, thinking the cat might be under the car seat. But no cat appeared, and Aunt Idalee screeched in alarm, "Roscoe, I can't find Miss Trixie. Did you take her out to go potty?"

"No, I thought she was with you," Uncle Roscoe answered.

Thump, thump, thump—the noise against the back door was unremitting. Simultaneously, Uncle Roscoe and Aunt Idalee realized what it must be.

"STOOOOOP!" Aunt Idalee shouted so loud her uvula

swung from the back of her throat to the front of her teeth.

Uncle Roscoe slammed the brakes so hard it caused their heads to ricochet off the dashboard. As quick as a flash, they jumped out of the car. There dangled Miss Trixie, her red leash caught on the door's locking mechanism. The constant knocking had rubbed half her hair clean off, and she was limp. Apparently, she had leapt out the window to make a rest stop of her own and gotten snagged.

The pulverized pussy was alive, but she was never the same. Repeatedly banging her head on the car door left Ms. Trixie permanently cross-eyed, with a tendency to loll out her tongue and a pronounced lisp: "Meowth." After the unfortunate accident there were no more road trips for either the black cat or Aunt Idalee and Uncle Roscoe.

Since Velveeta follows Della everywhere without a leash, she's in no danger of meeting a similar fate. But in other regards, Mavolyn's SUV was like the clown car at a three-ring circus. I swear Ringling Brothers and Barnum and Bailey couldn't compete. Our routine of packing an implausible amount of tennis gear and people into a 24 cubic foot vehicle is just as funny, but minus the big, floppy shoes, red ball noses, and maybe a little less makeup.

This particular match was about 45 miles away because the country club was in an obscure place near Granite Shoals. "I just can't figure out why we have to drive so far. That country club shouldn't be in the League," Norma bellyached. "It's not even a genuine clubhouse…more like an abandoned FFA pole barn. Besides, it absolutely *drives me crazy* that we have to play tennis in the middle of a dusty pasture. And even stranger, we have to share a water trough with cows, goats, and sheep. It's unsanitary!"

She bent over her cup, lapping up coffee like an animal in a mock demonstration. "There has got to be some USTA ruling about not drinking water with horned creatures on the court. Can't their club just install regular water fountains?"[1]

"*Drive me crazy?*" Inari lifted an eyebrow, not comprehending the slang term. "Where is this place called Crazy?"

"I'll tell you where Crazy is," Della piped in. "In Texas, Crazy is about 15 miles from Podunk, just southwest of East Jesus, and down a dirt road from Bumfuck."

"That's right! And just up the street from that country club we're driving to this morning." Norma was clearly perturbed that she had to drive to the hinterlands of the Hill Country.

"I don't know what y'all are griping about. My boys *drive me crazy* all the time. It's not that far from here.," Sonia murmured, more to herself than the group.

"No, Inari. Don't listen to them. Crazy is not an actual place. But crazy is drinking from a cattle trough!" Mavolyn put her two cents worth into the conversation. "I brought my own drinking water and I suggest everyone fill their bottles to the brim. It's going to be another hot day."

◇◇◇◇◇◇◇◇◇◇◇◇◇◇◇
1 To be fair, the water trough was actually equipped with two spigots, one for the animals and one for the players, and a barbed wire fence rigged up down the middle so the animals couldn't cross over and interfere with the game. So techincally, we weren't sharing the same drinking water with the animals. However, it was true that the location of the country club was quite a distance from Cedarway. But despite the long haul, I found it rather entertaining to have cows and other cud-chewing livestock quizzically standing by the fences, spectators at a strange farmhouse version of the French Open, watching us play tennis.

"Oh, I think I get it!" Inari chirped, a row of white teeth flashing, "It is one of those old Southern sayings."

Everyone nodded their heads, glancing back over their shoulders at the little figure stuffed in the third seat of the truck. Sometimes conversations were so fast paced and off-the-wall we forgot that our accents and vocabulary could befuddle anyone not born here.

"Damn it! We are always waiting for BR," Starr grumbled from the back. "What is her deal?"

Punctuality was not an attribute all our team members share. Seven o'clock "AIS" (Ass In Seat) was our scheduled "ETA" at the parking lot. For these game days, I traveled twenty miles on Hamilton Pool Road from our ranch in Cypress Mill. On early mornings, I drove the small, winding country road in a beat-up Big-10 pickup with Sheila, our blind pet kangaroo, the family dog, Fred, and my hubby, managing to be on time. However, it never failed; BR would always arrive late with some lame excuse as to why she was delayed. We had heard everything from "a tube of Vagisil looks like toothpaste at 6:00 a.m." to "chopping morning wood" with her husband. Despite BR's inevitable delays, we always managed to arrive at the matches on time.

"Remember last week? BR said she was late because her dog got sick. The critter got into the dirty clothes hamper and ate the crotches out of her panties," Della casually replied while sipping her coffee. "She had to take the poor thing to the vet and Roto Rooter its stomach out. Hell, I would have just let nature take its course and pulled out the underwear on the other end. Why waste money on a vet?"

Ignoring Della, Sonia muttered, "Well, I like to get to the courts early so we have time to warm up before the match," and tapped a caffeine-driven 60-beat-per-minute rhythm with her shoe.

Cradling her cup with both hands, Norma said, "All I know is…you should be grateful."

"Grateful? What should I be grateful for? BR is going to make us miss a match one of these days," Sonia replied, exasperated.

"You should be grateful because Starr is not driving carpool this week," giggled Norma, hiding her face behind her cup.

Starr's booming voice reverberated from the back seat, "Hey! I'm a good driver. Why don't you like me driving the carpool?"

"Starr, you drive well," Della said, jumping into the fray. "It's just that every time you drive, you make us listen to you caraoke♔ to ABBA."

"That is not true. I let y'all listen to other bands on the radio," countered Starr.

"Oh, yeah. You're right! Not only do we get to hear ABBA, we also listen to the Captain and Tennille." Setting aside her coffee for a big bite of a blueberry scone, Della reminisced, "I swear, last week when you drove us to Round Rock, my sphincter twitched for almost four hours after repeatedly listening to that song, 'Do That to Me One More Time.' The thought of Tennille and the Captain humping is just downright gross. Quite honestly, I don't get it. I had sex with my husband last month, why would I want to 'Do That to Me One More Time'?" Della said, nonchalantly wiping away crumbs. "The way I see it, having sex once a month should be sufficient for people married over five years." Della feels that God's gift to women was a vibrator. What's the purpose of mattress dancing with an overweight, middle-aged sweaty man on top of you?

"Yeah, Starr," exclaimed Mavolyn. "Just because you're a newlywed doesn't mean the rest of our libidos beat to the same song...I wonder if the Captain ever took that stupid sailor's cap off," she mumbled under her breath. "I bet he's balder than a bull's balls."

"The Captain and Tennille are a dynamo singing duo. They have had several gold and platinum albums, and I'm sure they have won one of those little gold megaphone-thingy music awards," Starr retorted, defending her musical repertoire and her favorite singing group.

"That little gold 'megaphone-thingy' is a Grammy," Della schooled her. "Grammy is the name my kids call their grandmother and she is old. That is exactly what the Captain and Tennille are—OLD. They play that geriatric stuff on eight track tapes for senile people in old folks homes."

"Well, you had to have least liked 'Muskrat Love'," Starr said earnestly.

"Oh, I remember 'Muskrat Love,'" Inari said with excitement in her voice. "In Japan we would sing karaoke to that song. It made a funny animal sound...*squeak, eek, eek, eek, squeak*...a Muskrat."

With a completely deadpan face, Della explained, "Inari, that isn't a Muskrat. It is the sound of Starr passing gas."

At that moment the huge SUV exploded with laughter.

Everyone cried with hilarity except Starr, who quietly chugged her Café Latte Vodka Mocha and muttered, "Y'all are mean. I happen to like ABBA and the Captain and Tennille. They never make me flatulent."

"Well, that's about the only thing that doesn't make you serve up air biscuits," Della cynically retorted.

A car horn blared across the lot as BR roared ninety-to-nothing toward us in her immaculately restored 1964 Toyota Land Cruiser. Screeching to a stop, she parked across two spaces; the gun rack mounted on the back window popped loose, and shotguns bounced inside. We all ducked, certain that one of them would go off. Oddly, fifty or so adhesive Kotex napkins and puss pads polka dotted the vehicle like an arts and crafts project from panty camp. The door opened and two long, tanned legs emerged. Agitated, BR grabbed her gear, locked the door, and bounded for Mavolyn's SUV.

"I wonder what her excuse is this time," Norma commented.

"I heard you, Norma!" BR said, annoyed. Quickly jumping in the front seat, BR tossed her racquet bag in the back and nearly hit Sonia in the head. "Let's go!" she demanded.

Mavolyn started the truck, and faster than a jackrabbit high-tailed it out of the lot. Five, four, three, two, one… we have liftoff! Our heads smashed against the headrests, drool rolling into our ears from the white-knuckled, G-force acceleration—zero to 75 miles per hour in 2.8 seconds. It was an instant facelift: lips, cheeks, and neck pulled back tighter than a cowboy's Wrangler jeans.

After the adrenaline rush of Mavolyn's rocket style take-off diminished, Della broke the silence. BR had been quietly sulking in the front seat, and in typical Della-style, she bluntly asked, "What's wrong with you?"

"What's wrong? What's wrong, you ask?" BR said, wavering on the edge of tears. Clearly, her dark Oakley sunglasses were an attempt to mask the previous ones she had shed. Pausing for a moment to gain her composure, she cleared her throat. A sense of anticipation came over us all. "Yesterday I got one of those online 'buy one get one free' coupons for a facial and a haircut at Inner Beauty. You know the beauty parlor I'm talking about? It's the place close to C4."

We nodded. Inner Beauty is Austin's most ritzy-titzy beauty salon; their motto is "Because everyone knows Inner Beauty doesn't always get you laid." This is where the elite discreetly meet for specialized treatments ranging from computerized haircuts to hemp hair tinting and follicle stimulation, as well as Botox, Restylane, micro-dermabrasion, and uterine rejuvenation.

"Well, while I was in the dressing room changing out of my clothes and putting on a robe, I bumped into 'Cindy with an S' from Capitol City!"

"Get out of here! What are the odds of that?" Starr frowned.

"Cindy with an S" is known to introduce herself at tennis matches and social events by extending her fingertips for a halfhearted handshake and announcing in a condescending tone, "Hi. My name is Sindy. Cindy with an S." The whole tennis community of the surrounding metropolis area calls her "Cindy with an S." Several years ago she first introduced herself to me at a local tournament, and I thought, *What kind of woman instructs a person how to spell her name?* Actually, the spelling is appropriate in her case: SIN-dy. Her sinful activities are so numerous and nasty, the *Austin American Statesman* newspaper regularly reports her wild dalliances. Articles on Sindy are neither "above the fold" nor "below the fold," but directly "in the fold" on the newspaper. You might have seen her driving around town in her red convertible Ferrari with a bumper sticker that reads: "Honk if you like WEINER." That bitch doesn't even own a dachshund!

BR continued, "Sindy had just finished dressing and was leaving, but before she made it to the door, she turned around and real persnickety-like said, 'I've heard about your new team of oddballs. Y'all haven't got a chance. Losers!' Then she walked out. I didn't give it much thought at the time. I was late for my first treatment. I threw off my clothes, stuffed them into the locker, and skedaddled."

"I would have loved to been there," Della murmured heatedly. "I'd given her a piece of my mind."

"Yeah! Not only is 'Cindy with an S' a ho-bag, she's meaner than a scorpion," added Norma.

"That's not the nastiest part," BR delicately touched the sides of her sunglasses, hiding the rage in her eyes. "After my hair appointment, I went to the dressing room to change into my clothes. When I opened the locker, only my purse hung on the hook. Needless to say, I was shocked. I asked the receptionist and a couple of the beauticians to help me find my clothes. We turned the whole salon upside down, but found nothing."

Sonia lifted an eyebrow incredulously. "'Cindy with an S' stole your clothes?"

"Well, I wasn't quite sure until I saw heavy-flow feminine

pads stuck all over my truck! Then I knew it was Sindy."

Bewilderment struck us all.

BR tried her best to explain the scene—wrapped up in nothing but a white towel the receptionist had given her, and walking barefoot to the parking lot, she discovered that her vintage Land Cruiser had been totally plastered with at least two boxes of sanitary napkins and panty liners. If BR wasn't already riled up about her clothes being swiped, the idea of anyone touching her precious truck had to have pushed her over the edge. BR loved that truck. Why, she wouldn't even allow her teenage kids drive it five feet down the driveway.

"I tried to peel off the pads, but the adhesive strips pulled off the paint." BR sighed with disappointment. "After the match I have to make a humiliating drive downtown to South Lamar Boulevard with my new paddy wagon, so to speak." Shaking her head in disbelief, she went on, "There's a mechanic at Lenny's Garage who swears he can remove them without messing up the paint job. He said that he has done it before and is an expert at scraping off the sticky goo."

"Who randomly carries boxes of Kotex pads with her?" Mavolyn didn't wait for an answer. "It had to have been Sindy...or some other woman with an out of control menstrual cycle."

"What a freak!" Norma crowed.

"Go figure. I guess Sindy makes a habit of this," said BR, attempting to make sense of the hateful prank.

Looking out the window with her mental wheels working

in overdrive, Della interrupted, "This calls for revenge! Sindy needs to pay. She needs to pay dearly. What she did to BR is absolutely NOT RIGHT."

"I agree," Norma chimed in. "'Cindy with an S' is a menace to society and she needs to be stopped, as well as her trampy little teammates at C4."

"What can we do?" Starr asked, taking her last sip of Café Latte Vodka Mocha.

Norma squealed, "I love revenge! Let's beat the bitch!"

"No physical harm!" demanded Sonia. "I'm all for retribution; but whatever we do, we can't get caught or thrown in prison. We don't want to set a bad example for our kids. Can you imagine if we got arrested and thrown into the pokey? The gossip would be flying around the league on a supersonic, lip-driven Concorde."

Inari agreed, "Yeah. I don't want my children to go to school and find out that their mother is a piece of 'jail bait.'"

"First of all, we are not going to get caught or go to a penitentiary for a college-style prank," Mavolyn explained. Honking her SUV's horn ferociously and weaving through the immaculate congestion which occurs daily on MoPac, Mavolyn drove with breath-taking disregard for curves, chuckholes, and human life. She once again engaged warp speed. Resuming her conversation, "And second of all, Inari, it is impossible for you to be 'jailbait.' The term 'jailbait' is slang for a person who is younger than the legal age of consent for sexual activity. You are 41 years old and well over the legal age for sex."

Norma countered in a sultry Mae West voice, "Sex is a

misdemeanor. The more you miss, the meaner you get."
She giggled at her own quip.

Inari missed the joke. "Oh! I thought 'jail bait' were the new
inmates: they are the bait on a hook for the older prisoners
called 'Jailbirds.'" Pausing for a moment to consider,
"After all, wouldn't jailbirds eat jailbait?" reasoned Inari.

"Hey. That is a very logical point, Inari!" Starr said.

"This won't be a college-style prank…it will be better!"
Della interjected. "Sindy needs a taste of her own medicine.
We need to think of a revenge plan minus any blood," she
concluded, nodding to BR.

"What about going to Barnes & Noble's, filling out all those
loose magazine subscription cards and addressing them
to Sindy? Within a week she will be inundated with odd
magazines like *Good Housekeeping*, *Popular Mechanic*,
and *Motor Boating*. And even more horrible, she'll be
obligated to pay for all of them. Boom!" Sonia punched
the air with proud affirmation. "Now that would be some
real financial retribution. Boom! Boom!" A few more sky
punches for added emphasis.

"Did you just snort a line of stupid? That has got to be the
worst idea ever," Della blurted.

"What about a reindeer game?" Norma exclaimed with a
broad radiant grin.

Mavolyn looked doubtfully at Norma in her rearview
mirror, "What is a reindeer game?"

"You know that Christmas song, 'Rudolph the Red-Nosed
Reindeer'?" Norma warbled, "They never let poor Rudolph

join in any reindeer games…Then one foggy Christmas Eve Santa came to say…" complete with off-key, operatic trills that sent chills down our backbones.

"Enough!" Starr stopped Norma's nerve-grating rendition of the beloved song. "And y'all think my singing is bad?"

"How do we play a reindeer game?" Fascinated and suddenly charged with interest, Inari seemed ready to participate.

Unflinchingly, Norma continued, sitting forward on the edge of the car seat. It was obvious her blabber infection* had another relapse. "First we need to collect plastic and inflatable Christmas yard statues—reindeer, Santas, manger scenes with Mary, Joseph, the three wise men, camels, sheep, and baby Jesus…I'm thinking fifty to sixty figurines. Then late at night, we sneak out, haul them over to Sindy's house and set them on her front yard in various sexual positions!" Screaming with a wild surge of enthusiasm, "Wouldn't that be a hoot? Can you imagine Sindy's neighbors driving by her front yard with Santa taking it in the butt from a reindeer? Or a camel riding one of the wise men?"

"Bestiality! Let's just leave out the baby Jesus," Sonia said reverently.

"That's no big deal," Starr gruffed. "Sindy's neighbors see that kind of crap going on at her house all the time."

"Now, I don't want y'all to get all worked up over this," BR said, feeling a twinge of guilt that she might have started a Hatfield and McCoy situation. "This is my fight with 'Cindy with an S', so let's just simmer down."

"Hell, no!" hollered Della. "This is our fracas too! Right, girls?"

A resounding "Yes" echoed throughout the Expedition. At that moment, I felt like a middle-aged gang banger, with a strong urge to "pull out my Nine and bust a cap"… except I don't have a 9 mm handgun and I'm not quite sure what a "bust a cap" means.

C4 had always been Cedarway's nemesis. Perhaps it's the condescending bitchy attitudes, or maybe it's the rancorous and spiteful demeanors, or even the garish displays of personal wealth. C4 is the most aristocratic private club in Austin.[2] The prerequisite for membership is a net worth of over $20 million dollars in liquid assets. (Vacation homes, jets, yachts or executive boxes at the Cowboy Stadium don't count, sorry.) It is where the elite meet for golf, tennis, cocktails, and other swanky events. The membership is so rich, the club actually has an onsite bank and a satellite Lamborghini dealership.

And the Alley Cats are the most condescending, materialistic of the bunch. Last year their tennis team's uniform was hand-tailored and designed by Michael Kors himself. They accessorized with coordinating Tahitian black pearls, Chopard diamond earring studs, black feather boa sweat bands, and nasty attitudes.

I'm telling you, these hussies are so malicious that they can visually sodomize you with one glare! I still remember the first time I laid eyes on them—looking as irritable as

◇◇◇◇◇◇◇◇◇◇◇◇◇◇◇◇

2 I actually have no bones to pick with most of the members of C4. In fact, many of the gals are my best friends. However in every story and every game in sports there has to be a rival—a ruthless adversary. Sorry girls! No hard feelings. After the season is over, drinks will be on me at the Mean Eyed Cat.

half-starved runways models, they casually sashayed onto the tennis courts with matching Louis Vuitton tennis bags carelessly thrown over their shoulders. The pompous prima donnas warmed up for a match by preening and pretending that no one was watching them. John McEnroe's voice reverberated through my head, "You cannot be serious!"

Individually, I'm sure the C4 women are nice, but collectively they morph into a pack of ferocious she-wolves in short skirts with no inhibitions about eating your face off! This ongoing rivalry is nasty and contentious—think Oklahoma University vs. University of Texas, the infamous "Red River Rivalry" of college. Actually, depending on the time of the month, the name could be synonymous for a Cedarway vs. Capitol City Country Club match.

If narcissistic bitches had a religion, C4 would be Mecca, and sex would be like hymn singing. Unlike normal church-goers, who think once a week is plenty, these women are on their knees at least once or twice a day at the Altar of Unholy Naughtiness. Currently there is an unsubstantiated rumor floating around Austin that these she-devils have rigged up their club's ball machine as a device they call "The Pounder." According to BR's Rumor-Has-It, the gossiprazzi® swear that these horny vixens use it all day long, even while working on their ball placement shots. I thought that was what tennis pros were for! Now this story sounds a little far-fetched to me, but I can verify that these women are looser than a clown's pocket. In fact, I've actually seen one dry hump the net post on a tennis court.

Unlike these skanks who play tennis and bed-browse all day, Cedarway members are average overworked mothers and housewives with part time jobs. Beauty queens we are not! If our hair is tousled and windblown, it is not from expensive product, but from driving football practice carpool with our heads out of the window because middle school boys haven't discovered deodorant yet. Then there's flop-sweat from running a half-marathon to catch the family dog across the highway, and the faint scent of Elmer's Glue from that science fair project on "Why Asparagus Makes Urine Stink," and booger-sugar encrusted on our sleeves. Looking sexy for our husbands at the end of the day is pretty much a non-starter. Over the years, that alluring come-hither look has become a facial grimace akin to a difficult BM. Still, we do love our families…most of the time.

There are no secrets on a Cedarway team. All the little excuses people use to hide behind are stripped away, because those defenses are of no use on the tennis courts. I suppose it is the nature of the game, or the common goal that brings together very dissimilar women. It's as if there is a cohesiveness derived from the sweat, the swearing, and the insanity of the sport. As individuals, my teammates have their quirks and idiosyncrasies, as well as different political and religious beliefs. But there is always a deep respect and an acceptance for each other's convictions and eccentricities. However, those same principles and peculiarities made us subject to ridicule from the bimbos of C4.

"STOP!" Inari screamed. "An armadillo!" Her nose pressed against the car's window, she pointed to the freshly smashed creature. She sounded like a child at Christmas, "You have to stop, Mavolyn. I need to get that armadillo."

"Okay, Inari. I'm goin' to pull over, but you have two

seconds to scoop up that dead varmint," Mavolyn insisted as she slammed the large vehicle to a screeching halt, dust billowing from under the tires.

A sunny smile broke over Inari's face. She reached in the back of the SUV, removed a can of tennis balls from her bag, and disappeared out the door.

Norma chortled, "Inari, you know you can get rabies for touching armadillos?"

"You can't get rabies from armadillos, you moron," scowled Della. "It's leprosy!"

Inari tossed the three yellow balls onto the highway and, with surgical precision, scooped up the remains of the armored creature. Lickety-split, she was back in the car.

"Inari, what do you plan to do with that?" asked Starr.

"I am going to examine and then send to my uncle in Japan. He is a traditional flute maker. He would like to make a flute from the armadillo shell."

"Lovely," Sonia wrinkled her nose in disgust.

"I think I have bad gas again," Starr announced. "Yep!" A large rumble vibrated the vinyl seat. "I believe it was that hummus and boiled crawfish I ate for breakfast this morning. NOT the Captain and Tennille!" This was said with a sharp stare thrown at Della. "I should get out of the car for a moment. The bottom of my Buick is gonna fall out!"

"You get your ass back inside this vehicle now! We are going to be late for the match, and you know USTA rules state that we only have a 10-minute leeway before we default," Mavolyn firmly stated.

The pungent smell of something like rotten eggs and canned smoked oysters engulfed the inside of the SUV. Mavolyn pressed the accelerator and we tore down the highway, windows down, blowing out Starr's nasty farticles. The car filled with the sound of voices complaining about everything from feminine napkins to bad music choices, flatulence to revenge against Sindy—except Inari. The sweet thing quietly sat in the back of the vehicle, gazing at her can full of armadillo guts, Velveeta peering over her shoulder with equal curiosity. I always thought that carpooling was a great opportunity for our team to bond; that day it felt more like bondage.

At this point, you might be asking, "Why in the heck would you put yourself through this ordeal? Tennis is just a game!" But there's where you're wrong. It is the Battlestar Galactica of suburban women's sports. If an EMP, nuclear warfare, or other world-ending event struck, or if aliens came from another sector of the universe arriving to kill us for our brain matter, you would unquestionably want a tennis player in your survival group. So don't judge.

Our ragtag band decided that our rivals would not beat us this season, come hell or high water. Sure, we might not have the monetary muscle to trounce these affluent Jezebels off the court, but we had resolve and fortitude on the court. This season was going to be different; we were going to use our intelligence and energy to focus on a new tactic. Let's be honest, we hated the hoochie mamas' guts and we wanted to show them up! What better revenge than to win?

7

Don't Eat Chili and Exercise

Her name was Wilhelmina von Helmina, a strange name for a German. I heard she was good, that she would get me into shape in no time. What no one told me was the torment she would inflict in the service of that goal.

For those of you who do not know, Pilates is not for fatties or the "faint of heart." Sorry, but that's the God's honest truth. I should know. Before I began taking Pilates classes I was at least twenty pounds overweight, and a crybaby pussy. Standing in the foyer of her studio for the first time, I gazed upon a beautiful Zen-type décor appointed with moss green wallpaper, a babbling water fountain, a delicate Jewell orchid situated on the reception desk, and sandalwood incense providing aromatic *feng shui*. Then I noticed the framed black and white photographs of what looked like 1940's torture apparatuses with leashes, hooks, and gears mounted to posts, and my relaxed inner *chi* state of being evaporated. Several weeks later I learned these were pictures of Joseph Pilates's first experimental exercise machines, but at the time I thought, *What the HELL?* I was afraid I had stumbled into some amalgamation of a medieval torture chamber and an exotic Las Vegas sex lounge.

I poked my head around the corner, peering into the main part of the studio. There, several women were lying on mats: bent over, legs twisted behind their heads, pretzel-like with their behemoth buttocks stretched up toward a bamboo ceiling. I stood flabbergasted as five synchronized hineys gyrated to a methodical beat of what sounded to me like leather smacking against flesh.

A faint shadow fell across the floor of this sanctum, silhouetting a tall, womanly being. "Von, too, sree…" It was a booming, ogre-like voice, punctuated by the smack of a whip, a counterpoint to the heavy breathing of exercising ladies—all inhaling and exhaling swiftly, in unison.

Horrified, I wondered, *Was that creature spanking those ladies on their twirling, airborne keisters?* I was troubled by the idea of these middle-aged housewives reaching a collective spankasm⊛! Suddenly "whippin' your ass into shape" took on a whole new meaning.

At that point I had seen and heard enough. I turned to high-tail it (no pun intended) for the nearest exit, but a stern hand grabbed my shoulder from behind.

A voice asked, "Vhat may I helpz you vith?"

I wanted to bolt, but now the ogre was between me and the door, so I played possum. I clasped my hands over my face and hunched over into a ball. Frozen solid…except for my bladder, which tried to make a run for it down my leg. I was perversely grateful that it was that time of the month, and I was wearing what my grandmother called a "white padded pony" in my undies.[1]

Apprehensively, I turned around and found myself looking straight into rippling six-pack abs. A 6'2 blonde, in black spandex tights with matching jog bra and wooden clogs, holding a leather riding crop under her armpit—it was Wilhelmina! Fear consumed my body like a forest fire. I could feel the sanitary napkin fill to capacity!

"You doez not likez vhat you seez?" she asked, staring down at me. Strong as her body, her words were like a sledge hammer.

I tried to compose myself, but could only manage a panicked, "Uhhh, uhhh, uhhh…". *What exactly is she asking me?* I wondered, *You does not like what you see? What, the Pilates studio or your musclebound body?*

"Come," the beefy woman said sternly. "I vill show you around." Grasping my forearm with a vise grip, she led me to the back of the studio. "I am zee head Pilates instructor and proprietor of zeez establishment. My name is Wilhelmina von Helmina. Butz youz may callz me Villa. And vhat iz youz?"

Still incapable of articulating, unable to pull my eyes away from this Terminatrix, I grunted, "Uhhh, uhhh, uhhh." It was a simple question, but I couldn't spit out my name to save my life.

Willa ignored my inarticulate response. "Youz are vaiting for Starrz Noelz and Norma? Yes?" she asked.

◇◇◇◇◇◇◇◇◇◇◇◇◇◇◇
1 It was one of the many Kotex pads we salvaged from BR's truck. What the heck—they were clean and unused, why not save a little money and get something out of Sindy's mean prank?

Eyeballs ratcheting off the walls like pinballs, I searched for my tarty friends. *Where in tarnation are they? I am going to kill them.*

"Uhhh, uhh, uhh," I stammered again, as though my mouth was filled with dried saltine crackers. Perspiration began to run down my back, though I hadn't even begun to workout.

"My granz uncle is Joseph Pilates. He was a German immigrant and invented all zees machines," the Aryan goddess was pointing to oddly constructed equipment with elastic cords, steel springs, and hooks. The place looked like an eccentric porn movie set.[2] "I too am a German immigrant. My fadder and mudder came from Monchengladbach, Germany and settled in Fredericksburg when I was twelve years old."

Holy crap! I'm with the dynastic queen of this kinky calisthenic cathouse. How in the world am I going to get myself out of this situation?

I know what you are thinking—"What are YOU doing in a Pilates studio?" Staying in shape is very important for competitive tennis players, especially with this year's grudge match looming. Like most self-respecting women, I don't like gyms. I'm intimidated by the whole idea of them: sweaty female bodies pumping, grunting, and grinding with picture-perfect make up and coiffed hair. It's comparable to a bitchfest at a Junior League luncheon.

Starr and Norma suggested that I investigate Pilates, an alternative body-changing workout. They agreed to escort me to a preliminary exercise session.

◇◇◇◇◇◇◇◇◇◇◇◇◇◇◇

2 I am not saying I have ever SEEN a porn movie set.

Prior to my introductory class, we met at the Texas Chili Parlor downtown on Lavaca Street for some chili enchiladas. Starr decided to order up a "Green Bomb," a mixture of Chartreuse and Monster Energy drink. Norma concocted her own drink, self-named "The Brainchild"— Tito's vodka mixed with a grape flavor Emergen-C grape vitamin packet and a slash of Smart Water. I ordered a glass of the brew—brewed sweet tea, that is. The plan was to take separate cars after and rendezvous at the Pilates studio. Obviously Starr and Norma RSVPed "late" and I was stuck at the party without wingwomen.

"Let me showz youz more." Still clamping my arm with a plier hold, she steered me in front of what looked like a contraption the Spanish Inquisition used to interrogate Protestants. Willa reverently said, "Zeez is zee… Reformer!" A muscled arm unfurled like a Teutonic Vanna White.

When Willa said, "Reformer," I swear I heard J.S. Bach's *Toccata* organ music start. You know, that scary-ass background music you hear in old horror movies. I was looking at a horizontal platform/bed that slides back and forth, featuring several detachable heavy-duty leather straps and chains. Just laying eyes on it made my knees buckle. In my parents' Episcopal household, sex was never talked about; I learned everything by secretly snatching porn magazines from under my big brother's mattress. I still haven't outgrown the notion that the tubesteak fandango is taboo, so this was beyond any Freudian fairytale I had ever read or seen.

I had no time to stare; Willa goose-stepped me past more frightening contraptions with names like "The Tower" and

"The Cadillac," pausing to point out "Teaser bars" and the "Magic O-Circle."

Her voice filled with pride, Willa said, "My grandz uncle sayz that zeez machines resists your movements, in just zee right way, so zose inner muscles really have to work against it. Zat way you can concentrate on zee movement! You must always do it slowly and smoothly…zen your whole body is engaged."

Seeing sweaty women exercising with Velcro ankle cuffs attached to vertical poles and rubber balls clinched between their legs, I had an unsettling sense that the wings on my Maxi-pad pony were going to let loose and gallop away. It was like a twisted version of Cirque de Soleil. I had seen enough.

"Well, thank you for showing me around your studio," I smiled weakly, squirming from her grasp. Clinching my legs tightly together, I hobbled my way for the door, hoping my crouch mop wouldn't slosh out of my panties.

Just as freedom was in sight, Starr and Norma walked in the door, faces shiny as newly minted pennies. "Oh good, you're already here!" Starr whinnied, giving me an affectionate hug.

I hissed, "Where in the hell have y'all been?"

They were too tipsy from their noon toddies to notice my exasperated expression, and each hooked one of my arms, corralling me between them back into the studio.

"Doesn't it look like fun?" Norma's eyes twinkled with excitement. I responded with a firm stink eye, but my disapproval did not register.

Starr continued without taking a breath, "Norma and I are having a blast in Pilates! Plus, we have lost so much weight." Modeling her curvaceous figure, she said, "After six months of class I have dropped 10 pounds! Also, I have reduced one cup size in my right breast and two in my left breast." Cupping a boob in each hand, I thought she might improvise a puppet show, starring her lopsided meat bags.

For a brief moment, I was tempted to ask Starr how her mammaries became catawampus, but I had ogled enough bizarre things for the day.

Norma hollered, "Hey, Willa!" and then pointing towards me, "Can she do class with us?"

"Yah! But she must signz zee legal release formz," instructed Wilhelmina, her tone businesslike.

Before I could object, Norma yelled, "Yahoo!" Slapping me on the back, she gushed, "This is gonna be a hoot!"

"Uhhh, uhhh, uhhh..." I groaned, the needle of my moral compass spinning like a helicopter blade. After Willa's introduction, I really didn't want to be here. But my friends had trapped me in a barbed-wire pen; there was no escape.

After signing "zee legal release formz"—confidentiality agreement, medical release, disclaimer, and Power of Attorney—Wilhelmina von Helmina began our class.

The *fraulein* instructed Starr, Norma, and me to stand on black, padded mats facing a large floor-to-ceiling mirror. Willa started with a repertoire of stretching drills to warm up our muscles. Then we commenced a series of animal-themed exercises: The Elephant, The Weasel, The Monkey, The Seal, The Frog, The Butterfly, and The Swan.[3]

Willa repeatedly commanded, "I vant youz to engage your core," while smacking her crop and clicking the heels of her clogs together. "Engage your core!" Whack! "Your core!" Slap! At the time, I had no idea what a "core" was, and I sure as tarnation didn't want to personally "engage" anything on my body that was associated with hard "core."

Over the next hour, we performed the "Zip and Hollow," "Pelvis Elevator," "Vacuum Cleaner," and the most demented exercise of them all, the "Rectus Femoris Stretch." At that point a high-pitched sound trumpeted from Starr's rear end like a Bratwurst bugle. The whole studio of women turned and looked at us. I wanted to stand up and scream, "It wasn't me! It was Starr," but I was twisted into a ball. She began to emanate a green haze of "colon cologne" that smelled like cooked cabbage. We had nowhere to hide! As the foul smell spread, our sophomoric sense of humor got the better of us. Soon we were crying with laughter. Willa, however, was unimpressed with Starr's musical buttocks and aromatic Chanel No. 2. She had heard that tune and smelled poofume many times in the studio.

Suddenly Starr's giggles ceased, and she gasped, "Oh, my goodness! I think I'm crownin'! In fact, I know I am!" Getting up off the mat, pulling taut the waistband of her spandex yoga pants as a makeshift butt hammock, she shuffled to the restroom. "I gotta go…I gotta go, NOW!"

◇◇◇◇◇◇◇◇◇◇◇◇◇◇◇◇◇

3 I can attest, there is nothing graceful or appealing about an exercise called "The Elephant": bent over like a sandwich, ass in the air, face crammed into my poontang. A few inches and I could have literally pulled the wet Kotex pad off my panties with my teeth. I don't know about you, but I have never seen an elephant doing anything similar to this exercise either in its natural habitat or in captivity.

Laughing like a braying burro, Norma inquired in between loud hee-haws, "How many centimeters dilated are you?"

Starr slammed the bathroom door. Moans of muffled ecstasy could be heard, then thunderous vibrations like the horsemen of the Apocalypse, causing the other women to stop and cock their heads with uncertainty.

Bottom line (no pun intended) at the end of class, Starr and Norma shamed me into signing up for three months of classes. I walked out of the studio mortified, bow-legged, and sore from exercising muscles I had not used since my honeymoon. Riding a soggy white saddle for more than an hour, that old cowboy saying "ridden hard and put away wet" seemed to have more meaning and significance.

Apparently, there is an unwritten Pilates rule—don't eat anything that might cause intestinal gas within 24 hours of class. No beans, broccoli, prunes, onions, or spicy foods! Really, Willa should put it down in "zee legal release formz," before the section on "groin pulls" and "neck lacerations."

We quickly said our good-byes outside the studio. Starr had cleaned herself up and changed clothes before heading out to her secret poker game, hidden on a deserted dock on Lake Travis.[4] Norma was bounding downtown to a local orphanage, where she volunteers on Mondays and Thursdays.[5]

◇◇◇◇◇◇◇◇◇◇◇◇◇◇◇◇

4 Her addiction to gambling always had Starr sneaking around on her husband, Cedarway's police chief, hoping he wouldn't find her hiding behind five cards and a pile of poker chips. Starr started her own underground poker club. She seemed to enjoy the thrill of living on the edge, though she knew her own spouse might have to cart her off to the state penitentiary.

5 Norma's latest cause was an eight-year-old named Pearletta, a little girl whose migrant worker parents had shipped her off to an aunt in Austin who lived in an AMC Gremlin.

I felt like I had busted out of a prison. I tore off to the ranch driving Old Blue, an old four-door Chevy pickup, where Sheila and Fred were waiting for me, as well as over 150 exotic animals.[6] Now that our son and daughter were off to college, the job of feeding the animals was mine.

Now, I can grudgingly admit that Starr and Norma were right. I can't claim I'm now abdominally gifted like Wilhelmina, but within three months of starting classes, I was stronger and more limber. Those naughty-looking exercises and racy machines don't seem so ominous to me anymore.[7]

If you want to attend Willa's Pilates classes, you can find her studio in Cedarway, at the end of a shopping center, next door to the neighborhood liquor store. The main workout room has an expansive, picture frame window that looks out on the shopping center's asphalt parking lot. Every morning, between 9:00 and 11:30, rows of beer trucks arrive. The drivers time their deliveries for when Pilates classes are in session. Local drunks straggle from the liquor store with their little brown bags and sit in front of that window, similar to De Wallen, Amsterdam's red-light district. To my knowledge, it is the only Pilates studio in the state of Texas with a bleacher stand for spectators.

◇◇◇◇◇◇◇◇◇◇◇◇◇◇◇◇

6 I don't mean animals that wear edible underwear, fishnets, or pasties. Our family's ranch outside of Johnson City is home to several species of African hoofed mammals: Scimitar oryx, kudo, black buck, fallow, barasingha, and zebra, to name a few species.

7 BR's Rumor-Has-It.net tells how I lost an additional 10 lbs. at the "Cambodian weight loss clinic."

8

Dancing with the Devils

There is something special about the popping sound of a freshly opened can of tennis balls. I can't quite figure out why. Perhaps it is the gaseous aroma of formaldehyde expelling from the canister—evoking a rhapsody that only a tennis fanatic would understand. For most players that sound is akin to the exploding pop of champagne. Unfortunately, the beginning of the tennis season was not cause for celebration. No champagne for our team...our performance was more deserving of Two Buck Chuck from a brown paper bag. We were in tenth place by the end of the first half of the season; it was going to be virtually impossible to win from a third-to-the-bottom spot on the roster.

Fall Season – Austin Women's Team Tennis Schedule	1	2	3	4	5	Subs	6	7	8	9	10	11	Subs	Total
Volley Girls						0							0	
Match Makers						0							0	
Southern Slice						0							0	
Alley Cats						0							0	
Point Taken						0							0	
Sweet Spots						0							0	
Get A Grip						0							0	
Kiss My Ace						0							0	
Mood Swings						0							0	
It's a Ball						0							0	
Net Results						0							0	
High Strung						0							0	

It seemed like we had somehow angered the tennis gods; we lost more matches from bad luck than any other cause. A few examples:

"Volley Girls" versus "It's a Ball" – (12-4)

On our first official game day, Inari was injured in a scuffle with a team of Latinas. Yearning to assimilate into Texas culture, she had recently begun taking Spanish classes at Austin Community College. Resting on the side court between the first and second sets, Inari attempted to impress her Mexican-American competitors with small talk and proudly said, "Me caca es su caca." She mistook the "s" for a "c," producing a statement that they interpreted as some serious smack-talk. One mamacita pushed her into the net; Inari bounced off, landed on her caca outside of the service line and injured herself. Sonia jumped into the tangle, an attempt to defend Inari. First, emotional, high-pitched Spanglish insults were exchanged. Then after three minutes or so, arms intensely began flailing in the air, an indication the rhetoric was beginning to boil over until one of the Latina teammates grabbed Sonia in a headlock. Tantamount to a Mexican lucha libre (less the colorful masks) the three women began kicking, biting, and pulling hair until Mavolyn jumped into the middle and broke up the skirmish. As you might have guessed, the game was defaulted and we were summarily escorted out of their country club.

In addition to that, the day before the match Norma had fallen asleep while sunbathing. Four hours later someone found her in the scalding Central Texas heat, and she spent the remainder of the day in a hospital with third degree burns. Needless to say, she couldn't play tennis, so we forfeited her match. Norma spent the next three days stark naked on her sofa, smeared with aloe vera gel and shiny as a pomegranate, whimpering in pain...not from her burns but the loss of the game.

"Point Taken" versus "It's a Ball" – (15-1)

The following week our team was slated to play Point Taken. Three days before the match, Della chased down a streaker at the high school's Friday night football game. The late 1960's fad was having a resurgence among the teenagers, so parents were called to volunteer for "Booty Duty" on the sidelines, preventing likely nudie runs. That particular Friday night, a sneaky one got past the weenie watch and onto the field. Sprinting down the middle, Della tackled the kid on the thirty yard line and spanked his naked hiney raw. She twisted her ankle, but it looked as though Della enjoyed giving the young man a thrashing! Still, three days wasn't enough time for the sprain to heal.

The League's official rules allow teams to use four substitute players during the season. We invited a sweet older woman from our country club to replace Della for that match. She looked like Yoda—the same pale-green skin tone, sparse gray hairs, and pointed ears. Weirder still, she smelled like roquefort cheese and wore Crocs to play the match. Yoda-lady was partnered with BR, who wasn't impressed with the plastic clog-wearing Jedi Master. Some doubles players just *click*. They have an instant connection and intuition, playing with a natural rhythm. It was quite obvious Yoda-lady and BR were not simpatico. BR missed a simple crosscourt shot, and the squatty woman schooled her openly in front of their opponents. A big tennis etiquette no-no! Without a word, BR grabbed a water bottle full of

Gatorade, squeezed the cold contents on her substitute partner, and walked off the court, leaving Yoda-lady alone and drenched in orange. Another match forfeited.

"Net Results" versus "It's a Ball" – (10-6)

On the day we were to play Net Results, Sonia had yet another date in juvenile court, thanks to her three boys' pranks. They were always in trouble. It's ironic that the nerdy Jesus freak birthed these spawns of Beelzebub; they are like something from a Stephen King novel. Obviously those mischievous traits were inherited from their paternal side. Unfortunately, this practical joke would have got them thrown into juvie jail if it were not for the legal influence of Mavolyn's husband. In this instance, they had collected 50 or so discarded boxes from the back of the Whole Foods loading dock. Over the course of a month, they painted the boxes grey to resemble tombstones with RIP inscriptions of teachers' names and witty epitaphs. Late at night they sneaked on school property and positioned the boxes in the middle of the track field, creating a mock graveyard. The following morning, the student body and facility arrived on campus and saw the sun rising over the makeshift cemetery. Score one for the heathens! Criminal charges of vandalism and harassment were filed. After their legal ordeal was over, Sonia hauled those poor boys to church every day. On days when services weren't being held, they worshiped in the parking lot of the Holy Saints of Perpetual Indulgence Church.

As a result of the judicial court date, we had to "bench" the line—Inari and Sonia.

"Hot Flashes" versus "It's a Ball" – (16-0)

The fourth match was against the Hyster-sisters from the Hot Flash team.[1] That day I suffered from plantar fasciitis in the worst way. Crouched and hobbling around the court with excruciating pain, I looked like a member of the other team…who, by the way, hammered the crap out of Mavolyn and me. It was a singeing double beagle loss and quite honestly, we considered ourselves lucky to have scored the two zeros. That day, we couldn't even win a coin toss.

Needless to say, it looked as though the season might be a lost cause. It was truly pathetic. Our renegade team had not congealed the way Mavolyn and I thought it might. Doubts cast little shadows over our early enthusiasm. I knew there had to be a way for these eight talented women to win the League. But how?

I needed a strategy to rally these eccentric ladies. Although we were an unusually cohesive group, something I would have never expected when Mavolyn and I put the team together, we were each completely nuts … about something. Beulah Rose and her entrepreneurial inventions, Inari with her peculiar armadillo fetish, Starr's underground poker club—the crazy list goes on. I wouldn't say that my interests were nutty or odd. Since my children went off to college, my husband and I spent more time on the ranch and volunteered at a few benevolent organizations around Austin. One of these was the Orchestral League.

As a new member of the Orchestral League, I was elected chairwoman for the year's annual fund raising ball. Little did I know, the League always hands off this stressful, time consuming responsibility to rookies. Fortunately, I

---

1 My pet name for the uterine-exempt biddies on the Hot Flashes team. Hey, I'm not knocking the old gals, I'm soooo over pads and pons and PMS, I could scream!

was well acclimated to organizing big shindigs as a past sorority president, PTA school carnival councilwoman, and captain of our tennis team. Same headaches and bitchiness, different settings.

Unfortunately, the benefit was scheduled on the day my husband and son were dove hunting in Uvalde. I was set to tag along with Mavolyn and her husband, but I didn't want to be a third wheel, so I invited Starr to be my date for the event. Her husband was working the night shift at the police station in Cedarway, so she was available to play.

By normal tennis bitch standards, martinizing[2] is completely acceptable. However, for Starr, too many drinkie-poos opens Hell's gate, allowing madness and mayhem to run amok. And Lord knows Starr had a spare set of keys to that particular gate. As head of the committee for this hoity-toity party, I didn't need any embarrassments for the evening. She was therefore required to hold my hand throughout the function so I could keep an eye on her. This was a huge social ball, and the elite Who's Who of Austin was in attendance to raise money for the fine arts. I had methodically planned everything to the minutest detail. It was necessary that everything go without a hitch because as chairwoman, I would be blamed for any mishaps.

I used to be intimidated by these fancy-schmancy shebangs. I'm not the kind of girl who drifts on the prevailing winds of societal norms. Most socialites are aloof and give off an air of superiority. With very little eye contact, they often greet each other with their "air kisses" and "hate hugs." You know, those halfhearted hugs that have trivial affection and

2 Socializing combined with copious amounts of vodka martinis. Martini + socializing = martinizing.

almost no physical contact, a mere pat on the back to obey the standard social graces. And what really irks me is that the aforementioned ladies don't give compliments to other women. What's with the petty posturing? I always give other women compliments. If I notice a piece of jewelry or an article of clothing that looks spectacular on a gal, what is the big deal about giving them kudos? Then one day I came to the realization that I put my brassiere on one boob at a time, just like all those bitches. I don't care what they think. I hand out compliments like Halloween candy, give big lipstick smooches on cheeks, and strong booby-smashing hugs!

During the first part of the soiree, Starr Noel behaved herself and stuck by my side. She looked absolutely stunning. Draped in a gorgeous, shimmering emerald-colored gown with a plunging neckline that, of course, accentuated her famous Super Big Gulps. Starr Noel loves the color green because that's the hue of the felt on a poker table. And I must say, the color suited her. She looked like a million bucks that evening. How she managed to get her size 14 curves into a size 4 pair of Spanx was perplexing. Inadvertently, I held my breath all night, worried that one fatal gastric toot would blow her high-heeled shoes right off her feet.

Across the crowded ballroom stretched a panoramic scene resembling the energetic floor of the New York Stock Exchange; a vivacious consortium of social climbers, jetsetters, debutantes, and avant-gardists finely dressed in glittering gowns and tailored tuxedos buzzed to and fro. The soaring noise of festive how-do-you-dos and polite introductions folded into rapturous laughter, clinking glassware, and reverberating music from a twenty-piece big band jazz ensemble. The sound was almost deafening.

I was surprised at how many people Starr knew, mostly wealthy businessmen from her underground card club. We are not tennis partners, but she insisted on introducing me as her "partner," which caused a dog-like, confused tilt of many heads. Like a high voltage live wire, it tickled Starr to fill men's minds with the notion of women scissoring.

We spotted Mavolyn and her husband in a huddled group across the swarming ballroom, so I took Starr by the hand and we made our way through the maze of people. I could tell the conversation involved something intense and secretive: it was all Austin politicos, pressed shoulder to shoulder and whispering.

I quietly murmured over Mavolyn's shoulder, "Hey! What's going on here?"

Trying not to disrupt the talk, Mavolyn spoke softly, "One of our state's senatorial candidates has unexpectedly dropped out of the upcoming November election."

"Which senate race?" Starr piped up.

"Shhh! The state! The 24th District!" Mavolyn put a finger on her lips.

"What area is that?" Starr apparently didn't get the hint.

"Where we live," Mavolyn said crisply, flashing Starr a would you shut up look under a furrowed brow.

Without a second thought at all, Starr stepped in and with a half-smile said, "Have y'all considered Mavolyn?" I couldn't tell if she was just buzzed from the numerous vodka tonics or if she was serious.

Everyone looked up from plotting to stare at Starr. I am

not sure if her audacity or her mammaries were making the biggest impression, but their wide mouths and saucer eyes meant something.

She tried again, "Have y'all considered Mavolyn?"

The trance broke, and a man who looked like a shark in reading glasses asked, "What are you talkin' about, 'lil' lady?" He had to be the one running the show here. (Later I found out that he was a respected, long term Attorney General and leader of several congressional committees. A real bigwig in the political community.)

"I beg your pardon, sir. But there ain't nothin' little on me," Starr purred.

Nervous giggles started in the group…they all knew that debating, even in jest, with this man was like locking horns with an angry longhorn bull.

Starr was undeterred: "Last year, 59% of Texas women voted. Women are the only candidates that can statistically 'cross-over' and capture Hispanic and African American voters. If y'all want to win the 'gender gap' and the minority vote then I suggest you run a woman. Mavolyn understands women's issues, and in my opinion, she's far better qualified than most of those men running for political office. I think she would make a wonderful gynotician."

"Gynotician? What the heck is that?" inquired one of the male lackeys.

Quickly, Starr explained, "A politician with a uterus!"

The esteemed politician said nothing at first. He couldn't quite figure out what kind of a critter he was dealing with, and like most hunters, he knew it's important to know where to grab a wild thing so you don't get bit.

After a few minutes he spoke, "This position historically has always been occupied by a fella. Not a housewife, but a *man* with a college education." He gave a sinister chuckle.

"Excuse me! Where is it written that a person has to have testicles to run for this...male dominated District 24?" She put her hands on her hips. "That type of LBJ, 'good ol' boy' politickin' has been gone since the invention of boxed wine."

Hands were covering mouths to muffle snickers, and I yanked Starr's green sequined gown. I shot her a zip your damned lip expression, which of course she completely ignored.

"Mavolyn may not have a penis, but she's got a set of cast iron huevos that most men wish they owned. And she graduated from the University of Texas with double major undergraduate degrees in finance and political science."

"She can't run!" another minion said, "She doesn't have any experience."

"What's that got to do with the price of tea in China?" A high octane, vaporous sigh rose from deep in Starr's well-endowed chest. "Most of you assholes don't have the know-how or capability to run a dishwasher much less the state's business. Besides, Mavolyn's been involved in the political circus since her husband ran for judgeship ten years ago."

Mavolyn's expression showed she was torn between utter mortification and surprised gratitude.

Starr pointed the tiny plastic sword from her empty martini glass at the group, scolding, "You people are so arrogant. That's why folks hate your type. Silver-tongued windbags, that's what y'all are." This was punctuated with a small hiccup.

"For cryin' out loud, lady! Who in the hell are YOU anyway?" the leader guffawed loudly.

I dug my high heel into her toe, but she carried on. "I'm the *person* who voted your butt into office. And I'll be the same *person* who'll vote you out of office next term, you jackleg! Also, I'm a Daughter of the Confederacy!" I wondered if the last comment made it clear to everyone else that the booze was talking.

Turning from Starr dismissively, the Attorney General directed his attention to Mavolyn's husband. "Well, what do you think, Judge? Do you believe your wife would run for office?" Now, politicians and attorneys never ask a question they don't think they already know the answer to, so clearly he thought the Judge was an ally who would never cross the political Rubicon of dissension.

Everyone in the small congregation stared at the Judge's face, waiting with a look of vivid interest.

He was between a rock and a hard place; I could tell by the way he shifted his feet...but the Judge looked earnestly into Mavolyn's eyes, "Well...I do think she is more than capable of handling the pressure cooker of politics. She definitely has the intelligence and I believe a sincere passion to help people." I thought I detected an unfamiliar note of concern and tenderness in his voice. He took a deep breath, "I think Mavolyn would be a terrific Senator in the 24th District."

His reward was the expression on Mavolyn's face.

Starr's reply was a celebratory whoop of "Cheers!" She slapped Mavolyn on the back, crowing, "Now this is what I call a real 'fun raiser'! It calls for another drink!" She whistled for a waiter and signaled for a vodka tonic.

No one else was celebrating, but after a few moments of stunned silence, a quiet patter of applause started. I wasn't sure if it was for Mavolyn, or for the Judge standing up to the AG.

Mavolyn looked at her husband's face, which was beaming confidently. This show of respect wasn't common; the Judge isn't lavish with praise, and I don't think he had done anything that loving since the birth of their children. Mavolyn's job up to now had been as a stay-at-home mom and supportive political wife. At the time I thought, *This just might be a door to something new.*

"Dad-burn it!" barked the Attorney General, causing heads to turn in the direction of our little pow-wow. The old man was not taking kindly to the notion of losing control.

"What do you think, Mavolyn? Would you like to run for office? It may be too late to make a successful campaign. We are in late September and that's just not a whole lot of time to stump or build up a financial war chest." The Judge took Mavolyn's hands and cupped them into his own. It was a sweet, honest moment.

Everyone stared at Mavolyn, even the Attorney General, who was angrily gulping a recently-served Jack Daniels on the rocks.

"If I do run," she said a bit breathlessly, "and I'm not

saying I'm gonna throw my hat into the race. But if I do, I want to run the campaign MY way...no interference." I saw a familiar resolve emerging from beneath her Southern genteel exterior. "It's so late in the election cycle, I don't have time to squabble with our affiliated party. I need my energy to canvass voters." Turning to the legislative leader, Mavolyn looked straight into his craggy face, eyeball-to-eyeball, and declared with surprising authority, "Not only do I get to organize my own campaign without meddling, I also get to pick my own campaign manager."

The tension in the air was ominous. It felt like an old-fashioned gun duel from the pages of a Zane Grey Western novel. Then sinister laughter came thundering from the depths of his belly.

"You certainly can run, I'm not gonna stop ya. But you'll get none of MY support. And that goes for you too, Judge. Good luck, little lady." A gnomish grin stretched across the old politician's mouth, and as he turned to leave, he spitefully swatted Starr straight on her sugar buns. "Won't this be fun, little Miss Daughter of the Confederacy. I hope you'll be ready for battle. Say hi to Cedarway's police chief for me when you get home." Starr's eyes widened... *he knew who she was!* With that final note, he turned and walked off, disappearing into the throng of socialites, dancers, and waiters.

Someone broke the silence: "I beg your pardon, but you never answered the question. Will you run for the 24th District?"

A long, quivering sigh came from Mavolyn, and she let her eyes travel all the way around the circle. "I need to give it some quiet consideration away from the Hoop-De-Doo and rigamarole of this place." Gently squeezing the Judge's hand, she continued, "It's a big decision and I need to talk it over with my husband and family. But I'll give y'all an answer soon. I promise."

The congregation of politicos disbanded, realizing that a remarkable shift in power had occurred. Needless to say, Starr celebrated by getting completely hammered on vodka tonics. I knew I was in trouble when she started blowing cocktail onions out of her nose. Before I left to handle a situation in the kitchen, I hitched her to a table by tying the strap of her knock-off Chanel handbag around her leg, and backed that up with "Irish Handcuffs" (a cocktail for each hand). Tethered up and bound with manacle martinis, the only thing I didn't have was a Hannibal Lecter mask to prevent her from talking. I thought she would be fine for at least five minutes.

But when I came back, there was no busty beauty sitting at the table. I spotted her on the dance floor; "Midnight at the Oasis" had lured her out to shake her groove thang, and she was busy doing her own special disco boogie-down— something between a convulsing seizure and spastic twerking. Grinding away with her two martini partners, sloshing the liquid contents on the dance floor, Starr bootie bumped between dancing couples to get closer to the band. I figured she'd be okay there and prepared to head back to the kitchen…and then I spotted Sindy and her harem of hussies up front, scoping out the brass section.

Before I could get there, Starr was encompassed by all eight C4 team members. I could see the conversation getting snarky, and the claws were already coming out. When I heard Starr slur, "We could beat y'all with our racquets tied behind our backs," I started pushing people aside. But the dance floor was completely packed.

Sindy nonchalantly pushed back a strawberry blonde tendril from her updo; it pains me to admit it, but she looked gorgeous in a shimmering black evening gown and a rockin' pair of Joan Crawford "come-fuck-me" pumps. I comforted myself by thinking that the red hourglass tattoo on her back was hidden by taffeta ruffles and hand-sewn Swarovski crystal beads.

She shrugged pityingly and said, "I've seen the rankings. Sorry, but your team sucks this season, sweetie!"

Starr was so stunned that for a moment she was silent. Sindy went on, smirking cooly, "Cat got your tongue? Or to be accurate, vodka got your tongue?"

Starr belted the last of her second martini and growled, "We are gonna stomp you and your little horny toads. In fact, I'm so confident we'll beat the crap out of y'all, I'll bet one thousand dollars per member that our team wins."

Nodding confidently to her teammates, Sindy replied without hesitation, "I think we'll take that wager."

With an unflinching, deadpan expression, Starr moved the two empty glasses into her left hand. Presenting her right, she said "Fine! Let's shake then."

(Later that night, Starr confessed that she hoped Sindy wouldn't call her bluff. Even blind drunk, she knew the statistical odds for our team weren't good.)

A 15 carat, emerald-cut, yellow diamond ring introduced the arrival of Sindy's right hand. The two women shook and sealed the deal.

There was nothing I could do. I got there just as Sindy dropped Starr's hand and turned with her friends to glide poisonously away. I was all set to give Starr a hell of a lecture, but her expression was shocked and morally deflated. She knew she had just made a mistake that could end her friendship with our entire team.

9

I Have an Announcement

The next week, after our usual Tuesday practice, we picked up to-go barbecue and headed to the Texas State Cemetery for a picnic. Usually, dining with the dead is not allowed on the premises. However, being a history aficionado, Mavolyn has made friends with the groundskeeper, and he lets us sneak in the occasional chopped beef sandwich. I know that may sound a little creepy, but the 22 acres of manicured lawn and landscape is beautiful. We usually lay out an unzipped sleeping bag near the Gold Star Mothers' memorial, because no one is buried there, and Sonia thinks its important not to disturb any souls.

This was a particularly beautiful day for a picnic. Under the oak trees, some of the girls were meditating on the deep, universal questions: *What does Siri look like? Why is 'bra' singular and 'panties' plural? What is wine weenie?* BR brought a new invention: a mechanized ice chest that converted dry ice vapors to shoot out cold cans with a push of a button. It was loads of fun to watch it launch beer bullets…although one ejected a little forcefully and shot out the window of a car passing by the cemetery. BR has since worked out most of the kinks, and the new Gatling

Beergun is being manufactured in her Cedarway garage in anticipation of the beginning of the next tailgating season.

From a distance I could see Velveeta rubbing against Ann Richards's unique gravesite; that orange cat is strangely attracted to the ex-governor's tomb—a white marble headstone resembling her emblematic swirl-high hairdo. Back and forth, back and forth, gently polishing the carved monument. I imagine it was Velveeta's tender way of showing her affection to the past governor. I was thinking about her famous quote: "I've always said that in politics, your enemies can't hurt you, but your friends will kill you," which seemed particularly true after that recent, infamous night.

Norma sighed, "UMMMMM! This barbecue brisket is to die for." She has an addiction to puns.

"You are being so disrespectful," Sonia chided, her eyes rolling with disapproval.

"This isn't as good as my husband's barbecue," BR complained. "His little roadside trailer serves up the best smoked meat in town."

Mavolyn interrupted the bantering from across the sleeping bag. "I have an announcement."

Everyone looked up.

"I have been asked to replace a Texas senatorial candidate for the 24th District." Mavolyn's face beamed like an incandescent bulb.

"Oh, Mavolyn! That is terrific!" Sonia exclaimed.

"A real, honest-to-God Texas senator?" Norma gasped

behind a mask of barbecue sauce.

"That is wonderful!" BR shrieked. "It will be useful to have a political endorsement for some of my inventions and business ventures."

Inari said, "Will you be on the television? I've never known a person that has been on the television."

"Other than my family, y'all are the first people I've told," Mavolyn said in a hushed tone, pensively reflecting on a long-ago, youthful aspiration. "It has always been a dream to work in politics." The forgotten goal was now resurrected. Even though the odds were against her in this senate race, she felt inspired to take on a new challenge and perhaps reinvent herself. "It will be an uphill battle, so I will need y'all's support and help for the next two months."

"Well, of course you'll have our support and help, plus anything else to spare!" Norma said without reservation. "Won't she, girls?"

Everyone nodded with genuine acceptance.

"Well, thank you. I honestly mean it." Mavolyn continued, "Part of the deal I made with my affiliated party was that I got to choose my campaign manager." Pausing for a brief moment for theatrical effect, "And guess who I have picked?" Without waiting for an answer, a slender long finger pointed in my direction. "I'm asking J. Morgan to be my campaign manager!"

I sputtered, "Mavolyn! I'm quite flattered, but I've never run a political campaign. I know nothing about it."

Waving a hand, Mavolyn said, "It's just like organizing a

society ball combined with managing a ranch."

Well, she had me there. I do know how to coordinate community shindigs, parties, and jamborees. And ranching has been in my blood for generations. Parties, rallies, and wild animals…seemed like my skills and politics could go hand in hand.

"Y'all will make a great team," BR declared with a glint of delight in her eye, shooing ants away from the onions with a *swoosh*.

A burst of congratulatory handshakes and hugs were passed around the sleeping bag along with the barbecue, potato salad, beans, and pickles. It was a wonderful picnic.

It wasn't until we were piled in Mavolyn's SUV and headed back up the MoPac expressway that the others noticed how quiet Starr had been.

Norma turned in her seat to say, "Starr, you sure are silent back there. I'm surprised you haven't insisted on playing one of those Abba or Tony Orlando & Dawn songs on the radio. Are you okay?"

"No, I'm feeling alright…I guess." She knew she had to tell the girls about the bet with Sindy last weekend. Between this secret and her three-day hangover, Starr felt like a red coal had been smoldering in her brain.

To tell you the truth, I thought the girls would have heard by now, since Sindy and her cronies are all experts at using BR's Rumor-Has-It on their smartphones. But by some miracle, that hadn't happened.

During the car ride home on Saturday night after the soiree, she had cried as she realized the consequences of what she had done. Losing a bet was one thing, but losing trust and friendships was quite another matter.

I gave her some advice: "Don't hem-haw around and go into the details, just tell them plainly and quickly. It hurts at first, but then it's over and you're relieved. Afterwards just give it some time, the wound will heal. Trust me."

I heard Starr take a deep breath, "I have something to tell y'all." She murmured so low that the words seemed to lose themselves in the big car.

"What is it? I can't wait to hear!" Inari gleefully said. "We've had one exciting thing happen today. Maybe we will have one more and then another! What is that saying, good things come in threes?"

"No, Inari. It's bad luck that comes in threes. It's in the Holy Bible," Sonia stated.

Della pounced. "What? Now, where is that written in the Scriptures, Sonia? I don't think the word luck is even mentioned in the Bible."

Before Sonia could rebound Starr interrupted, "Excuse me, y'all, but I really need to say something. It's about last Saturday night…"

Diving headfirst into the deep abyss, she revealed the whole episode. It took her 30 seconds to explain the truth; the ensuing freakout lasted 30 minutes. I won't go into a detailed description of the wailing and gnashing of teeth…I don't think my friends would allow their kids to read this and learn the kind of words their mommas actually yelled.

"You did WHAT?!" Mavolyn boomed loudly, causing the windows in the truck to vibrate. The SUV swerved across three lanes traveling southbound, crossed the median and juddered onto the Missouri Pacific railroad tracks. I thought we were going to end up in the ditch on north MoPac! No one could catch their breath until the car was back on our side of traffic again.

Mavolyn continued, "Never mind the fact that gambling is illegal. But did you ever stop to consider us? After all, we're teammates!" I've never seen Mavolyn so peeved. "Besides, you know I'll be running for public office. Remember, that was YOUR idea! I can't be associated with some type of gaming scheme."

"I'm sorry! I don't know what got into me!" Starr wailed, slouching down in her seat. "Sindy just made me so angry. She was eyeolating[☙] me. I was watchin' her across the ballroom, gigglin' and whisperin' with all her other country club clits. I knew she was talkin' about us." A small remorseful sigh. "Sindy's like a mule. Mules have no self-confidence unless there's other horses around. So, all I was plannin' to do was corral Sindy off to the side, by herself and give her a good tongue-lashin'. But I couldn't cut her away from the herd. I guess I got frustrated and the wager just slipped out of my mouth without asking permission from my brain. Besides, I know we can beat those slapdicks," Starr added, trying to sound upbeat.

For a moment, we sat dumbfounded, silently staring out the windows at the road with eyes that did not really see.

Mavolyn broke the silence and snapped, "I'm not sure what a slapdick is…much less what a slapdick does, but I am sure that $1,000 multiplied by eight teammates is $8,000!

Do you realize we have only a 12.5% chance of winning? Those are not great odds for our team. That would have been a nice-sized chunk of change for my campaign, I might add!"

Norma roared, "Mother-flippin' pancakes! I hadn't done the math in my head until you mentioned it. $8,000!"

"Sweet Mary's ass and the donkey she rode on!" Sonia yelped, her face like Judgment Day. "$8,000! How could you do such a thing without asking us?"

"WTF!" shrieked Della. "I don't have that kind of money just sitting in a cookie jar for a rainy day."

It was as though Starr had woken a den of sleeping bears. "Now, Della, don't get all pissy on me," she said defensively.

"Pissy? Pissy? I'm about to reach over this seat, put you in a headlock, and punch you in the throat. How's that for getting all pissy?" Della said.

"Starr, you let your mouth write a check that your ass couldn't cash," Inari said, shaking her head.

We were all shocked by Inari's clever turn of phrase, but not as shocked as we were by the reckless bet.

I'm sure Starr felt everyone's eyes boring holes into her head. Looking remorsefully around at our traumatized faces, she sniffled, "Fine! Just toss me away like an empty beer can in a ditch beside Highway 71."

She went on, pleading, "I don't know what more that I can say other than I'm sorry. I'm truly sorry. I know I shouldn't have made that bet with Sindy and the Alley Cats." I know she longed to disappear, the thought of hiding in the back trunk with Velveeta and the nasty kitty litter box I'm sure crossed her mind.

There was nothing more to say. Money and time were tight for all of us. None of us had regular working jobs, let alone the extra cashola to cover an $8,000 wager. She was always doing something a little edgy and potentially illegal—including underground poker games and multi-level, pyramid gambling schemes. I suppose it is in Starr's outlaw DNA (all those nooses in her family tree), or perhaps she liked the cat-and-mouse chase with her husband. I haven't entirely figured out how that marriage works. I suppose he reluctantly turns a blind eye to her financial monkeyshines. Or perhaps he just loves her for who and what she is.

A hush draped the SUV like a wet blanket. Ten minutes passed without a word being spoken, which was a first for our group of Chatty Cathys.

Della spoke first and bitterly, "No use kidding ourselves. It's all over!"

"Della, it's just tennis. Oh…and $8,000," BR said, with a scornful glare at Starr. "We'll try and figure out a way to raise the money. I've already been thinking of a couple of marketing ideas. Bake sale, car wash, and…"

"It's not tennis," interrupted Della. "It's my marriage! I need to tell y'all something, too."

Inari said, "Wow! Three announcements in one day!"

Ignoring her, Della continued, "Number Five and I got a legal separation." (She's been married so many times, Della never calls her husbands by their names, just the numerical sequence in which she married them.) She confided, "Yep,

Number One cost me a future in the tennis industry and got me pregnant with my first kid. Number Two cheated on me. Number Three ran off with my heart and my inheritance. Number Four didn't want another baby and left me with one more kid to raise on my own. And now Number Five, well, he'll probably leave me, too. What do I do?"

Struggling for months with their conflicted relationship, she and her husband had separated and had begun attending marriage counseling meetings, hoping to resolve their discord. Solitarily brawling with her personal demons, Della's thorny as a thistle personality never revealed her personal feelings. She just kept everything bottled up inside and lips as tight as Tupperware. She would never say it out loud, but I'm sure Della was frightened by the thought that she might be a divorcee for the fifth time. Evidently things were not looking bright. The separation was not making her heart grow fonder, nor her husband's. The sad part of the situation was that she truly loved him.

Up to that moment, I had wanted to suggest we disband the team. The situation had turned into one big rusty, gnarled ball of barbed wire. One prick could cause tetanus and terrible pain. And I'd had enough pain; thoughts of the quarreling and backbiting of other teams combined with the hectic schedule and new financial problems clouded my mind like a heavy vapor. I thought, *I've had enough!*

Now, as if it were an out of body experience, I heard myself saying, "We all struggle with our marriages sometimes. But, Della, it shouldn't be those failed relationships that define you. It's the way you responded to those hitches in life. Choose them as learning opportunities instead of losses. Ultimately you've got to pull yourself together, pick up the broken pieces, and look at them—hard. The only question is how you let the experiences of those five marriages define who you are. Plainly put, you can either wallow in your thoughts of failure...or you can be happy. Della, what do you want for yourself?"

She paused for a while, letting my words sink in.

I asked, "Are you happy?"

From the depths of Della's core, a troubled sigh fluttered from her lips. "Not really," she murmured. And then she confessed, "I believe life can be better than this. I'm ready to try something different, but I'm petrified about my future and how I'm going to provide for my two kids." Della buried her face in her hands, obviously exhausted from the stress of her dilemma.

There we sat in Mavolyn's SUV, seething. Steam fogged the windows from our fuming tempers. Della's confession was kerosene on the already blazing fire of heated emotions. Everyone was pissed off or felt like they were being pissed on. It was a quiet ride home, everyone preoccupied by the questions on all of our minds: How in the HELL was the team going to dig out from the bottom and stop our losing streak? Where were we going to get eight thousand dollars? What would become of Della's fifth marriage? How would Sonia rein in her feral boys? And how was I going to run Mavolyn's political campaign?

I didn't know. But I was sure disbanding the team wasn't the answer! We were "in shit deep," up to our noses in sublime stupidity, and there was no way to climb out of our predicament other than with teamwork. It was obvious we needed each other.

10

A Voodoo Doll, Lucky Thong, and other Superstitions

That anything lucky or even magical could emanate from an inanimate object—rabbit's foot, horseshoe, four-leaf clover, or a Texas toothpick[1]—seems to any *normal* person an unlikely notion. Think again! Maybe none of my team members are in the Mensa Society, but we are smart and sophisticated women; logic should tell us that luck can never dictate the outcome of a tennis match. However, in the pockets and dark recesses of racquet bags nestle charms, talismans, rock crystal amulets, and gnarly wishbones from decades-old Thanksgiving dinners—all hidden from view until their energies are needed to endow good fortune or curse opponents on the court. The Racq Pacq is well-equipped to combat evil spirits and/or ensure victory over our enemies...I mean competitors.

I admit I feel a little weird about them. After all, one of the Ten Commandments addresses this subject: "Thou shalt not make unto thee any graven image...." Although Moses isn't around to expand on the list, I'm sure it would include dream catchers, lucky pennies, lady bugs, evil eye medallions, acorns, and scarabs, too. Besides, does

1 A specialty item made from a male raccoon's genitalia.

any rational person believe that an object can logically influence the outcome of an event? Mavolyn refers to the team's charms "Stupid-stitions"! But I know for a fact, Mavolyn carries in her tennis bag a green bumpy plastic pickle that yodels. Talisman or sex toy…who is to say? But it's in there!

I'll let you in on a secret: I have a lucky charm, too. I'm not proud to admit it, but I have an article of clothing that I wear every time I walk onto the tennis court. I've owned this garment for three years: a worn and tattered, pastel yellow pair of underwear. It's my lucky thong! The color of the lingerie has faded, as have its shape and form. It was once a very lacy and sexy panty, full of elasticity and feminine mesmeric power; now it sags like something from Edith Bunker's underwear drawer. It only hangs on my hips because I haphazardly sewed a hair tie to the waist band. It may be totally psychosomatic, but during last year's spring and fall tennis seasons, I NEVER lost a match!

Della's talisman is a bit more ominous. She actually has a voodoo doll dressed in a little fuchsia tennis outfit and cap that resembles a rival player. I've only seen it a few times; it never emerges from her bag until mystical assistance is needed during a challenging match. But I know it has dark green stains across its face, exposed tufts of cotton stuffing, and puncture wounds on lugubrious places: knees, elbows, feet, and even eyes. Della swears the voodoo doll works. I had my doubts…until that season's tennis match against the Circle X Ranch team.

There is a rumor around the league that Circle X Ranch, a neighborhood in southwest Austin, is where the town's swingers reside. They say the subdivision's H.O.A. includes access to an exclusive website: www.4sumkinkyshit. org. Consequently, my girls have nicknamed this spousal sexchange® country club, Triple X Ranch. According to Rumor-Has-It, there is an international sign that couples use to covertly announce their proclivity to *swing*: three stacked rocks on top of or at the base of the mailbox.

I don't know if it's really true…but driving through the streets of Triple X, we surveyed a terrain of xeri-scaped yards with stacks of three boulders!

"I don't understand why couples swing," Della gruffed. "Hell, I don't like having sex with my own husband. Why would I even consider having sex with some other woman's hairy-assed husband?" Not only was her comment accurate to most women's thinking, but it was an insightful disclosure regarding the status of Della's crumbling marriage.

"That is just disgusting and unchristian," Sonia crossed her arms in indignation. "Those people will absolutely go straight to H-E-double L!"

"You know, Sonia, you can say that word without actually being cursed to go there by God," Mavolyn told her flatly, voice quivering with annoyance that we were once again late for the match due to BR's tardiness. She was driving ninety-to-nothing, tightly gripping the steering wheel, zigzagging through the master plan community. Hairpin turns caused the tires to screech as Mavolyn honked at anyone that got in her way, flying down the road at delirious speeds. As always, we arrived on the courts within minutes of defaulting all four matches.

Since the beginning of the season, we had never won three lines, but that day looked to be the end of our losing streak.

Inari and Sonia (6-3, 6-1), Norma and Starr (6-1, 6-1), and Mavolyn and I (6-4, 6-4), took our matches. After, we sat in the filtered shade of a Burr oak for the last match: Della and BR vs. the Raunchies (as we liked to call them). Ripples of hallucinatory heat radiated off the pavement, the sun's waves baking like a reflector oven, melting soles off rubber-bottomed tennis shoes and our very souls.

To calm herself, Norma was rearranging her collection of racquets in her bag. That woman has more gear than any other player I have ever seen, and she names each one. The "masculine" racquets have names like Jack Pot, Tommy Gun, and Spanky. A few of Norma's feminine ones have been called Anita Roddick, Dixie, and G-String. Even though I knew I was making big mistake, I asked Norma why she did this.

She replied very candidly, "Well, the game of tennis is 55% physical, 40% mental, and 5% equipment. If I should make a bad shot, which of course is highly unlikely, I certainly wouldn't blame myself...that would encroach upon my 55% physical and 40% mental."

Here we go, I thought.

Norma's symptomatic RLS (Restless Lip Syndrome) kicked in. "You see, I hold my tennis racquets fully responsible for those poorly executed shots. That is why I name them...It takes all the guilt away from me and deflects it to someone else."

I could tell she was prepared to explain in a LOT more detail...but I was saved by the sound of angry footsteps approaching. Everyone else was excited and nervous, but as she climbed the bleachers to join us, Mavolyn looked distracted and upset.

"What's the matter, Mavolyn?" I asked, sitting next to her.

"I think I just threw up in my mouth." Dazed, eyes glazed with distress, Mavolyn whispered, "I went to the ladies room at the clubhouse to wash my hands and one of those Triple X Raunchies solicited me to spouse-swap. Do I look like a woman who puts out that sign? I'm not walking around with three rocks on top of my head. You think the Raunchy would know that my husband IS a Texas state judge? That behavior might be accepted on the national level of politics, but NOT at the local level."

Obviously, I thought, *Mavolyn doesn't know about The Cloak Room bar near the Capitol on Colorado Street—* the infamous, seedy watering hole where state legislators, lobbyists, and lawyers wet their whistles, so to speak!

Mavolyn put her head on my shoulder and cried, "I'm not that kind of a woman. Why would she ask me to do such a thing?"

Patting her back, I answered, "Honey, don't worry about it. In fact, you should be flattered."

Abruptly lifting her head from my soggy shoulder, Mavolyn snapped, "Flattered? Why in the hell should I feel any flattery? It's absolutely disgusting and not right. Those folks need to be thrown in jail."

"It's a compliment, Mavolyn," I said, trying find a better spin on this aspect of the sexual revolution for my very traditional friend. "It might have been a kinky-ass question, but she was basically telling you that she admired your beauty. Think about it; she wouldn't have asked an unattractive woman to swap with her. You are a gorgeous, lovely woman."

After a moment, Mavolyn concluded, "In a weird kind of way, that sorta makes some sense." It occurred to me that, despite her efficiency and stalwart demeanor, Mavolyn had a lot of insecurity deep down. She's an iron cactus flower, the Texas equivalent of a steel magnolia. But she'd had a whirlwind romance after college, gotten married, and then started popping out kids shortly afterwards. She had always defined herself as a judge's wife, a supportive stay-at-home mom. Any of her own ambitions as a political wonk had been put on the back burner until now.

On the tennis courts I meet so many women like Mavolyn who have lost their identities, unsuspectingly bamboozled by society to conform and accept the grown-up expectations of being a woman. I should know, because I was one of the Baby Boomer generation who mind-numbingly followed that path until I woke up and smelled the coffee. Suburban housewives' existences are usually wrapped up in their kids, a mortgage, and being a dutiful spouse. In this fast-paced world we live in, some of them have lost their identity simply running around being who they are—moms. They want a little recognition, a simple pat on the back. That is why I see so many gals on the tennis courts desperate to win a match. You see, winning brings the feeling of self-worth and respect. And as strange as it may seem, in the minds of these housewives, it is a part of regaining their value and importance. After all, there are no awards for being a good mother and wife, aside from the macaroni necklaces and handcrafted refrigerator artwork proudly given to us by our adoring children. However there is prestige, albeit a smidgen artificial, in winning a tennis match, and a collection of championship plastic medallions draped on a tennis racquet bag.

I gave Mavolyn a big hug and clasped her hands in my own. "Everyone who knows you, knows you are honest, responsible, ethical, a great mother and wife." I paused to let the words sink in. "Now, are you sure that Raunchy didn't see the lucky yodeling pickle in your tennis bag? That might have been the reason why she asked you…"

The dimple in Mavolyn's cheek registered her amusement. We both giggled, and turned our attention to the match that was about to conclude.

It was an intense match. Della and BR split sets—6-2, 4-6. The final set was a flurry of sweating and swearing, both flung across the court with the same passion as the ball smacked from side to side. Top-spin profanities smashed near the baselines, volleys of yells, down-the-line curse words hit in the alleys, and foul expletives were shot with wide-angled underspin. Some would argue that tennis is a "non-combative" sport because there is no direct contact between the players. However, the game can be anything but civil.

This match had the morbid fascination of an MMA (Mixed Martial Arts) cage fight like you sometimes see while channel surfing—the same 8-foot cyclone perimeter fence, just with a 3-foot net splitting the middle. By this time, things had gotten ugly: Della yelling "Hey, you BAMF-ers ! This isn't a dodge ball game we're playing here!" and the responding, "You know where you can stick that racquet, ass wipe."

At the switch-over, as Della sat on a bench near a water

cooler, I saw her jerk her duffle bag open and fumble inside, hunching over. I knew what she was looking for. I saw her exasperated mumbling, sweat dripping off her lips, as she covertly performed a pin-sticking ceremony. Sitting high on the bleachers, we could all see her jabbing feather-adorned needles into the mouth of the doll. (Later she swore her hocus-pocus spell was merely to cause an unspecified vocal affliction—i.e., Strep throat, tonsilitis, or even chronic phlegm—to prevent her Triple X opponents from spewing vile threats and bad "line calls.")

The heat felt like religious conviction; I'm sure the mercury knocked the tops off countless thermometers that afternoon. Even Velveeta got out of the roasting sun, leaving her customary umpire position at the net post to watch from the stands. We were all surprised at that, and I could see Della was crestfallen; it was the first time her precious pussy had abandoned her side. We knew there was nothing left to do but pray...and reach for our lucky charms!

Sonia rubbed her baptismal beads, which she kept around her neck like a noose during matches to ensure that it would not fall off. Inari wore a beautiful, sterling silver koi pendant on a red silk cord, her *omamori*. Inari said it provided a specific power: *yaku-yoke*—avoidance of evil. Starr's talisman is a pair of dried piranha earrings from South America, which she wears to every match. Whenever she needs to conjure some good fortune, she will swing her head back and forth, causing the fish to flutter and her boobs to bobble. She was wagging her head vigorously now.[2]

◇◇◇◇◇◇◇◇◇◇◇◇◇◇◇

2 She also wears them whenever she ante-ups at her underground poker games. Starr does win quite a few mixed doubles matches, as well as many poker pots. I doubt the piranhas are endowed with enchanted powers, but her bodacious ta-tas... now those might be her true lucky charms!

The score was 5-6 in the last set and a tie-breaker would ultimately decide the winners. Della and BR were visibly losing their mental mojo. All competitive sports games ebb and flow with the athletes' mental stamina, as well as their physical conditioning. It is what separates talented competitors from the true champions. The heat was overbearing, BR's energy was obviously waning, and Della was out of profanities. It seemed our team was going to lose. But then, call it fate, black magic, or some kind of kismet, a dirt dauber flew into a Raunchy player's mouth. These little wasp-like bugs almost never sting, but this one repeatedly stung the woman's tongue, tonsil, and uvula. Hysterical screams and hollers reverberated across all 24 tennis courts at the Circle X Country Club. The woman ran around the tennis net about thirteen times (we counted), arms frantically waving in the air. The hullabaloo stopped every match going, and players watched the berserk one-woman race with complete confusion.

I have only seen this much commotion on the court one other time—two tennis seasons ago. During a very cutthroat USTA final doubles tennis match, a C4 member smashed an overhead with such physical force it caused her IUD to pop out, shoot over the net like a bullet, and hit her opponent smack-dab between the eyebrows. The sheer power of that catapulted contraceptive caused the poor player to fall backwards and hit her head on the green pavement. After waking up, the woman dazedly said, "I saw twinkling illuminations just like the Marfa Lights dance across my body like little fairies." USTA officials were called to the court for a ruling. The C4 doubles team was disqualified due to a technicality (Rule 26, USTA Comment 26.4): "deliberate hindrance with an object other than the tennis ball which may cause physical harm to the opposing side." It was all anyone could talk about for weeks. In fact, *Sports Illustrated* and *Stanford Medical Magazine* published huge articles on the event, calling it "...a new aerodynamic breakthrough for use in the medical science of prophylactics." The human cannon herself is now a local celebrity and is currently negotiating a television contract for the new series "Housewives of Austin." Who would have ever guessed that a projectile-popping coochie could earn such notoriety and command a six-figure income? Hell, if I would have known that I would have been practicing a long time ago!

After the dirt dauber situation simmered down, the wounded competitor spat out the smashed insect parts and signaled that she would not forfeit the match to Della and BR. Play continued, but her lips and cheeks bloated to unnatural, Melanie Griffith-type proportions. She looked like she had overdosed on a mélange of Botox, Restylane, and Viagra. No longer able to swallow, green Gatorade dribbled from her engorged lips, staining her mouth an incandescent jade-color, as well as discoloring her chin and neck.

"Fourubbi Lovbbi," she shouted.

"What do those words mean?" asked Inari.

"I think she meant 40-love," replied Mavolyn.

We might have been willing to chalk it up to a random accident...then the situation got *really* interesting. The Raunchy woman glanced over to the clubhouse and saw the club's handsome tennis pro. As strange as it may seem, the bug-afflicted player had not realized her face had swollen into the shape of an unripened acorn squash. Her own partner was afraid to point it out, knowing the match would be forfeited.

Squash-face flirtatiously waved her hand and began to trot towards the tennis pro, cooing "Stebbia, babbeee. Itebbi istha mebbi, Sthhhepppanheee!" (Approximate translation: "Steve, baby! It's me, Stephanie!")

It was as though we had front row seats at the Alamo Drafthouse for a bad zombie flick in 3-D. Stephanie had no idea she looked like a caged creature gawping at the dazed tennis pro between the links of an eight foot fence. I'm sure he felt grateful that a steel barrier stood between himself and Stephanie. The hurt was plain even on her bloated face.

"Wabbis thaba mabber?" (What's the matter?)

Frozen with terror, the young tennis pro stared, unable to flee. Finally, he whispered, "Oh, Stephanie! I am so sorry!" and covered his eyes with his hands.

Every tennis match on the courts at the Circle X had been stopped by her previous screaming; now the other players watched with amusement. Racquets in hand, they walked closer to the scene as Act Two commenced.

"Wabbis thaba madder?"

Slowly bringing his hands down, the pro tearfully explained, "I'm sorry, Stephanie. I was told that genital warts couldn't be transferred orally."

Her answer was a shriek so loud it was heard clear across Highway 360 and caused the water in Town Lake to ripple. Then, a second high-pitched sonic boom echoed across the court, from Stephanie's partner, Candy. Apparently (and as Rumor-Has-It.net would later confirm) they had been getting doubles coaching from Steve in a different sport. Wink! Wink!

Their thundering cries echoed across the club's 1,000 acres of beautifully manicured property. Every golfer dropped their putter, every tennis player dropped their balls, and every bridge player in the clubhouse dropped their cards to cover their ears from the deafening noise. Even the squirrels that lived on the fairways dropped their nuts and stood on their haunches, paralyzed. The melodic singing of the cicadas stopped mid-chorus, and birds perched above us in the shaded boughs of the Burr oak trees stopped chirping, beaks open aghast at the sound.

In the silence that followed, Stephanie and Candy grabbed their bags, turned with indignantly swiveling hips, and marched off the tennis court. Della and BR won by virtue of default!

Screaming with delight and joy, we jumped from the bleachers, hugging each other and giving celebratory high-fives. It was our first four line victory!

"Hurry y'all. I gotta get out of here!" said Norma, anxiously cramming her numerous christened racquets into an oversized bag. The delays in this last match were going to make her late for her volunteer work at the local children's home. Helping the orphanage brought Norma a sense of completeness. She especially enjoyed spending time with her new friend Pearletta. Norma's childhood anxieties and fears of abandonment still haunted her. She didn't want Pearletta to have those same feelings of neglect and emptiness Norma experienced as a young child.

We would have loved a leisurely victory lunch, but Norma

was chomping at the bit to leave. So we settled for a handful of the obligatory snacks the Triple X's provided as the hosting team—pigs in blankets, fish tacos, HoHos—and we hightailed out of the country club. The interior of the SUV rang with cascades of laughter, nauseating examinations of blistered feet, and boisterous tales of mishaps on the court. We were so elated by a potential end to our five-week losing streak that even the loud reverberations of Starr's "Love Will Keep Us Together" caraoke🐚 enhanced the festive mood. I sat shotgun, while Della and BR sat behind me, slamming premixed Cosmopolitans out of a large thermos. Inari sat beside them with an empty tennis ball can in her lap, face pressed against the window, watching for smushed armadillos. As usual, Sonia occupied the third row, applying Sally Hansen brush-on hair removal goop while on her cell phone with the boys' school principal, discussing their water balloon condom fight in the hall during lunch break. Velveeta was in the rear trunk area scratching around, hiding a fresh batch of stinky brownies in her traveling cat box.

Mavolyn left Norma at the orphanage, Della at the marriage counselor's office, and Starr at her clandestine poker palace off of Comanche Trail. It was the our typical, twisted Texas version of Mr. Toad's Wild Ride.

11

The Daily Dish

I've always kept a journal. By jotting down private thoughts, funny anecdotes, and crazy stories, I hope to remember and pass on a few life lessons for my children—the little gems of knowledge I've learned from my experiences and the things that have shaped my outlook on life. Like pressed, preserved flowers between the yellowing pages of a leather-bound volume, capturing their ephemeral color and beauty…though many of my daily entries preserve a different kind of blossom.

Diaries are also like confessional booths, and even though I'm not Catholic I get embarrassed and sometimes even ashamed admitting some of these things on paper. But after the fact, I occasionally question the authenticity and truthfulness of certain incidents, and that's why I write them down. With this in mind, I started keeping a separate journal for the dumb-fuckery that our team went through that season. These were stories that people who aren't familiar with competitive women's team tennis would never believe. I was there, and sometimes I still don't! But the journal entries have it all in black and white:

Sunday – September 23rd

I have reluctantly become accepting of the chaos swirling around me. I suppose I have come to believe that if I don't embrace it, the bedlam might kill me. After all, it's not every day you post bail for a teammate who has chained herself to a moonlight tower on the corner of 9th Street and Guadalupe with ten other people to protest the demolition of a Texas State Landmark. Or escorting another teammate to the hospital for "hubby elbow," which has all the same symptoms of tennis elbow, but is the painful result of a different type of stroke all together, if ya know what I mean! I have found that binge tennis and hanging around seven women every day except weekends, can be a little overwhelming at times. Comparable to living on campus in an all-girls' dormitory, with all the same drama—PMS, relationship problems, money issues, and assorted emergencies—mixed together with one jigger of insanity, a splash of crazy, and a slice of wild-ass. I've come to the conclusion that this experience is preparing me for the Zombie Apocalypse. Why else would God have put me with these seven women?

I've also come to the realization that a recreational women's tennis league ain't for weak tits. I guess I discovered this about eight years earlier when I first joined Cedarway Country Club. Playing in high school and college never prepared me for the type of aggressiveness exhibited in otherwise normal ladies. And just for the record, I have played against some serious hard asses who would not hesitate to eat your face off! I often wonder how a little yellow ball can cause so much conflict.

Monday – September 24th

Under the right circumstances, when the stars align just perfectly, magical occurrences unfold as if things were simply meant to be. One of those special moments occurred today!

Mondays are the League's official match days. We played against the Match Makers, and there was serendipity involved. We won all four lines with only <u>one</u> small injury.

Mavolyn and I were playing our match next to Inari and Sonia's court and I saw the whole scene play out like a Three Stooges movie—minus the buttered popcorn and Milk Duds—a comedy in cinematic, vivid color.

Inari and Sonia were in the middle of their second set, when Inari spotted a long black, curly hair glistening in the midmorning sun on Sonia's lower jaw. "Oh, Sonia! You have a wisdom whisker!" I heard Inari exclaim.

Obviously, Sonia had never heard of a "wisdom whisker." She was plainly annoyed that Inari's head wasn't in the game, and curtly responded, "I have a what?"

Inari explained that in Japan the old men in her village let long facial hairs grow out on their black moles. They called these chin hairs "wisdom whiskers." Tradition says, the longer the whisker, the more wisdom the person possesses. I could see Inari staring through her Coke bottle glasses at Sonia's dark, two-inch, corkscrewed hair and heard her gleefully announce, "You must be very smart!"

Mavolyn and I giggled. Sonia smart? With all that unwanted facial hair she must be a frickin' genius!

It was evident Sonia was completely grossed out by the thought of such a long hair on her face, regardless of Japanese tradition. She usually referred to unwanted whiskers as "confused eyebrow hairs that lost their way." From my vantage point, it looked as though the wiry hair traveled from a more southerly direction!

"Inari, at the switch-over you have GOT to pluck that hair from my chin. I'm not sure I can continue to play tennis if that darn hair is on my face."

Mavolyn and I were both worried that there wouldn't be enough time; USTA rules only allow you three minutes. But Sonia insisted and handed Inari one of the numerous plier-like tweezers stashed in her racquet bag. I heard her tell Inari "Mexican women have strong follicles, so you might want to yank a little harder than usual." Tightly holding her racquet in both hands with a death grip, Sonia pushed forward her chin and closed her eyes. So Inari grabbed hold and gave a powerful jerk, causing Sonia's head to heave forward and slam her right eye into the butt of the racquet she was holding. Cupping her injured eye with one hand and holding her chin with the other, Sonia looked up at Inari, who was standing over her and holding a six-inch coiled hair tightly clamped in the large tweezers. Nasty! They went on to decisively win their match. It was a great example of teamwork.

(I'm pretty sure Sonia kept the hair to show her Bible study group.)

Tuesday – September 25th

Norma wanted to score some Weight Watcher points and asked me if I wanted to attend an afternoon Pilates class. I agreed with hesitation. Why? One word: Edgar!

The only man in our Pilates' group is a 70+ year-old named Edgar! He is a regular at the afternoon classes. A nice enough gentleman with a cordial demeanor, he looks similar to KD Lang, but with hairier legs. And one other exception…

Strangely, no one seems to notice but me. Bending over in the downward dog position, Edgar's oyster🦪 always rolls out of his loose-fitting gym shorts. And each time my eyes gravitate in that direction. It looks like it is made of gray, wrinkly Play-doh. When he goes into plank, it flops onto the padded mat with a muffled thud. I find myself oddly mesmerized, which scares me.

I'm not bashing old people, but personally, I think nutsacks are overrated after the age of 70. First of all, they're ugly! Balls lose their sex appeal after they drop below a man's knees. What use do they have at that age? They are only used three times a year for ABC sex.⁕ Thirdly…well, there really is no third reason. They are just hairy and gross after male menopause. Yes, I think men go through menopause. They just call it by a different name—"midlife crises." What bull crap! Look at the etymology of the word—MEN-opause. Just like MEN-struation and MEN-strual cramps. Men over 70 years old should consider getting a HIS-terectomy and chop those shriveled-up Nutellas!

Wednesday – September 26ᵗʰ

The past two weeks have been an all-out sprint. From the moment the alarm clock goes off in the morning and my feet hit the ground, it's "balls to the wall" every waking hour (I now think of Edgar whenever I hear that term!) It feels like only yesterday we were eating lunch at the cemetery and Mavolyn asked me to be her campaign manager. Since that moment I have been desperately running around in Old Blue, spearheading the campaign—setting up fundraisers, posting yard signs, mailing fliers, and scheduling speeches. The election is only five weeks away—ironically, the day after our final match against C4!

I am responsible for the overall organization of her campaign, which takes more energy and gumption than I ever imagined. Needless to say, at the end of the day, my giddy-up is gone. It's easy to wonder where time went and whether I really have it in me to do it all again tomorrow, but I'm too brain-dead tired to think, so I flop into the bed, instantly falling fast asleep.

Mavolyn, however, seems to thrive on the stress and long hours. She is in her element and glows like a pregnant woman…then again, Mavolyn might be glowing because she is sweating to death over this election. It's a tight race with little margin for error. And typical of her fastidious nature, everything has to be perfect. Regardless of the political pressure cooker, she has found strength in her cause. The election has liberated her. I am amazed at her self-transformation, finding her identity and hidden talent as a politician after all those years just accepting the traditional female role as a housewife—cooking, cleaning, and breeding. I see her passion and resolve grow with every speech she gives, every hand she shakes, and every interview that is aired on local TV. After years of supporting her husband's elections, Mavolyn has now found her voice and is stumping for her own political goals.

Mavolyn's opponent is a carpetbagger from Palestine. Della calls him a "douche bagger" and rightfully so. He is one of those typical scuzz-bucket political parasites with an over-inflated sense of worth. Deep pockets and part of the good 'ol boy boss system, his reputation as a scoundrel is known far and wide; however, he seems to get elected to everything he runs for.

Monday through Friday after playing tennis, the girls run off the court, shower, dress, and head out to the unofficial campaign headquarters at Kerbey Lane Café. In a corner of the restaurant, we have set up a makeshift office with a couple of extra cellphones and laptop computers. Coffee, coffee, and more coffee is the fuel that has sustained us. The restaurant provides us with plenty of fresh java juice, which Sonia loves. Jacked up on caffeine and able to talk up a storm (a Cat-5 tornado, that is), I appointed her chairman of telecommunications. Norma helps with the phones, too. Inari desperately wanted to be on phone duty, but her thick accent made it difficult for people to understand, so I gave her the title of Chief of Staff. She loves it and brags to everyone at the club. BR is head of marketing and research. And Starr is the CFO, responsible for keeping the finances on a shoestring budget. (I know that sounds a little strange, appointing SN as "keeper of the books" in light of her gambling, but she is a mastermind when it comes to numbers.) The toughest job was given to Della and Velveeta. They tool around the voting district in a rented U-Haul truck with posthole diggers and ready-made bags of cement, installing plywood signs along the miles of major roads and highways. It's amazing; despite all the hard work, the election has brought our team even closer together.

Notwithstanding the long hours working on Mavolyn's campaign, Starr's outrageous bet still weighs heavily on our minds. Where are we going to get the money? We're all scared that we haven't thought of anything. Mavolyn is just downright petrified that someone will find out about the illegal wager before Election Day. I've told her time and time again NOT to worry, but my words don't seem to give her comfort. Some way we have to raise that money and not let anyone know about the gambling stake...but HOW?

Friday – September 29th

"Girls Day Out"! On Fridays the Racq Pacq has regularly scheduled "lady lunches" after morning tennis clinics. These outings are more than just blabfests; they are healing rituals—a ceremonial exhale, if you will, after the week's end, a way to stop the clock, buoy the spirit with rousing smack-talk conversation, and treat ourselves to good food and drink.

As unrepentant foodies, we don't go to the regular glam palaces. We like the off-the-grid hidden gems that very few know about. Living well requires that we indulge in pursuits that are unique and peculiar—this has always been my mantra…and my sisters agree. So our "lady lunches" demand distinctive food, high-voltage libations, and some type of calorie-burning activity all in the name of "exercise." Our workout-themed luncheon this week was "Shoots & Shots" scheduled at Red's Shooting Range. Make no mistake, the shoots came before the shots! Drinking and firing guns is not a good combination, even though it is common practice in most rural counties in Texas.

Last month at our "Girl's Day Out," we took a group class and got our CHLs (Concealed Handgun License) near the ranch. It was a very educational outing in spite of Starr nearly shooting her left nipple off.

Regardless of what others may say about guns, I think it is important for a woman to defend herself and at least have the knowledge to properly fire a weapon. I've never understood why people say, "Guns kill." I saw a bumper sticker that stated: "If guns kill people, then pencils misspell words." The same logic would apply to shot glasses. Because shot glasses make tennis ladies drunk! And indeed, after target practice at Red's, the gals slammed down a few shots of tequila at a local bar. So who's at fault for getting them drunk? The shot glasses! Because it certainly couldn't be the ladies' fault for sitting at the bar!

Monday – October 1st

Game Day! It's autumn and the first day in October, but the temperature was in the 90's. Heat shimmered off the sweltering courts like the Mojave Desert. It occurred to me that tennis players have other opponents besides the person across the net. One foe is the weather. Austin's climate is unpredictable. In summer the heat indexes can reach well over 110 degrees, wind can blow to gusts up to 40 MPH, and golf ball-sized hail can come crashing down. One year we had 31 straight days of temperatures of 100+ degrees and over 100 days with absolutely not a drop of rain.

You know that foamy froth that collects on the backs of horses after a long day of riding with a saddle? Today, that same lathery spume began to ooze from under the arms, necks, and the back of the knees of our opponents, the Volley Girls. I've got that Howard Hughes "don't touch the weird funk" germ syndrome. I could handle my own kids' crappy diapers and crusty nose boogers when they were small. I can even squeeze my wiener dog's anal glands without getting squeamish. But when it comes to someone else's biological schmutz…that just puts me over the edge. My germ phobia especially kicks in after matches. It has always been a tennis tradition, win or lose, to shake the opponents' hands at the end of all matches. Not doing so is considered unsportsmanlike.

Today Mavolyn and I won our match against the Volley Girls. Even though I was excited about winning, I didn't want to shake hands. I stood in the middle of the court, trying desperately to figure out an excuse to get out of touching those sweaty women. Huffing and puffing from the heat, white stuff now collected in the corners of their mouths and that horsey butt lather oozed from the fat rolls on their bellies. I considered sticking my finger down my throat and barfing, claiming I had the flu.

Hurry and think, think, think! My brain was in gridlock, imagining those germy hands and the disgusting possibilities of where they had been. It was all too awful! So I ran off the tennis court, screaming like a half-crazed banshee woman! I mean, really now. What was my alternative? I'm a Southern woman. And Southern women are always supposed to be lady-like, polite, never hurting anyone's feelings and sensibilities regardless of the situation. So, I figured hysteria trumped bodily secretion and unhygienic crap anytime.

Regardless of my ~~mental breakdown~~ hissy fit, the whole team won again! High fives, hoots, and hollers!

Tuesday – October 2nd

I bumped into the Alley Cats at Chuy's this afternoon. Dressed in matching chartreuse Vera Wang tennis outfits with fluffy feather boa sweatbands and chunky turquoise necklaces, they stoically sat together at a round table, collectively looking like a surprised Don Knotts. Permanently raised eyebrows and puffed-up lips, it was obvious they had just come from a neighborhood Botox party. Peroxide and plastic, the blondtourage❀ sipped beer through straws, barely able to articulate vowels much less one syllable words. I'm not slamming medical cosmetology. I'm one of those aging Texas debutantes, too! It sucks getting old. Gravity and time are a woman's worst enemies. Like the Alley Cats and most mature women, I want my skin to be as firm, shiny, and smooth as an Airstream trailer, but I'm not into the needles and pain necessary to achieve that ageless look.

Last winter, my sister made a huge decision to go under the knife. She was only 49 years old, and I questioned her motives. I couldn't understand: Why such an aggressive preemptive strike against age? After all, she really didn't have many wrinkles or that wiggly iguana-like dewlap neck. She simply said that she didn't want to wake up one morning looking like she had a throw down with physics and lost.

"Facial plastic surgery is not only fantastic to stave off the 'wrinkles of time', but it is great for a 20-year marriage. After all, you want to look beautiful while faking an orgasm!"

She had a complete facial overhaul. It was a 3 ½ hour surgical operation with blepharoplasty, a neck lift, and Lipotransfer. Blepharoplasty is equivalent to a circumcision. It is a surgical procedure which removes the foreskin-like tissue from the eyelids (minus the **brit milah** religious service). Lipotransfer extracts fanny fat and transfers the globular tissue to the face. As kids I always called her a "butt head." Well, I guess I'm now anatomically correct.

Don't believe the malarkey they tell you about plastic surgery. It f-ing hurts! And NO, you will not be "up-and-at-'em" in a couple of days. She was in bed for two weeks. When she was wheeled out of the operating room after the surgery, I couldn't catch my breath. She looked like she had been wrestling with a tractor and lost. White gauze was wrapped around her head like the mummy of Nefertiti. Peering out from under the shroud were two Hop Sing eyes, puffed up and shimmering with a bluish tint. Remember Hop Sing? He was the Chinese cook for the Cartwright family on the 1960's television show **Bonanza**. On several of the episodes, Hop Sing chased Hoss Cartwright around the house with a cast iron skillet for stealing food from the kitchen. She didn't just look like him; I think during the medical procedure, the Chinese cook snuck into the operating room and whacked her a couple of times with a modern day crock pot along with the electric cord.

After I carted her home from the hospital, she woke up four hours later, crawled from the bed into the bathroom, and looked into the mirror with total disbelief. The reflection was a person she didn't recognize. At first she thought she was still jacked up from the anesthetics and hallucinating. "Who in the HELL is that?" she mumbled out loud.

For one week after the surgery, I played Nurse Ratched at the Cuckoo's Nest. I attended to all her needs: served her meals in bed, washed her clothes, and even got in the tub with her to shave her legs. Thankfully she could take a crap by herself, or I would have been changing bedpans, too.

The times when she wasn't sleeping off the double-dose painkillers and extra Xanax I administered, she was in the bathroom, freaking out. She would gaze into the mirror for hours, holding herself upright against the sink, knees buckling, faint from the sight of her swollen face. It made me wonder if the doctor accidentally gave her a frontal lobotomy, inadvertently poking the scalpel a little too deep into her face. "Please, dear God," she would beg, "Just don't let my face turn out like Donatella Versace. I promise I will NEVER have plastic surgery EVER again!" I told her it wasn't wise to make compromises with God or promises you won't keep. NEVER have plastic surgery again? Come on. Statistically women who have had cosmetic surgery once will inevitably have another procedure. It's like potato chips. You can't just eat one.

I don't think my warnings about not making promises with the Almighty impressed my sister. She sat in bed with an emotionless stare. Then again, her face was stitched up tighter than a trampoline, so I'm not sure she was capable of an animated reaction. Or it could have been those five codeine pills I crushed up and blended into her noonday smoothie.

Despite my dubiousness, today she looks great. But, it taught me a good lesson about cosmetic surgery and why I don't do pain or needles or stitches. It's simple: I don't want to be in the uncomfortable situation of making God a promise I can't fulfill.

Monday – October 8th

Game Day!

The first half of the season, Mondays were filled with disappointment. At that time, our team's proverbial fat lady was backstage warming up her vocal cords, but she had yet to sing. From the look of things, It's a Ball is pulling up from behind in the ranks. We won all four lines today!

I don't understand why women get all gussied up to play tennis. Fully coiffured, complete with face paint (lipstick, mascara, eye shadow, and blush) they walk onto the court ready for a glamour photo shoot. Honestly, I can't figure out who they are trying to impress! After all, we're just a bunch of women chasing down a stupid yellow ball. You don't need to look beautiful to win a tennis match. Hell, most of the time when I walk off the court, I look like I've been run through the wringer.

Of course, as a late bloomer, I have always thought looks aren't everything. Sweet sixteen and never been kissed.[1] Never asked to homecoming, prom, or even a single date during high school. Living in a mini-warehouse didn't help either.[2] I stayed at home most weekends, watching reruns on TV by myself, learning about humility. But I think I developed a sense of humor and a unique perspective I wouldn't trade for anything.

When I did finally "bloom" in my college years, the door to FUN finally opened...along with my legs! I wasn't a slut, I just had

◇◇◇◇◇◇◇◇◇◇◇◇◇◇

1 I practiced French kissing with our family dog, Peanut. That is until Peanut contracted cold sores. My mother said it would be a good idea if I stopped kissing the dog. My mom didn't understand. I wanted to be prepared for the day when a real boy wanted to kiss me. I didn't want it to be an awkward situation like it was the first time I kissed Peanut.

2 Yes, you read correctly. My dad was a real estate developer and built the first mini warehouse in south Houston. In the back of the project he constructed an apartment where our family lived and managed the business. It was a BIG turn off to boys who were even slightly considering asking me out on a date. My front door was a chain link fence with a padlock—a pubescent penitentiary, so to speak.

some sexual catching up to do! After all, I only got to second base with Peanut.[3] I learned quickly that my bang-bang was capable of more than just bleeding once a month. It turned out it was a virtual funhouse the other three weeks out of the month.

Tuesday – October 9th

After our morning drill with the tennis pro, Sonia requested that we meet for lunch at the club. She needed some advice about something troubling that had happened over the weekend.

Turns out, Sonia found a huge stash of marijuana in her eldest boy's backpack. She knew something was odd when she went into her son's room and found the family dog, a teacup Chihuahua, duct-taped in a file box with a tinfoil chimney. Scrawled in Sharpie pen on the outside was "Hap's Bong Box." Fortunately, the dog was okay, contently cuddled in the corner, looking as though it had been lobotomized. Still, Sonia took Hap to the vet to insure he would not have permanent brain damage.

Up until this day, Sonia had always been that nerve-grating, enabling mom who thinks her precious little monsters are <u>never</u> wrong or <u>never</u> liable for the bedlam. She was always the one pointing the finger at other kids or making excuses for her sons' misbehavior. Seems that we have a generation of those mothers. I told my kids at an early age that they better own up to their mistakes, because if you can't learn from them then you'll be left in the dust by those who <u>did</u> learn from their f-ups.

Sonia was in a bit of a quandary. Not only is she a Religipoo, but also a tree-hugging, animal rights, save-the-planet wacko. She needed to get rid of the illegal drug, but didn't know how to

---

3 I never even had one of those famous "sex talks" with my parents. I was too damn ugly in high school, so they never worried about me getting preggers. Everything I learned about sex, I learned from my dog. Thanks, Peanut!

environmentally dispose of the "devil's lettuce"—that is what she called it. In our youth, we had all known how to consume it, but unfortunately, none of us knew how to throw away pot, either.

Hashing over, so to speak, the proper way to dump the Willie Weed, an idea came to us like a puff of magical smoke. We can get rid of the ganja and earn the $8,000 for Starr's bet. We're having a 4/20👑 Bake Sale!

Thursday – October 11th

We are absolutely flirting with insanity. Desperation makes people do stupid things. And indeed, we are desperate to raise $8,000 with only a couple of weeks before our match against the pussy posse. Although the reward ratio is high, the risk is another factor. I'm not sure the team carefully thought through the chance we are taking. Selling marijuana-spiked confections is obviously NOT legal, but our backs are up against the wall. It may be the only way to earn the $8,000 ante quickly.

Our 4/20 Bake Sale is scheduled on Saturday at the semi-pro tennis tournament sponsored by Cedarway. Let me state for the record, Mavolyn has NO part in this scheme. Due to the upcoming election, she recused herself from our moneymaking project and made the whole team solemnly swear on Sonia's tiny traveling Bible never to discuss the incident.[4] Oops!

Before we start baking tomorrow, everyone has been given "marching orders" to do a little internet research for some

◇◇◇◇◇◇◇◇◇◇◇◇◇◇◇◇

4 Did you know that keeping a diary or journal can be dangerous? Such memoirs can be legally subpoenaed and used in a court of law. This is the very reason politicians like Mavolyn and CEOs of publicly traded companies never write journals. If the Feds ever subpoenaed my journals for incriminating evidence, I'm afraid my private notations would be far too racy and perverse to be read in court.

hippy recipes to camouflage the nasty taste of the cannabis. The usual culinary mass-market chefs—Betty Crocker, Mrs. Field, and Little Debbie—don't strike me as the kinda gals who would be sharing a kitchen with Bob Marley, much less toke a fat doobie. So I thought Martha Stewart might be better acquainted with Mary Jane and the two of them could hookah me up (sorry, bad pun) with some hemp recipes. Considering Martha has been locked up in a federal penitentiary, I figured she would have a whole section on jailhouse cuisine and tips about "buffin'-the-muffin" or do-it-yourself sex tools. I trolled her website and I couldn't find one marijuana recipe, not even a pot roast, or a single article about scissoring.✠ What the HELL?! Martha spent five months in the slammer for several criminal counts—conspiracy to obstruct justice, committing perjury, making false statements. Pretty heady indictments for a woman who considers herself the queen of home economics and a marketing guru of the twenty-first century. You can't tell me that Martha's stint in the big house, hanging around a bunch of horny prison bitches, teaching them to crochet jock straps for their homeboys, that she didn't get anything in exchange. No packs of cigs. No gunning✠ in the shower. No wacky weed recipes. Nope, Martha is just not that kind of a woman. She doesn't do anything for free. Under that cool and calm veneer, brass ovaries are hanging just above her skirt line. I know that bitch has a special recipe box, and she won't share. She really pisses me off! So I am improvising…and creating my own damn recipes. SCREW YOU, Martha!

Friday – October 12th

Have I completely forfeited my immortal soul? What's next? If baking pot brownies and selling them isn't bad enough, what will the team do next for money? Start a subdivision bordello like the police recently busted in Westlake? (Ironically, the neighborhood chicken ranch was just down the road from Capitol City Country Club. Hmmmm…coincidental? I don't think so!) My conscience is beginning to rub a hole in my brain.

We clandestinely met at BR's house. She has a big kitchen with two double ovens, the ideal spot to get all the baking done in one day. Also, her high school-aged kids are in the marching band and had an away football game in Lampasas, which gave us more time to bake the illegal sweets.

In BR's kitchen, all seven of us made an assembly line: mixing ingredients and marijuana into large bowls, shoving pans into the ovens, then pulling them out to cool and repeating the process over and over again. Every treat got a seven-leafed figure in green icing on top. It was a covert sign to clientele who would actually understand the message…our repeat customers!

Apparently the secret to disguising the skunk taste of grass is butter, butter, and more butter. How would we know? Well, the team does have <u>high</u> standards! We anointed ourselves as our <u>own</u> official "taste testing" panel just like the Food Channel. The only notable difference on this particular episode is the special ingredient was whacky tabbacky. And although I wouldn't vow that MY recipes were the best, I think they were damn de-fucking-licious! I just can't remember. The whole thing is a blur.

Over the afternoon, we baked and decorated 1,600 individual deserts. While we were waiting for something to come out of the oven, BR gave us a tour of her garage, a makeshift laboratory. Her husband had built an addition onto their garage to shelter all of her experimental gadgets, gizmos, and thingamabobs. The team stood in awe at the staggering view—Bunsen burners, test tubes, welding equipment, pulleys with ropes and chains, dry erase whiteboards with incoherent scribbling, computers chirping away, and odd mechanical devices whirling around. Dr. Jekyll would have felt at home in BR's garage.

She has been working on several new inventions, one of which she calls the "Power Pon," an oversized double absorbent tampon. Another, the "Vaginal Vacuum" or "Vag Vac" as BR calls it, is a douche-like disposable vacuum. BR says that every month her panties look like a TV episode during Shark Week, and she is trying to minimize the menstrual carnage not only for herself, but for others who experience the same heavy periods.

Quite honestly, I was impressed with BR's creative contraptions and her marketing gimmicks. While she was giving us a tour of her invention factory, BR came up with our 4/20 Bake Sale marketing slogan: "Our treats will put a SMILE on your face… GUARANTEED!" The advertising gimmick was provocative and bold. In spite of this, we reckoned most folks wouldn't understand the joke. And if they did catch on to the promotional witticism, people wouldn't think in their wildest dreams our team would actually sell spiked Scooby snacks at the club…the idea was just preposterous. After all, we don't look like employees at Planet K.

At last, we finished. Hazy plumes of green smoke hung in BR's kitchen like a cloudy coffee shop in Amsterdam. But, thankfully, the musky smell of marijuana was concealed by the aroma of freshly baked cookies, cakes, and muffins. Blurry-eyed and strangely dry-mouthed, we felt a euphoric silliness. Flinging chocolate chips, hurling eggs, and throwing handfuls of flour, an impromptu food fight left us laughing on the kitchen floor. For some reason it didn't occur to us that we were BAKED!

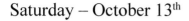
Saturday – October 13th

God help us!

Normally we devote our weekends to family time, but today we woke up early and set up two folding card tables in front of Cedarway's tennis pro shop. Inari made a poster which read:

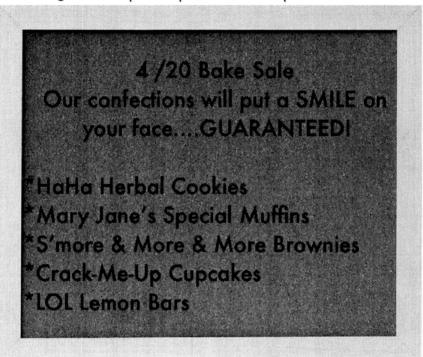

4/20 Bake Sale
Our confections will put a SMILE on your face.....GUARANTEED!

*HaHa Herbal Cookies
*Mary Jane's Special Muffins
*S'more & More & More Brownies
*Crack-Me-Up Cupcakes
*LOL Lemon Bars

We sold our freshly baked goods for $5.00 a pop, I mean a dessert. (I sound like a drug pusher!) We needed to sell all 1,600 deserts to earn $8,000. I was so nervous, fearful we were going to get busted. Clenching my teeth and Kegelling my butt cheeks, I tried to contain my nervous laughter. I unknowingly do that: laugh when I'm nervous. Today, I giggled like a high-pitched hyena for two hours straight until we closed down the 4/20 Bake Sale.

Starr sold more treats than the rest of us. I think it was because she felt remorseful about putting the team in this predicament. She wore a very low-plunging blouse and two of Mavolyn's campaign buttons strategically placed on each boob. She called them her "promotional puppets," an eye-catching way to sell the goodies, so to speak, and campaign too. In fact, Starr's advertising ploy really worked. Most of the men who walked by our ~~pot dispensary~~ table, niplashed their heads for a second look. (Mavolyn was across town at a fund raiser. If she would have seen Starr flaunting campaign buttons on her Pointer Sisters...all I'm saying is boy howdy! Mavolyn would have had a shitfit.)

The fruit of our labors—Cannabis confections

The green icing we used to make seven leaf decorations was another advertising winner. Most people thought they were lucky four leaf clovers! But those customers who understood the P.R. stunt, they were our target audience and bought lots of our cannabis confections.

Call me stupid, but I had no idea regular suburban folks were secretly into marijuana, especially those women who wouldn't dare touch a 500 calorie cake. With disregard to the nutritional value or the high sugar content, skinny bitches were lining up ten-deep to purchase our pot pastries. I know selling marijuana-laced desserts to unsuspecting people crosses the line. You don't have to tell me that it is inappropriate, but in our defense no one got hurt and everyone enjoyed their treats. At least that is how I justified it. In fact, we had many happy customers. They came back again and again, again and again to buy more.

The tennis tournament was a success, as well as our 4/20 Bake Sale. We sold 1,357 deserts! Even though I felt a twinge of guilt, it was good to have collected $6,785. WOW! I'd like to see the Girls Scouts pull off a cookie sale like this one! Yeah, put that badge on your green sash!

We still needed to sell the remaining 243 deserts and collect the balance ($1,215) of the bet. Figuring we could hawk the rest of our stash on the UT campus, once again, the team pulled together and we got it done...at least 85% done!

Monday – October 15th

We won again!

We played against the Mood Swings and I'm telling you, their name is appropriate. What a bitchy group of gals! There were arguments on all four courts regarding numerous infractions— bad line calls, "sound interferences" (USTA rule 31:1-5b) from cellphones, foot faults, and even a "let" call for a rattlesnake that slithered across the court while a point was being played.

Additionally, Starr and Norma's opponents claimed several "hindrance(s)" (USTA rule 34:12a) during the course of their match. Evidently, Starr had eaten her famous "breakfast of champions"—leftover chicken livers combined with a typical game day concoction she makes of bourbon, bitters, and green Gatorade. (She says she plays better when buzzed. Whatever!) The combination didn't settle with her stomach. Between the loud tooting and the hazmat gas wafting over the court, Starr and Norma's opponents complained about "distraction" and that they couldn't play. Honestly, I didn't blame them. I was a little upset too. Starr should have known there is a "burn ban" in effect. We haven't had rain in weeks. One fiery ember from her ass and south Austin could go up in flames!

Thursday – October 18th

If "apathy is the glove into which evil slips its hand," as Bodie Thoene claimed, then can you conclude that perversion is the cheetah-printed panty into which lustfulness slips its legs?

Today at the club's round robin practice match, we saw Norma's cheetah-printed panties. And not only did we see her underwear, we saw it catch a tennis ball. The funny thing, it looked like she enjoyed catching that ball with her Gucci. Now I know that Norma's husband has been out of town traveling quite a bit, and she seems pretty upset by his absence, but honestly, she can't possibly be that hard up?!?!

Friday – October 19th

"Antiques and Absinthe" was the lady lunch theme today. We traveled to the Round Top Antique Fair for a little "retail therapy" and along the way drank some high octane booze. Absinthe is anywhere between 110 to 144 proof. They say it's a hallucinogen…and I'm inclined to think it is true!

In an inebriated stupor, Della got in a fight with another shopper at Marburger Farms over a Black Forest carving. The story goes like this: Della was in the process of buying a unique wooden art object from Germany. She placed the antique down on a display table to dig in her purse for her wallet so she could pay the vendor. All of a sudden another women whooshed in and snatched the antique from the table. One thing you never do is F with Della if she wants something! In the middle of Tent B, Della and this random woman started screaming at each other, then began slapping and hair pulling, followed by wallering on the ground with some serious punching. They caused such a ruckus, the brawl had to be stopped by the County Sheriff.

Needless to say, we were thrown out of Marburger Farms. I thought Mavolyn and Sonia were going to crawl under a rock and hide from embarrassment. Norma, Inari, and I thought the skirmish was rather entertaining. I hadn't seen a "chick fight" since high school. Starr stood on the sidelines and made a few bucks placing odds with the other shoppers who were gawking at the tussle.

Maybe the absinthe was merely the fuel and the conflict with that random shopper was the ember which ignited Della's raw emotions regarding her failing marriage.

Monday – October 22nd

Chest bumps and high fives! (Okay, maybe not chest bumps... that might have hurt a little.) We won three of our four lines. We are moving up in the ranks quickly!

I think I've heard about every lame excuse under the sun for playing tennis poorly. Bizarre justifications from festering blisters to underwear wedgies, broken racquet strings to blinding sun, and pulled hamstrings to chafed inner thighs. However, I've never heard of "TS" until BR. TS is an acronym for tampon slippage. Apparently it was her time of the month, and as we all know, she flash floods like a Category 5 hurricane. Today, BR was at high tide. She couldn't use her patent pending Vag Vac. Something about not meeting all the FDA regulations and a battery malfunction with the sucking mechanism. So, she used her experimental Power Pon!

Working out the little kinks before mass producing the device for human use seems a logical thing to do. Experimental testing on small rodents or rabbits would have been an option. However, since Guinea pigs don't have large enough vaginas to test the Power Pon, BR decided that she would be the Guinea pig!

Unfortunately, the absorbent material used for the oversized tampon expanded ten times the estimated size she had calculated at her household laboratory. Her tummy swelled up like a pumpkin, with her bellybutton poking out like the shriveled up stem. Indeed, the jumbo period plug did stop her menstrual flow, as well as stopping the game, too!

We rushed her to Brackenridge Hospital emergency room, and the doctors popped the rag from BR's vag like a pimple. She wanted to keep the bloated tamponator in a discarded mayonnaise jar, but the doctors wouldn't let her take it home. Something about it being bio-hazardous.

Friday – October 26th

We had a choice: bowling at The High Ball on Lamar or swimming at Barton Creek Pool and looking for salamanders. Starr wanted to drive to Pflugerville for a Mexican cock fighting tournament. Of course, Sonia was absolutely appalled by the idea. Starr told her that it was no big deal and that the losing (i.e., dead) roosters were not summarily discarded, they were fried up and served with French fries and coleslaw at the concession stand next door.

Unbeknownst to us The High Ball had been demolished for redevelopment, and the pool was closed due to high levels of bacteria, so we just hung around the Cedarway country club. After all, Girls' Day Out is just an excuse to "bend an elbow" and get a little drunkiggle.

Monday – October 29th

We had a bye this week, so the team didn't play our usual weekly match. Yeah!

Instead of playing tennis today, we canvassed subdivisions, knocking on doors and asking potential voters to support Mavolyn. Oh, my aching feet!

I think I'm going to completely lose my marbles…though I can't claim to have a big marble collection. I hate to admit it, but I'm actually counting down the days until the season is over. Earlier, I thought the team might have been too far up that well known creek without any paddles. In fact, we have made a complete comeback.

Thursday – November 1st

The early voting poll numbers have come in from the County Clerk's office, and it doesn't look good for Mavolyn. There is a 20-point spread with the challenger ahead. Despite all Mavolyn's hard work on the campaign trail, her opponent's benefit of a big financial war chest and political clout have played a large part in his lead. Although all signs point to Mavolyn losing the election, she never once gives up hope. I marvel at her grace and courage.

Friday – November 2nd

Only three more days until the last match and four until Election Day on Tuesday. Everything is finally winding down...

Sometimes it's about the little things, those small pleasures that elevate your mood—a hug from a friend, a handwritten letter in the postbox, or a smile from a neighbor that make the day better. After three months of grueling foot pounding and ball busting on the courts, tennis season is coming to an end. I thought I would organize a celebratory outing, or even better, a Girls' Weekend! Although the shindig would only be for two days—Saturday and Sunday—I consider it to be a small pleasure, if you will, to lift the spirits and bid farewell to the year's Austin Tennis League.

12

A Pink Taco Spa Treatment

We were in second place! We had climbed out of our tenth place hole and staged quite a comeback! The Hot Flashes were four points behind us in third place. The Alley Cats were in first place, of course, but with only a one-point lead. It was still exasperating to have the C4 team ahead of us in the ranking. However, second place was nothing to sneeze about, even in the middle of cedar fever season! It was still just possible to take the victory if we brought out the howitzers[*] for one last, brutal match. As luck would have it, our final match of the season would be against the Alley Cats!

The team had been practicing and playing almost every day—cross training drills, local tournaments, round robins, and strategy clinics. As team captain, keeping the girls' attitudes positive was my job. I was a cheerleader of sorts, minus the perky pom-poms and STDs. Therefore, I thought we should take a little break and have a Kool & the Gang-style Ladies' Night (per Starr's musical suggestion).

Of course, coming to a consensus regarding the *what, where, and when* was always a challenge with eight opinionated women. Some of the saner ideas ranged from traveling to San Antonio and partying on the River Walk to fishing on Matagorda Island and staying at an old fishing camp. Mavolyn, of course, wanted to do something a little more economical and stay close into Austin—maybe a cultural experience like visiting the Blanton Museum followed by a night at The Mansion on Judge's Hill. Sonia vetoed that, as anything having to do with education or judges brought her sons to mind.

Inari suggested camping at Hippie Hollow.[1]

"Oh, my sweet, gentle Jesus! We can't do that!" Sonia gasped. Drenching a hand towel in icy water from a nearby cooler, she wrung it on top of her head in a kind of christening. "The people who go there are living on the dark side!" She looked like she was ready to start quoting scripture.

A patronizing chuckle burbled from Della's throat: "For crying out loud, Darth Vader! Hanging around our team all season long, what side do you think you are living on, Sonia? Because you sure aren't on the angelic side. Hell, I'm surprised none of us have gotten arrested for some of the crap we've done." Apparently she was in a mood to pull punches, because Della didn't bring up the fact that Rumor-Has-It had reported Sonia's boys had been caught throwing poop bombs at cars in the pickup line at the junior high school that week.

"Guess what?" BR announced, moving to change the

---

1 Inari had no idea that Hippie Hollow was a clothing-optional public beach and mostly a Sausage Fest. ☻

subject. It is a little ironic that, as the inventor of an e-rumor mill, BR actually avoids verbal conflicts. While we have a no-holds-barred policy on conversation—including politics, religion, and our individual ovulation schedules— she didn't want to get into another Kinky Friedman-type discussion while standing on a hot tennis court. BR had a recent "ear-to-the-ground" anecdote to broadcast. "I heard that the hellcats just got back from their girl's weekend to Napa Valley." She jealously huffed, "They rented a quaint four bedroom house in a vineyard and hired a limo, plus a personal culinary and wine tour guide."

"Geez Louise! That had to cost them a pretty penny!" Norma exclaimed, standing on a sizzling slab of asphalt, slamming a grape energy drink that stained her teeth purple. Of course, thanks to her love of wine, her teeth always seem to be that shade of violet-red, especially during the cocktail hour.

"Who is Geez Louise?" questioned Inari. "And Pretty Penny, who is she?"

Actually we were stumped by Inari's question. Geez Louise! No one could answer because we didn't know ourselves. It's funny how certain homegrown sayings creep into our everyday language without our knowing their origins.

Norma jumped in, "Perhaps Geez Louise is a distant cousin to Golly Molly. A quick criminal background check or Google enquiry might give the answer. As for Pretty Penny, very few people have seen her around these parts for months since the Bush tax cuts expired. She left town with Scott Free when inflation kicked in and Uncle Sam and Debbie Downer took over the joint. And until the Buck Stops Here, all we have now is Saving Grace."

Starr thought Norma's longwinded explanation was hysterical and loudly heehawed, accompanied with a few swinish snorts. The rest of us found no humor in the pun and glared at Starr, except Inari. She was still confounded by Norma's witty play on words.

Nobody said it…but if it hadn't been for Starr and her $8,000 bet, we probably could have taken a fancy trip. We tried to peddle the remaining 243 desserts on the UT campus, but unfortunately, that didn't happen. While we were in the middle of a big score, selling the balance of the sweets to a hipster near Union Building, Sonia thought she saw the campus police.

"FUZZ!" she screamed, voice echoing off the university's buildings. Sonia dropped the desserts, and we all scattered like roaches. Even after the 4/20 Bake Sale, we still had $1,215 to pony up before Monday's match. Needless to say, we were still Hulk raving mad at Starr, though the remaining balance was a manageable amount (about $150 each).

Maybe she knew we were thinking that very thing, because Starr broke in, "How about Lake Austin Spa? About two weeks ago at my poker tournament, I won four Mother-To-Be Indulgent Spa Package coupons for this weekend. If we split the cost eight ways between us, it would only be half the price."

"I can't believe I am saying this, but I think Starr's plan is brilliant!" BR offered Starr a big high five.

"I like it too!" Della threw her approval into the conversation. "I could use a day or two of relaxation."

I wasn't so sure. While I love the woman dearly, this spa

scheme sounded like it was going to be another one of her screw-ups, and I didn't want to be tricked into thinking otherwise. BR and Della might have been seduced by Starr's Tony Robbins-like charm, but I wasn't sure how our team of pre-menopausal women could get away with redeeming "Mother-To-Be Indulgent Spa Packages."

"I hate to be a buzz-kill, but there is just one little problem. We're *not* Mothers-To-Be," Mavolyn pointed out. I can always count on her TSA-level veracity; in her mind, regulations are never broken to accommodate a particular situation. "The coupons don't apply to us," Mavolyn continued.

"What is a Mother-To-Be?" Inari queried.

"It means you've had sex!" Norma exclaimed. Clearly, she was getting frustrated with the lengthy absence of her husband. As a broker of fine and rare wines, he had been away for three weeks in upstate New York, working for Sotheby's auction house. "I haven't had sex in so long, I think my *cherry* has grown back."

"We are too mothers!" Della firmly stated, "Every one of us is a mother. It's just that the 'To-Be' part might not be completely accurate." Her mental cogs were in overdrive trying to figure out how we could get around that requirement. "They aren't going to turn us away. What are they going to do? Make us all take pregnancy tests at Lake Austin Spa's front reception desk? I can see us now, peeing into eight cups in the foyer. I don't think so."

"Inari has a valid question," Norma argued, "What is a 'Mother-To-Be'? A mother-to-be what?" she said, an almost theatrical Shakespearian quality in her voice. "A mother-to-be…a teacher. A mother-to-be…a doctor. Even a mother-to-be…a plumber. It's seems like an open-ended designation. Besides, I doubt there are any disclaimers that state a mother-to-be has to be pregnant."

"Hey, I won those spa coupons legitimately. They are mine to use, and I think we should go!" Starr validated. Starr was hell-bent to claim this poker prize; I am sure she meant it as an apologetic gesture to the team for roping us into her wager.

"You can't win a poker game lawfully in Texas. It's illegal to gamble. You know that, Starr!" Mavolyn warned. "Besides, aren't spa gift certificates kind of a weird way to ante up? Most of your poker partners are men. I think…"

"So there it is!" BR said. Cutting off Mavolyn's attempt to filibuster, she put the motion to a vote. "All in favor of redeeming Starr's vouchers at Lake Austin Spa for this weekend say, 'Yippee'."

Six joyful "Yippees" were squealed in unison.

"And those against, please give us a 'wet raspberry' with your tongue: *Pppphhhttt*!"

"Pppphhhttt!" But Mavolyn and I were out-voted—two to six.

"Well, it looks like the 'Yippees' have it!" said BR, "Mothers-To-Be at Lake Austin Spa, here we come!"

"I just don't want us to get caught," Mavolyn said reluctantly. She didn't want us to be the party poopers. I had other reasons—related to a harrowing experience in Turkey—for not wanting to go to a spa…which ended up on Rumor-Has-It.net. You can read about it there.

"Aw, come on, y'all," Starr said. "We'll have great fun! Besides, it will be an adventure." She pulled out the spa's printed brochure from her tennis bag, and the girls gathered around to discuss the luxurious procedures they wanted to schedule: lavender aromatic body scrubs, seaweed facial wraps, and hot-stone massages—what more could a woman ask for? An adventure...?

So we made plans to have our "girls' weekend" on the following day, Saturday. Now we had to figure out how to look like we were actually preggers. Prior to making the appointment, Della, BR and Norma concocted a plan to "*legitimately*" redeem the spa vouchers as "mothers-to-be." They calculated the appropriate stages of pregnancy for each teammate according to our respective weight and size and gave that information to the receptionist when booking.

There is a NO alcohol policy at Lake Austin Spa. But as BR has said, "Friendship should be celebrated with champagne, caviar, and chocolate." Ingeniously, she and Norma had devised a way to smuggle libations onto the property and simulate a third-trimester pregnancy costume for themselves. They had rigged-up a "booze bong": three insulated bottles of Veuve Clicquot, each duct-taped around their waists. An attached section of green garden hose worked as a siphon. The "hooch pooch," as we called the contraption, fit underneath a one-piece bathing suit, the kind of XXXL swimwear advertised in a Sears catalog.

Mavolyn and I were summarily instructed to pose as first trimester mommies because we carried a little more weight than some of the others and still exhibited our "mother's apron"—the fatty, stretch-marked extra skin from previous child-bearing days. This little flabby flap never went away, and I have since claimed it as a souvenir from kids. We too sported one-piece Speedo type swimsuits.

The elaborate operation had Starr and Sonia play the parts of mothers in their second trimester. However, considering Starr's portly figure, she was expecting twins. She wore a flower printed, grandma-style bathing suit, purchased at Goodwill, as well as a Bjorn Borg red sweat band around her head. Sonia dressed in a modest tankini, her usual conservative swimwear, since in her mind any exposure of the midriff is too erotic. Before meeting the team at the spa, they had gone over to the Golden Corral and chowed-down at the all-you-can-eat buffet for an early lunch. Their belly baskets full of redneck roast beef, hillbilly hash, and senior citizen bean salads protruded like they were at least four months pregnant.

Della had purchased EPT pregnancy test kits for herself and Inari, the two smallest and thinnest women on the team, thereby appointing them as newly expectant. Somehow she had gotten the test sticks to register positive for pregnancy, and stashed them in her tennis bag for proof of their fertilization status.

"These urinary tests don't lie," Della said to the attractive female receptionist at the front desk, waving the two sticks in her face. The woman pulled back from the preggo-meters, obviously grossed out by the thought of being near an object that had been previously peed on. Without any hesitation, the receptionist allowed Della and Inari to pass as mothers-to-be…along with the rest of us!

In the sauna, aromatic mist heavy with eucalyptus and

spearmint billowed from the cedar hot box. The humid haze was so thick, it was almost impossible to see the faces of our teammates. It was so relaxing, I was glad that I had organized this final "get together" before the tennis season ended. We congregated around BR and Norma on tiered, wooden benches, sipping champagne from garden hoses, exchanging jokes, and raucously carrying on. We laughed at the total nonsense of our condition. *Eight pregnant ladies in a sauna! How did we ever pull off this shenanigan?*

Inari had volunteered to be the "snack lady" for our weekend soirée and brought appetizers, a welcome relief to Mavolyn after being responsible for the hors d'oeuvres all season.

"I made different rice dishes," Inari said proudly. "You know, you can make lots of things with rice. There is brown rice, sticky rice, jasmine rice, rice pudding, fried rice, white rice, even Spanish rice and Mexican rice, rice cakes, rice pilaf, chicken and rice, almond rice, broccoli rice casserole, red beans and rice, rice crispy treats…"

Starr interrupted, "Inari, you sound like the rice version of Bubba Gump."

Unimpeded, Inari exclaimed, "Oh, and I made a new recipe for you! Japanese style peccadillo rolls. Remember the jarred peccadillo at your Piggly Wiggly store when you were a young girl?" She unveiled a large platter of unique sushi, beautifully displayed with garnished green bean sprouts and little balls of wasabi.

Starr gulped, "Oh, Inari. That is so sweet of you to name a Japanese dish after me. What's the ingredients in a peccadillo roll?"

"Well, there is rice, of course. Cilantro, avocado, cotija

cheese, pickled armadillo, and a sprinkle of cayenne powder!" Inari said, confidently.

"Armadillo? Did you say, armadillo?" Mavolyn bellowed.

Sitting in the steam bath, we were a homely bunch of garage-sale gypsies. Salty perspiration dripping off our noses, mascara melting down our cheeks, and terrycloth towels twisted tightly on top of our heads like large cinnamon rolls...except for Della. Owing to the high humidity, her curly Shirley Temple ringlets began to frizz straight up like a troll doll. The day before, BR drove one of her franchised dog grooming vans, "Doggy Style" to Della's house and gave her a "Brazilian Blow-Out." Della was desperately trying to rekindle what little was left of the romantic passion in her loveless marriage, and thought a makeover might be the solution. Unfortunately, the beauty renovation didn't quite work out. BR had tried a new canine grooming invention—an unusual contraption combining a blow dryer, flatiron, and shears that looked more or less like a Benjamin Franklin printing press. In the kitchen, a makeshift beauty parlor, BR was busily working on Della's coiffure when the heat intensity of the machine caught her hair on fire. Flames shot from her head like a Fourth of July Roman candle, setting off the fire alarm. The Cedarway fire department came to the rescue to find them—one with scorched finger tips and the other whose smoldering hair looked like it was put out, or rather beaten out, with a wooden rolling pin.

None of us looked very beautiful marinating in the thermal crockpot, all wearing dowdy swim wear and drinking fine sparkling wine dispensed from two duct-taped faux baby bumps. But we didn't care. The heat and the aromatic scents began to melt away the stress and anxieties.

"So, what beauty treatments are everyone getting?" Norma enthusiastically inquired. "Unfortunately, BR and I can only have facials and manicures," gesturing to her booze belly.

Sonia replied, "I'm having a coffee scrub and massage, getting my girlstache♛ waxed and my ears too…plus a Bushwacker."[2]

My husband doesn't like the Brazilian look on me," said BR. "So I 'ladyscape' myself to resemble a more European country. I call it the German! A small little patch that looks like Adolph Hitler's mustache. Sometimes I look down there at my bush-tache and I have the unsanctionable urge to click my heels and give my twat the 'sieg heil' salute!"

Amused, Norma interjected, "Hell, I think I should rename my jewel box and call it the Ethiopian. I haven't had sex in so long, it's starving to death."

"TMI," huffed Mavolyn. "Enough with this talk, y'all," scrunching up her face. "Can we discuss something different than shaven chinchillas?"

Della and Inari were having something called Bamboo Bliss massages. It had something to do with shiatsu, but in my mind, there was only one way a massage could be even slightly blissful if it involved a bamboo shoot. No way I was going there. I was very cautious about choosing my treatments. I wasn't about to have my taters mashed during a massage. So I focused on my feet and face, scheduling a basic pedicure and something called an advanced

◇◇◇◇◇◇◇◇◇◇◇◇◇◇◇◇◇
2 I think you can figure out that one on your own.

resurfacing facial.

"Did you know that before the invention of nylon strings, the material that was used in wooden racquets was cats' gut?" Starr offhandedly asked. In addition to her other qualities, she possesses a plethora of abstract knowledge that could only be useful to a contestant on a twisted television game show. And she tended to show this off at odd moments. Like in the sauna.

"That is so disgusting!" Sonia cried.

"I wonder how many cats it would take to string a racquet?" Norma asked, wiping her damp brow with a towel.

With a deadpan expression, Inari quickly answered, "Probably two."

A collective "What?" rolled out of our mouths. *How would she know that?*

"Yes. Two cats. One to hold the racquet and one to string it," her smile was like a beacon. Inari made a joke! She was finally catching on to the colloquial humor. Everyone laughed out loud.

All at once, with cinematic *air de mystere,* a whoosh of hotter steam entered the sauna and caught us all by surprise. Our laughter gave way to horrified gasps. It was the Alley Cats! They stood framed in the doorway—*NAKED*—a pink taco buffet line! A faint glow from an overhead light accentuated their curvaceous, coppery bodies. We were a school of wide-mouth bass with dumbfounded expressions. It was a direct punch to the gut.

I knew I wasn't the only member of our team wondering,

Is this possible? How did they know we were here? Is this a strategy to psych us out? With only two days to the match, stakes were high, and all means of winning were on the table, including mind games.

Even nude the C4 team looked chic with perennial red lips[3] and beautifully coiffed hairdos, especially Sindy's stawberry blonde locks, which seemed to glow more intensely red than ever, like a mood ring. They possessed that certain *je ne sais quoi* attitude—that elegant haughtiness which can be so annoying on some women. Each one had a body like Barbra Eden from *I Dream of Genie*, less the gem stones in their bellybuttons.

One of the bimbos had a small tattoo. I wanted to look closer, but was afraid of having my face eaten off. I thought it looked similar to BR's ladybug, which was hidden on her right buttock, just below her panty line. BR had it inked during college, but passing time and the birth of two children caused it to look less like a cute little bug and more like an over-baked chicken pot pie. Three of the other meatslappers had bellybutton rings attached to three-inch gold chains that led somewhere I couldn't see. (A year later, walking by a skanky novelty shop on Bourbon Street, I discovered what those gold chains were attached to…) *What were 50-something year old women doing with pierced belly buttons and chains?* I quietly contemplated.

The contrast between the two teams in the steam room was as vast as the Gulf of Mexico. On one side were bronzed, nude, statuesque women and on the other, frumpy old nanny goats in grandma bathing suits. It was embarrassing. Who

---
3 Let me clarify, I mean the set of lips on their faces. At the time I was trying hard not to look *down* at their other sets of lips.

wouldn't be psyched-out by the visual disparity? I know Norma said that 55% of the game of tennis is physical, and 5% equipment, but that mental 40% might be the most important part of the sport. The cuntachos[*] had once again trumped us with a clever ploy.

Della's rich, throaty voice rang through the mist, "So, who let open the door at the weasel farm?"

I edged up close and grabbed the elastic band on the bottom of her suit. I saw the faces of my teammates, which reflected my own paralyzing fear.

At the front of the pack, I heard Sindy's velvety, toxic tones, "Well, well, well. If it isn't the Ballers." Rumor-Has-It had sent out an e-blast last week stating that the C4's had given our team the derogatory name "Ballers." Normally, I would be a little taken back by the juvenile name-calling, but in this case I didn't mind. I didn't see what the big deal was...I've been playing with my husband's ball sack for almost thirty years and consider myself a real *ball*erina of sorts. "We're just here to have a little relaxing break before our tennis match on Monday."

The other seven look-a-likes—skin unblemished with a smooth, almost synthetic appearance, void of any stretch marks or cottage cheese cellulite—stood sentinel behind Sindy. It was creepy. They seemed not from this world, more like extraterrestrial beings: plastic and peroxide Barbie doll fetuses from outer space.

Della, unflinching, asked, "What are y'all here for? Having your assholes bleached?"

I gasped. Like a hermit crab, I wanted to retract into my fastidious little shell. I really wasn't in the mood to wrestle with a posse of bare women. *Besides,* I thought, *I'm supposed to be at least three months pregnant! I can't do any brawling. I've got my baby to consider.*

Inari chimed in with a deadpan, tart expression, "Oh, no Della. Can't you see? They've already been to the hairdressers." Once again, Inari made a joke! She was turning into George Carlin right before our eyes, but there was no time to congratulate her wittiness.

Popping out the green hose to sip from the bottle under her swimsuit, BR chortled, "We heard about your little pornament🔸 last week. I posted about it on Rumor-Has-It." This was a reference to a supposed invitational tennis tournament, but played only with balls and boys...and no racquets.

Sindy stared at BR's odd-shaped, green-colored areola. It was clear she couldn't comprehend the weird nipple or why BR would be breastfeeding herself.

Sindy gave a patronizing laugh and curtly replied, "Oh, I'm sorry. Did you want an invitation to play?"

Then her voice took on a demonic tenor, "I'm giving y'all a fair warning. Keep it up and I'll sue y'all for defamation and slander." She pointed directly at Mavolyn with her perfectly manicured finger, "And Mavolyn, considering your upcoming election on Tuesday, in the minds of several voters in your elective district...I'm thinkin' that isn't befittin' behavior of a senator." Scorn sizzled on her lips. "Y'all've🔸 been spreading rumors about us bein' immoral and slutty."

"The only one spreading anything...is Y'ALL spreading Y'ALL'S legs," Inari said, "In my country, Confucius says,

'If it looks like a slut, talks like a slut, and walks like a slut—then it is probably a slut.'"

"Wow! I never got that fortune in any of the cookies I've eaten," Norma said under her breath.

The heat of the sauna was reaching a boiling point. I was fearful the situation would escalate. Between naked women, champagne bottles, duct tape, and violence I could just imagine the scandalous headlines on the front page of the *Austin Statesman*.

"We heard about your little sideline bookie operation, Starr," Sindy crowed, glistening with perspiration.

"What? Sideline what…?" Mavolyn stared with disbelief.

Sindy continued, "Yeah, according to the spread, it looks like the odds are in our favor to win. I believe we have a statistical three to one probability for victory."

Our team didn't know if we had been sitting in the heat too long or we had heard right. A gambling ring? Unbeknownst to us, Starr set up an online *sportsbook* for the championship match. We were still statistically considered the underdogs, so by using reverse logarithms Starr calculated the parlay payouts, and was collecting sideline bets to subsidize the remaining $1,215 from the 4/20 Bake Sale.

Sindy's comment constituted fighting words for Starr. She was already drunk as a skunk from too much boob bubbly. The level of sobriety aside, in her mind, nobody was going to hornswoggle her or get the best us. We were the better team!

Rising from the cedar bench in her flowery, secondhand

swimwear and red sweat band, Starr got face to face with Sindy and growled "I tell you what. Why don't we make it double-or-nothing?"

"Done!" Sindy pronounced, sticking her hand out straight. Starr shook.

Our team was silent with shock. How could Starr do this? Double or nothing? The prize pot would be $16,000! Where were we going to get that kind of cashola if we lost? According to the spread, our odds were not good!

Just as the silence grew unbearable, one of the C4s sniffed the steamy air like a hound dog. "What is that God-awful smell?"

"Yeah, I smell it too," another Alley Cat confirmed, "It smells like a gas leak or something!"

The repugnant odor was familiar. It singed the nose like snorting Drano. There was a team epiphany—it was, of course, Starr's famous paint-stripping farts. Her eat-athon trip to Golden Corral had begun working through her cast-iron plumbing. It was time for the femme fatales to make a dramatic exodus before things ignited into an even crappier situation.

Still unaware as to the source of the reek, a kitty cat urgently said, "We better get out of here before the place explodes!"

I never thought I would say it, but I was grateful for Starr's perfectly timed gastro-bomb detonation.

The Alley Cats filed out, but before the diva demons vanished into thin air, Sindy purred, "The spicy sushi rolls here are absolutely delicious. You should try them." She grinned at us wickedly. And, with a poof, they were gone!

"Hey, those were the peccadillo rolls I made for our team!" Inari screamed. "I put them outside by the lockers near the sauna." She rushed out, and in a moment she was back holding an empty platter. "Those Capitol City women ate our rolls. They are all gone!"

Needless to say, the team was deflated. The potential humiliation of an anticipated bitch-slapping on the courts, as well as a $16,000 bill at the end of the game…

"Could it get any worse?" my teammates moaned.

But while sitting in the steam box, I had secretly devised a plan that would be the ultimate "payback from hell" and a way to win the Austin Tennis League championship.

13

Game On, Bitches!

We met for the last time at our usual checkpoint—the Brewed Awakenings parking lot. It was going to be a beautiful morning for the final match of the season—threads of sunlight poked through clouds laced with peach and rust. The majesty of the sky seemed a heavenly endorsement, a kind of big, divine high five. I thought it was an auspicious sign: God was smiling down on our little band of misfits, and despite all the crap we'd been through it was going to be a good day!

Per norm, the team was waiting for BR. It would also be the last time for her late, grand arrivals and lame excuses. We stood around Mavolyn's SUV, sipping hot coffee, clearing the morning brain-fog in a quiet, bittersweet moment. Everyone was worn out from the long tennis season, as well as Mavolyn's grueling election. Balancing those with our regular motherly and wifely chores, we had all been burning the candle at both ends. It was beginning to take a toll on everyone's nerves; the backseats of our cars rattled with discarded Red Bull cans. Secretly, I was grateful the season was finally coming to an end.

But it was obvious that neither the sunshine nor the

upcoming match were the things on everyone's minds. It was Mavolyn who finally broke the silence...by nearly bursting into flames. She suddenly unleashed a slew of cuss-combos and f-bombs in a nuclear meltdown that lit up the middle of the parking lot.

"Starr, I friggin' can't believe you did it to us once again! What the HELL were you thinking? A double-down bet with the Alley Cats? Have you gone completely mad?" None of us had ever seen her so angry, and the team took two collective steps back. Della actually put Velveeta in the back of the SUV, thinking Mavolyn might drop kick the cat.

Mavolyn did not allow Starr to answer, though we all would have liked to hear what she had to say for herself. Foot stomping and arms whirling, screaming and yelling—her natural, placid demeanor and polite manners suddenly fell away to reveal a freaking scary monster, a creature that I had only seen a few times on the tennis court.

"Your boozing and gambling have absolutely turned this team upside down for the last time. You know, those skanky Alley Cats have told *everyone* in Austin about our team and that ridiculous bet YOU made with them... AGAIN!" Clearly, in Mavolyn's mind, the friendship was over. "Not to mention destroying *MY* reputation as a viable political leader. I already know I'm not going to win the race tomorrow, but at least I could have had a chance at a career in politics in the future."

"Don't forget selling the marijuana!" Inari added.

Demurely, Starr stepped into the middle of the circle. "I know what y'all are thinking: 'Why in the heck did I make that second bet with Sindy?'"

"Thinkin'?" Norma echoed the word incredulously. "No, that's NOT what I'm thinkin'," she squealed. "I'm thinkin' how in the HELL are we going to get the additional eight thousand bucks for yet another wager you made by drinking too much of that…that…that mammary juice at the spa?!" Throwing her hands in the air, she moaned, "It just doesn't seem real to me!" With her eyes scanning the parking lot, she went on, "I know there must be hidden cameras somewhere…I feel like I'm living in a damn dramedy on HBO."

"Oh, this is going to be mother flippin' good, " Della chimed in, "What is your line of BS is going to be this time, Starr?"

Sonia piped up, "I have already heard every stupid excuse in the book with my boys. Just try me. I've heard it *all* before, and it *all* stinks to high heaven. Saint Malo! Alabado sea a la patro san del cerdo. Aye, yai, yai!" and threw her arms in the air, exasperated.

All eyes were fixed on Starr as she stared remorsefully at the asphalt. "Well, first…let me tell y'all that I'm truly sorry. I apologize with all my heart that I put y'all through this whole mess. I know I'm a horrible teammate and I don't deserve your friendship or your trust. I'M ONE BIG HOT MESS!" Pausing for a moment to regain her composure, she went on, "I've accepted the fact that I'm an alcoholic and addicted to gambling. I've known for a long time that my bad behavior has hurt my health, my marriage, and my relationships with y'all." She tipped her face up, tears rolling down her cheeks, and looking at us searchingly. "I have a confession to make."

"Here we go…" Sonia said, rolling her eyes.

"I played at my usual Friday underground poker tournament the day before we went to the spa." So far, it sounded like the same story we had heard before.

Mavolyn interrupted, "Starr, I'm not sure I want to hear this story. Quite honestly, I'm just fed up with the whole thing. I really don't care anymore." She turned to walk away, shoulders hunched, deflated by everything that had happened.

"Wait a minute, Mavolyn! I think you'll want to hear this. Please listen. STOP! I'm begging you!" Starr earnestly pled.

We all stared at Mavolyn's back for what seemed like an hour. With infinite effort, she reluctantly turned around and shuffled back.

Nervously, Starr tugged the hem of her shirt. "As I was saying, last Friday night I went to my regular poker game. I've played cards with the same ol' fellas who have attended my club for years. This time a guy the boys and I call Mr. X[1] was there; he occasionally comes as someone's guest. He's one of those jovial, backslapping kind of dudes, nice enough, but always seemed a bit shady to me. I never knew his real name, but this time I paid closer attention to his face. He looked familiar, and I was trying to figure out exactly where I had seen him." She paused for dramatic effect. "Then it hit me like a ton of bricks…he's Mavolyn's opponent!" Looking directly at Mavolyn, she went on, "The same man running against YOU in the election!"

◇◇◇◇◇◇◇◇◇◇◇◇◇◇◇

1 The name of this dubious politician has been changed to conceal his identity.

Norma gasped. "You gotta be kidding me!"

"What was *he* doing at your sinful poker parlor?" Sonia queried.

Starr continued, "Like I said. I'd seen him at a couple of our card games, usually with a big wad of cash. Mr. X doesn't win much, that's why he's always invited back."

"Wait a minute. Let me get this story straight here," Mavolyn asked, "Are you telling me that this…Mr. X is *my* senatorial opponent?"

"Yep! That is exactly what I'm saying!" Starr's mouth pulled into a wry twist. "And not only that…I sorta *guessed* where he got the money for all his antes."

Della couldn't believe her ears. "Where?"

"He's been playing poker with campaign contributions! The money that was donated and supposed to be used exclusively for his election."

Marovlyn looked doubtful. "How did you know…I mean how did you *guess* the money was from campaign donations?"

"Well, this is where the story gets a little complicated," Starr hesitated.

"Please tell us it doesn't involve doing something illegal like selling more pot brownies?" Inari said, fixated on the notion that most of Starr's shenanigans included a dominator of illicitness…which wasn't far from the truth.

"No. But it does entail a plea bargain and some jail time," she confessed. "Oh, yes. And lots of gin and Dubonnet!"

"I don't understand," Mavolyn said flatly.

"Okay, here goes!" Starr started from the beginning.

Starr's poker hideout was located at an abandoned boathouse on Lake Travis, in a secluded cove near Hippie Hollow. It sat on a wobbly pier stretching over a shoreline now bone-dry from the drought, tilting to one side due to the lack of water in the lake. Starr said the angle made it difficult to keep poker chips and money from rolling off the tables.

It was about eleven o'clock at night, and Lady Luck had been sitting on Starr's shoulder. She had won several big pots thanks largely to Mr. X's extra "buy in" cashola. Depending on how many people were playing, cash pots sometimes exceeded $10,000. Folks traveled from as far as Temple to play at these secret Texas Hold 'Em tournaments.

No one would ever guess that Starr was human calculator, a real mathematical prodigy. The big yabbos, poofy hair, and seductive outfits that tightly covered her doublewide tail-end were a clever disguise. She always said, "God gave women a fishing box and two sparkly lures to seduce men," which Sonia would usually counter with a Bible verse about God's true fishers of men.

That night, across the table, Starr had eyeballed Mr. X carefully; between each shuffled hand, she plied him with copious gin and Dubonnet cocktails. Gradually, he lost about half his cash and made riskier wagers to recoup some of his money. Usually when players get desperate, they drop their guards and become vulnerable. Starr knew this and commenced small talk to distract him, making use of her twin booby traps.

Looking over a pair of Jacks, she flirtatiously asked, "So,

what kinda' business are you in?"

Pulling a stubby, chewed cigar from his mouth, hesitating while his eyes focused on Starr's mesmeric mounds, he slurred, "Well...you could say that I'm in the public relations business." A devilish grin took over his face.

"Hum! Making a pretty good livin', are you?" She slyly made a show of focusing her interest on the game.

Like most narcissistic politicians, Mr. X wanted to be heard. "You can say that, Sweet Cheeks. I get...I mean I earn most of my money from my admiring fans." A sinister chuckle, along with a puff of cigar smoke, left his lips.

And then Starr put two and two together: Mr. X was Mavolyn's rival in the 24th District senatorial race! It was the laugh that gave him away; she had heard it on one of his television spots.

Starr explained to us, "Then I started thinking about those folks who donated their hard-earned money to that scallywag's political campaign." Looking up as the morning sun broke through the remaining clouds, she proclaimed, "It wasn't fair! Even though those gullible people were backing the wrong candidate...sorry, Mavolyn...they deserved to know where their donations were going. Besides, there's a rule at my poker games: NO cheating! And Mr. X was cheating. Cheating those poor folks out of their money!" Starr looked directly into Mavolyn's eyes, grabbed both of her hands, and held them gently. She sincerely said, "Working on your campaign, hearing your speeches and the passionate promises you made to your constituents, I knew deep down inside that YOU needed to win. You would never steal anything from any voter, regardless of their political persuasion. And I had a strong feeling that jackleg was frivolously gambling away money that wasn't his. *Screwing* those donors, as well as *screwing* you out of an election."

"What did you do?" Della growled.

"Well, in between hands, I told the boys I needed to get into the Lotus Position.※ So I got up and left the table. It was an excuse to make a couple of phone calls," Starr said. "I called a man I had insulted at the Orchestral League charity ball a couple of months ago," Starr stated. "Remember him, Mavolyn?"

I recalled there had been a number of people Starr had insulted that night. So did Mavolyn. "No, not really. I do, however recollect you being lit up like a Christmas tree," she said.

"I'll give you a little clue," Starr teased. "He was once your husband's political ally before I nominated YOU as a candidate." Her eyes glittered. "Remember now?"

"The Attorney General?" Mavolyn gasped.

"The very one!" Starr confirmed, pride in her voice.

"Oh, my God!" Mavolyn's hands covered her gaping mouth.

"You know, I do have a few political connections myself. I called the Cedarway police department, and they scrounged up the Attorney General's home telephone number. Then I made a second call to the Honorable AG and told him who I was. He remembered me from the Orchestral shindig; he called me Miss Confederate Fighter. I explained that

I was currently at an underground poker tournament with Mr. X and identified him as a candidate for the 24th District tomorrow."

"Why would he believe you?" Della interrupted.

Starr playfully whispered, "When I snuck off to make the phone call, I took a few covert photos with my iPhone and texted him the pictures. The Honorableness verified right then and there that Mr. X was indeed the very candidate!"

"Holy Hairy Moley!" Inari cried.

"What happened next?" Norma asked, spellbound.

"Well, this is where it gets a little more complicated," Starr admitted.

"It can NOT get any more convoluted than what you've already told us!" Norma asserted, shaking her head in disbelief.

"Well, unfortunately, it does for ME," Starr confessed. "I made a plea bargain with the Attorney General for a lesser charge and reduced jail time in exchange for revealing the location of my poker party, handing over the moolah, and the arrest of Mr. X."

"Whoa! Just a minute here. Explain that one more time," Mavolyn exclaimed.

"You heard right. I agreed to disclose the whereabouts of my poker hideout, surrender my profits, identify Mr. X for arrest, and surrender myself for illegally gaming without a permit." Starr hung her head.

"Gosh, Starr. You sure did go out on a whim for Mavolyn,"

Inari said.

"The saying is: 'Out on a LIMB,' Inari. Not a whim!" Sonia corrected. "And it's 'Holy Moly,' not 'Holy Hairy Moley.'"

As I thought about it, I decided Inari was correct. Starr <u>DID</u> go out on a whim for Mavolyn; after all, it was one of those "gut" instincts (and not *her* typical gut instinct). Her biggest gamble was presuming without evidence that Mr. X was stealing money from his own political war chest.

When the local police and a team of ATF officers busted down the doors to the lake house, over $40,000 lay in the middle of the green felt. Dressed in pajamas, robe, and a pair of Hushpuppy slippers, the Attorney General came in behind the swarm of armed law enforcement officers. He scooped the gambling proceeds into an old Resistol hat box while the police handcuffed Mr. X and Starr. They were carted off to the Travis County jail for booking. Unfortunately, Starr's husband witnessed the whole raid. As Cedarway police chief, I'm sure it was embarrassing to watch your wife being hauled off to the slammer.

Starr was released later that evening on the condition she would appear for arraignment on Monday afternoon, the same day as our last match—today.

"You mean to tell me, you're going to jail?" Inari's eyes got even bigger behind her thick glasses.

"Yep. Right after the last ball is hit." Starr sighed, pushed back her baseball cap, and rubbed her forehead. "The Attorney General will be standing near the tennis courts at Capitol City Country Club, along with my husband, to escort me downtown to the pokey. And after they arraign me, the AG will make an announcement to the press, stating that he brought down a gambling operation and indicted Mr. X for illegally using campaign funds and participating in other corrupt organizations."

Starr's hunch had been correct. Investigators had been tracking Mr. X's money trail and his unlawful gambling schemes for several years. Evidently, he had been cooking his campaign books for decades. But Mr. X was slippery, so Starr's phone call had been the break they needed. It was a crapshoot that paid off for the Attorney General, as well as Starr.

It turned out the Attorney General's office had also known about the underground poker games on Lake Travis, which is why he recognized her at the Orchestral League Ball. Unbeknownst to Starr, she was under a secret investigation, too! Her plea bargain couldn't have been better timed, since it put her in a position to negotiate for a reduced sentence in exchange for her testimony against Mr. X.

Snickering under her breath, she said, "The officers at the Cedarway station later told me that Mr. X pissed on himself in the back seat of the squad car. He was so scared, he renounced his run for the 24th district senate race. Evidently he didn't want to embarrass himself in front of the public."

"Back up the truck here," Della said crisply, "if Mr. X is in jail now, then that means…" She paused for a moment to consider the implications. "That means…Mavolyn has WON the election!" she concluded.

Six of us stood in utter disbelief. It was a Salvador Dali-esque moment, when everything is out of whack and REALITY just got run over by a bus load of purple-colored pigmies, driven by Raquel Welch dressed in nothing but cellophane Twinkie wrappers.

Astounded, Mavolyn whispered, "I win?" A little shiver, half fear and half excitement, ran over her as she thought about the prospect.

"Yes, honey! You've won the race!" Starr said sweetly, throwing her arms around her neck. "I couldn't tell you until now. It was part of my agreement with the Attorney General."

"You've WON! WOW! Mavolyn, you're now a Texas state senator!" Inari gleefully trumpeted.

The group went into into ecstasies of congratulatory screams—hooting and hollering, jumping up and down, hugging one another, and carrying on. It was as if the weight of the world had been lifted from our shoulders. The election was over and Mavolyn won!

After the commotion settled down a bit, Mavolyn's bright, fawn-like face grew wistful. "Starr, I can't believe you did this for me. You're going to prison because of...me."

"Well, when you put it like that, it does seem rather magnanimous of me." Giggling a bit, Starr shook her head. "But seriously, it wasn't really a noble gesture on my part. It was one of those self-preservation things; I didn't want to turn out like my outlaw kinfolks: killed by a bullet in the back of the head like Belle Starr, or my wild-ass grandmother, Pearl Starr, a *poker madam* of a different kind. It was time for me to come clean. I needed to stop gambling behind my husband's back. I needed to stop drinking...as much. And I needed to start being a better friend."

Choked with emotion, Mavolyn squeezed Starr's shoulders.

"I think this is the nicest thing anyone has ever done for me." She dropped a kiss on top of Starr's head as a symbol of forgiveness.

Starr looked up with a rueful smile. "All things considered, it's a very minor punishment. The only bad thing is that I'm not able to see my husband or y'all for several months."

"Well, we're going to miss you, aren't we, girls?" Della nodded.

Another group hug ensued, though this one was more melancholy than the previous. Our friend would be behind bars in just a couple of hours! However, deep down, we all knew Starr was scrappy; she might even learn to enjoy the pinch of steel handcuffs.

"Oh, yes. There is one more thing I forgot to mention," Starr said, breaking up the lovefest.

"You've got to be kidding me! There's more to the story?" Norma threw up her hands. "I'm not sure I can take more!"

Starr concluded, "Before the sting operation at my poker parlor, I had time to roll up my winnings…the money that *wasn't* Mr. X's laundered stash," she qualified.

"How much did you hide?" Della pried.

Pausing for dramatic effect, she pulled from her cleavage a big roll of cash. "The exact amount for the double-or-nothing bet I made with Sindy, plus the remaining balance we needed but didn't earn at the 4/20 Bake Sale. $9,215!"

"Oh, my gentle Jesus!" screamed Sonia.

"Slap my fanny and call me Mable!" Inari gasped, quoting

an old spaghetti Western.

Unfurling the wad like a fan, Starr waved the money in the humid morning air. "The odds are WE are going to win the match today! That's why I doubled down with the Alley Cats on Saturday. Besides, we've got nothing to lose. BR is holding our proceeds from the bake sale and I have the rest. SIXTEEN THOUSAND SMACKER-ROOS! That's what I'm talkin' about, sisters! JACKPOT!"

"I'm not believing what I'm hearing or seeing," Norma shook her head.

"There's one more thing!" Starr continued, "Y'all haven't done the math, have ya?" She waited only a second for an answer. "WHEN we win this match against the pussy cats, at the end of the day, we'll have…$32,000! And after I'm out of prison, we're gonna have one HELL of a girls' weekend!"

Disbelief seemed to be the emotion of the day. Before we could consider the possibility, a loud tooting sounded from the other side of the parking lot…my "payback from hell" was coming!

BR was driving my Old Blue like a bat out of hell, pulling her husband's BBQ trailer. Loud music pulsated from two huge speakers in the bed of the truck, and whirling smoke emanated from the pit's stack. It was such a ruckus that customers at Brewed Awakenings came running out to see the bofunk extravaganza.

Everyone's jaws dropped in astonishment.

BR and I had been up to all hours the night before, decorating a hillbilly parade float with garlands of blue and gold streamers and colorful balloons. Additionally, as macabre as it may seem, we pilfered discarded funeral wreaths out of a dumpster behind the Texas State Cemetery, hanging the flower arrangements on clothes hangers and attaching them to the sides of the pit and on the door handles of the truck. I had also painted posters: "Kick Vagina!" We fixed them to the sides. It was a true freak show on wheels!

My plan was simple: pile the team into the BBQ trailer, drive down the Capital of Texas Highway and through the guarded entry of Capitol City Country Club, blasting the horn and blaring music. Our grand entrance would cause a hullabaloo sure to psych out the Alley Cats. Talk about a hell-raising start to the last game of the season!

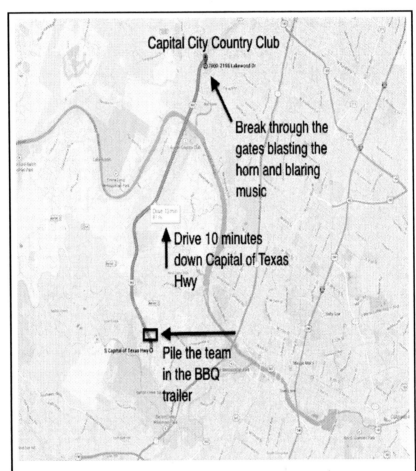

The battle plan: Drive up Capital of Tx Highway and storm the gates of C4.

14

Center Court

I wanted it to be one of those mind-blowing, earth-shattering grand entrances—you know the kind I'm talking about—like watching newlyweds leaving the reception, only more bizarre and over-the-top. We were playing the last match on the Alley Cats' home turf, so my plan was to do something that would downright unhinge the bitchitos and knock them off focus. Who in their right mind would waltz in (or rather *putt-putt)* into the finest country club in Austin in a beat-up ranch truck pulling a rusty barbecue trailer? (Disclaimer: I have never claimed our team was in their right minds.) The mental image of our team careening through the elegant C4 gates would surely cause the wildcats to quiver with anger from the tops of their heads to the bottoms of their feet. At this juncture in the season, it did matter if the pussy posse thought we were certifiably insane or just eight uncouth bumpkins. They had just spent a whole season calling our club a trumped up VFW, complete with faux Confederate cannons and cannonball pyramid decor. Well, if they thought we were a bunch of crazy, low-life carnie folks, by golly, let's prove 'em right!

BR and I had gotten up before dawn to hook up the BBQ trailer. Her husband had obligingly begun smoking pork ribs, a couple of briskets, and jalapeño sausages. Also, Norma's husband, who had returned early from a business trip to surprise her at the match, dropped off ten cases of Chateau Palmer, sixteen cases of Krug champagne, and the life blood and unofficial sports drink of all country club tennis mommas—vodka.

Of course, barbecue with all the fixin's wouldn't be a party unless friends were invited, so BR blasted out an electronic all-points bulletin on Rumor-Has-It.net to every member on the Austin Tennis League in our division. In total, we invited one hundred and sixty ladies to the Capitol City Country Club for free food and booze, and to witness the final smack-down with the Alley Cats. Most of the gals on the league hated the snobby wenches, so the majority RSVPed immediately. Imagine: one hundred and sixty rowdy, drunken cheerleaders in the bleachers, kindred spirits united to take revenge on their hated foes. It was going to be one HELL of a tailgate party that would absolutely pop the radiator caps off the Alley Cats!

It takes a special kind of crazy to drive down Highway 360 in the back of a decorated barbecue food trailer—festoons of brightly colored streamers and funeral flowers waving in the breeze, the aroma of chargrill trailing behind, and eight women dressed in short camouflage tennis skirts and velvety purple Crown Royal jackets[1] waving to passers-by like a bunch of bofunk debutantes. Preening over the sides, we were the mastheads on the front of a hillbilly tour

◇◇◇◇◇◇◇◇◇◇◇◇◇◇◇

1 Before we departed, Inari surprised the team with handcrafted gifts—eight matching vests tailored from Crown Royal bags, plus a small cape for Velveeta! They were quite the complement to our countrified camo uniforms and rubberized Justin Roper tennis shoes. It seemed logical to Inari's fashion sense: Wasn't Crown Royal for royalty? And why not? We were Queens of the Court, after all.

bus. To this day, I feel quite certain no one has ever seen a parade float quite like ours.

Driving to the proverbial Rich Bitch Death Star, excitement fizzed inside me like carbonation in a Shiner Beer. I was so intoxicated with anticipation, my bladder almost gave in to the excitement. You know that feeling? It's like walking into Neiman Marcus at the "One-Year Event Sale" with a new credit card and a high credit limit. Some of the girls were a little scared, but I felt no fear at all—only excitement at the thought of the end of a long struggle. Regardless of the outcome, I felt our team had had a winning season.

Or maybe it was just the champagne. Before we got underway, I had produced a frigid bottle of champagne and a gleaming ceremonial saber with gold cords and tassels… the same one my uncle used in the annual Knights of Columbus 4th of July parades.

"What's that for?" Inari flashed a quizzical look at the weapon.

"It's the last match of the season, and our team is still standing."

"Are we going to add murder to our list of illegal endeavors this season?" Inari giggled.

"No, Inari…while I would like to wring the Alley Cats' necks, murdering them isn't an option." I explained. "I'm going to *saber* a bottle of champagne. Have you ever seen this done?"

"No!" Inari exclaimed, aroused at the prospect of witnessing a bottle beheading.

I stood before the team, sword in one hand and bottle in the other, and announced, "Second place by one point! ONE point! Now this is cause for celebration. I don't want to get all sentimental and teary-eyed here, but honestly, I don't know how we came this far." Reflecting, I credited our success to that sometimes underestimated human attribute—tenacity. Most folks don't give that trait much respect, but I believe it was the unifying factor that held our team together. In large part, the girls were comically misaligned—an accident waiting to happen—but for some reason the combination worked. And the common denominator was tenacity. The resolve to win. This is what I wanted to celebrate.

With what my grandmother would call "Pomp and Circumcision," I drew the long sword back at a 45-degree angle. With a smooth, forceful motion I hit the glass throat of the bottle. Champagne spudded!

I poured the champagne into seven plastic cups and then slugged down the remaining bubbly directly from the bottle. Some of the sparkling wine dribbled down my chin until it was gone. A loud gutteral belch breached my lips, "Uuuurrrrpp!" I know it was rude and unladylike, but what do you do?

The girls collectively cocked their heads to one side with surprise. During the whole season together they had never seen me drink alcohol…not even one drop until now!

"What in the heck are you doing?" Mavolyn asked, gazing at me in amazement.

The stress had finally taken its toll, and I ended my 30-something years of sobriety. The sport had finally broken me and had driven me to drink.

After getting over their disbelief, everyone quickly slammed down their glasses of champagne…except Starr. She guzzled down a bottle of Milk of Magnesia before climbing into the truck with everyone and hitting the road.

When we rolled up to the CCCC gate, Ted Nugent's "Cat Scratch Fever" was pulsating from the speakers. To be frank, seeing us for the first time, I would have had the same awestruck expression that the guard had. Unable to speak, he opened the gate and waved us through.

Entering the parking lot, I looked across the gorgeously manicured lawn. There, in between the sprawling oak trees near the tennis courts, I saw a large congregation of women cheering and waving naked Barbie pompoms.[2] Every Austin team—the Sweet Spots, Kiss My Ace, Point Taken, and the Mood Swings to name a few—had come out to cheer us on, and were whipped up into a wolf pack-type frenzy. From a distance, dressed in their uniforms, the teams resembled different species of animals convening near a Serengeti watering hole on a TV episode of *Mutual of Omaha's Wild Kingdom*. They were howling and whooping, swinging those dolls around until a few of the heads flew off.

And there *they* were—the C4 team was lined up, arms folded, with matching pissed off expressions, longing to pound our asses into the hot pavement. Either my plan to get under their skins had worked, or they had attended

◇◇◇◇◇◇◇◇◇◇◇◇◇◇◇◇

2 These were Starr's idea. She went to a flea market in Pflugerville (just down the road from the Mexican cock fights) and purchased a big box of 100 knockoff Barbies. We stripped them all naked the evening before the match. Then BR and I drove out to meet with the captain of the Triple X team, who agreed to hand out the dolly pompoms at the game.

another one of their neighborhood Botox parties the night before. Below their frozen brows, hatred emanated like a shimmering heat mirage. Clearly they were annoyed about the crowd and tailgating, too. But I saw it as fair game. After all, there are no rules against inviting an audience… or bribing them to attend with barbecue and fine wine.

Clothed in nothing but their skimpy dresses and bitterness, the trophy wives stood on the court. I admit, for a moment, the Slutrons® had me rattled. It was their uniforms. It's true, they were spectacular! Finely tailored black pinstriped business suits with red accented sweatbands. Underneath the conservative jackets, bustiers peeped out, looking like sling shots that lifted and separated their breasts into deadly looking missiles. They topped off the ensemble with taut, rubberized skirts (complete with padded posteriors, and high-heeled Nike tennis shoes. It was a seductive yet menacing guise. I felt gooey inside, like a can of refrigerated raw biscuit dough. I hadn't felt this out of place since college, when my face spent 30 minutes smashed in a sorority sister's pusswuss during a fraternity "Bug Bust"[3] competition. The femme fatales had also bedazzled their racquets with Swarovski crystals.

BR muttered, "What a bunch of dominatrix douche bags!" Last year, she had a tent at Austin City Limits and sold bedazzled squirrel and nutria skulls. She had garnished them with multicolored sequins, and fixed little handcrafted ceramic cigars in their sharp, tiny teeth. While it might have been an example of Texas taxidermy gone amuck, she sold out by the second day—and later heard that several

---

3 A competitive sport at SHSU whereby sororities and fraternities cram members into a Volkswagen Bug. This activity is similar to "phone booth packing."

customers had up-cycled them into bongs. "Dang it! I can't believe they got the idea before me! Bedazzling tennis racquets!" BR kicked the dirt under her foot.

Pointing to one Alley Cat, who had bent over to grab a ball, Norma gasped, "Looks like that's not all they've bedazzled." Beneath her skimpy undergarment, *something* glittered, reflected the sunlight. It had not only caught the eyes of our team, but several male spectators on the next court.

"Ooh! I wish I hadn't seen that," Della groaned, "Is this a tennis court, or a Bangkok sex lounge?"

Starring at the gems winking from beneath the Alley Cat's panties, Inari questioned, "I wonder how she did that? Rhinestones, hot glue?"

"That's just wrong! W-R-O-N-G Wrong!" Sonia scolded.

"Come on, gals, let's grab our gear and start playing some tennis," Mavolyn said, corralling everyone and changing the subject at the same time.

I was busy with the Hot Flashes, who had volunteered to serve food. Sindy and her team sashayed up to the trailer, looking superior with that familiar cuntacious👑 attitude. But underneath the smoky barbecue, and behind their strong, musky designer perfume, I could still smell FEAR.

Sindy haughtily said, "Before we begin, I'm going to give y'all a chance to change your mind and concede defeat."

Della clenched her fists. "Ugh, you little shitster👑! I've had about enough of your games." Starr gripped her shoulders to keep Della from throttling Sindy (which was

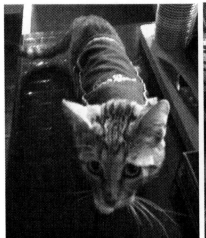

Velveeta in her purple Crown Royal cape

exactly what Sindy wanted). Every seasoned player knows it is impossible to play competitive tennis when you're pissed off. There was a whole chapter about it in Sindy's self-published playbook of nasty tricks, and she used the aggravating stunt to her advantage whenever possible.

"Oh!" Sindy continued. She looked down at Velveeta in her little cape, "Animals are not allowed on the country club's premises. You'll have to do something with...IT."

The red leaped to Della's tan cheeks, and I swear I thought she was going to come unglued. Sindy is the only person I know who would have the guts to push Della's buttons. Everyone in the league knew Velveeta was our unofficial mascot and Della's best friend. The thought of playing a tennis match without Velveeta sitting on the sidelines seemed almost impossible. No one seemed to mind the cat's presence until now. The adrenaline surging through Della's veins was making her visibly shake. This was not a good sign. Like I've said before, it's NEVER a good idea to get Della mad...NEVER!

"You know, Sindy," she whispered, "Payback's a bitch!"

Mavolyn gently pushed Della aside, and addressed Sindy in a warm, buttery tone, "Permit me to extend the same offer to *your* team." Pausing to eye her like a cowboy in a gun slinging showdown, "Let me make it perfectly clear: in no way will we forfeit this match to YOU."

"Well then, I guess we should get started with the ass whippings." Scorn sizzled from her lips as Sindy stalked toward the court, tossing her pale, shiny hair, posse in tow. Looking over her shoulder, she called "Oh, one more thing! My regular partner can't be here this morning. She's been a little under the weather. So I've drafted a substitute... per USTA rules and regs." A towering Amazon (she looked about 6'10") stepped forward from the sidelines. "This is Stilts." Like a panther stalking prey, the powerfully built woman strode up to Sindy. Her gaze was piercing, her dark hair done in short spikes. "She'll be my partner today." Sindy hooked her arm through the Amazon's and they strode away. Sindy had brought in a ringer.

There had been rumors that Sindy had done this before— "recruit" (i.e., pay) someone who is not yet ranked in the league, but has skills that far exceed the current level she is playing—like Maria Sharapova entering a high school tournament. Later that day, we found out that Stilts was an ex-volleyball player from UTEP. Clearly, there was absolutely nothing Sindy wouldn't do to win.[4]

◇◇◇◇◇◇◇◇◇◇◇◇◇◇◇

4 Actually, we later discovered that Sindy's regular partner really <u>was</u> ill. The Alley Cats had all been sicker than dogs, thanks to Inari's armadillo sushi rolls, which they had stolen during our spa day. Turns out the rodent had been a little ripe. At first, Inari was horrified that she had nearly poisoned us all with spoiled armadillo meat. However, the guilt was soon replaced by the satisfaction of knowing the Alley Cats had gotten what they deserved.

The two teams warmed up for thirty minutes, then convened on the side court where Sindy handed me the sheet of assigned match ups. As luck would have it, Mavolyn and I would play against Sindy and Stilts. We moved apart for one more private powwow. In the corner of my eye, I could see Della digging through the voodoo pocket of her bag; after a moment, she pulled out one of the Barbie pompoms dressed in a men's black dress sock. I guess it was meant to resemble an Alley Cat uniform. Sonia insisted we have a team prayer. All eight of us made a small circle and held hands. Sonia closed her eyes and tilted her chin toward the autumn sky, clutching her small "travel Bible" under her armpit.

"Please, dear Jesus, our Lord above," Sonia prayed. "Please give us the strength and stamina to take with us on the tennis courts today."

"Amen!" Norma interrupted, trying to break away and end the prayer quickly. Sonia gripped her hand even tighter, and jerked her back into the circle. "And dear Lord, may you give us the moral courage to withstand the struggles, disputes, and other conflicts that might…I mean, *will* occur. Help us to hold our ground, knowing that we are on the side of YOUR heavenly truth and YOUR protection."

"Amen!" Norma tried again.

"And Father, I know we should never ask for favors, but please, please let us win this tennis match against the heathenistic Capitol City Country Club women. Let us be victorious and glorify YOUR name. You know they are sinners and have offended and defiled all YOUR divine laws. May the wrath of YOUR scorn, dear Lord, come upon our enemy. And may the mercy of YOUR love be ever upon us during this day. Amen!"

"Amen!" Norma roared, yanking her hand out of Sonia's vise grip.

"Amen!" Della chimed in, jabbing a two-inch voodoo needle (a cocktail toothpick, actually) into the Barbie Doll's head, hoping to conjure up some juju magic.

Della's voodoo in action

"Whew!" Starr took a step back from the doll. "Remind me never to get in a fight with you!"

"Well, I would have preferred to use that sword, but it was in Mavolyn's SUV," Della countered in a serious tone.

"Okie dokie!" Mavolyn concluded in her usual businesslike tone. "Now that our souls have been blessed, I suppose...let's get out there and play ball! It's going to be a hot day! So drink plenty of liquids...preferably water." Mavolyn looked over at Starr suspiciously, hoping she wouldn't consume too much of her special *high voltage* sports drink. "And DON'T drink from the water coolers!" The Alley Cats were known to throw "roofies" into the communal water coolers on their opponents' side of the net.

Starr mused, "Remember last year, that woman at the annual C4 Power Players tournament? During the finals she drank from the water cooler, and five minutes later she was running around the club like a banshee. She lost the match and the EMS had to haul her ass off to the hospital."

It was now time to play. We ceremoniously raised our racquets in the air and hooted, "It's a Ball!" And with that, we disbanded and walked to our assigned courts.

We broke the huddle with two major concerns hanging unspoken in the air. First, no one wanted to talk about the calculated scores connected to the outcome of our matches. The Alley Cats were in first place with 154 points and It's a Ball was trailing with 153 points. To take the championship, our team had to win at least three matches in two sets or take a combination of several "split sets" (three set matches) and another two-set win. (If the math seems a little complicated, that's because recreational tennis can be complicated.) I'm sure we had all "run the numbers" in our heads, nevertheless it was something we didn't discuss. We knew the stakes were high! Second, the Attorney General had just arrived, with Starr's husband and two Texas Rangers in tow. The news about the poker bust hadn't officially broken, but my heart went out to the Cedarway police chief, understanding it must be a tremendous embarrassment to know he was there to arrest his own wife.

So the last game of the season began with the traditional "spinning of the racquet," which is much like a coin toss. Our volunteer cheerleaders were spread across the verdant country club grounds, eating free barbecue and drinking vintage wines and vodka. Plenty of VODKA. The pep squad waved their Barbie Doll pompoms in the air, obviously stoked on anticipation and alcohol.

Meanwhile back on the court, Mavolyn said to me, "Let's get this show on the road, shall we?" She was right. It did feel like a show. Our match with Sindy and Stilts got off to a relatively cordial start. Of course, they won the first the first set 6-4, so Sindy was oozing smug satisfaction from her pores. It was clear she had no doubt she was going to win; I wanted to jump over the net and smack that little snide smirk off her face. Then we split sets, and things got testy. Mavolyn and I got our mojo back and decisively won 6-2. Stilts's height and wide wingspan made it difficult to get balls past her, but we figured out her weaknesses and whizzed by several winning points. Sindy was as mad as a hornet. It was fun to watch her seethe.

We had a short ten minute break before the third set would begin. Sindy ran off to the restroom, so Mavolyn and I took a moment to scope out the other matches.

Sonia and Inari's match looked challenging, to say the least. They were playing a tie breaker in the second set. A strong competitive streak ran through both women. Inari's normally sweet expression, delicate as a handmade clover necklace, was replaced by an iron mask of steel determination. It was clear even at a distance that they were determined to win, make no mistake about it, but things did not look good.

Norma and Starr's match also looked tight and gritty. They were busy whacking the ball to and fro with powerful topspin shots, which made it difficult to follow. It looked as though the girls were going to pull it out and win in just two sets. But unfortunately for Norma, her husband picked the worst possible moment for his surprise. He walked out from behind the bleachers with little Pearletta holding his hand. He had promised me early that morning to wait until her match was over so she would not be distracted, but had gotten the timing wrong. Their appearance caught her off guard, and broke her concentration. As Norma peered over her sunglasses to confirm the image wasn't an illusion, the other team saw their chance. She and Starr lost the second set, and would have to play a third.

There was only one decisive victory: a landslide 6-1, 6-0 by Della and BR. Della, who rarely shows much emotion, was so excited she grabbed her C4 opponent and kissed her smack-dab on the lips. The C4 gal fell over backwards. She grabbed a bottle of Gatorade and washed her mouth out, spitting liquid on the court, thinking she had felt a little tongue action. It wasn't until much later that she realized she hadn't been chewing gum during the match, and the tutti fruity in her mouth had been slipped there by Della, during the PDA.

And as if on cue, out of Della's tote popped Velveeta's head. The precocious cat meowed, obviously excited about the victory, too. Screw Sindy—Della would never have left her best friend behind.

Then it was time for our third set to start, and we had to get our minds back on our own game. Now Sindy began pulling from her bag of dirty tricks. Everyone knows a can of tennis balls has three. In women's doubles matches, players usually secure the extras by tucking them into the leg band of their undershorts. Not our tawdry tabbies; they stuck the balls in the middle of their sports bras, where they peeked out next to their milk jugs. Boob. Ball. Boob. Boob. Ball. Boob. It was incredibly distracting. Sindy, clearly pleased at provoking us, crossed her arms across her now mounding chest and flashed a shit-eating grin.

Fortunately, I had planned ahead to counter any pranks. I

had concocted a batch of my homemade Tiger balm, adding a few extra herbs and spices like paint thinner and Tinactin. Right before the changeover, I covertly rubbed the balls with the salve, warning Mavolyn not to touch them. This was powerful stuff. I put the balls back on the court, ready for Sindy and Stilts's use.

It was Sindy's serve; sure enough, she and Stilts sandwiched the tainted balls in between their meat bags. It took about thirty seconds, then both of them started to howl, popping the balls out of their tops like pimples.

"What did you do to these balls? Damn it!" Sindy griped, frantically rubbing her singed mammaries with a towel, then squatting down under the water cooler to dowse them with icy cold liquid. By this time, the men playing tennis on the other courts were watching. Wet t-shirts and men...like moths to a flame. Our crowd of spectators was growing, the stands filled to capacity, and her numb nuggets were adding to Sindy's growing frustration.

"Oh, I'm sorry, Sindy." I said, looking contrite. "I pulled a hammy at the beginning of our match, so I had to rub on some BenGay. I must have accidentally got some on the balls. I do apologize. I have a new can if you want." I offered it to her.

Sindy snarled under her breath, cutting loose a string of profanities. She snatched the can from my hands, popped it open, grabbed the balls, and kicked the can off to the side. I knew from this point on it would be a PMS pissin' match.

During the commotion, I had time to glance at Sonia and Inari's court. Inari dripped with sweat, making her normally straight hair look like noodles. I knew things were getting tough when she pulled out her secret weapon, a move like an Australian doubles stance, but more effective and a little dangerous as the ball comes screaming across the net at 50 MPH. Inari calls her maneuver the "The Hari-Kari."

I watched Inari whisper in Sonia's ear and then scurry back to the baseline for the first serve. With a big SWACK, the ball catapulted across the net. Sonia made an excellent crosscourt return, triggering Inari to sprint for the net with a booming war cry, holding her racquet like a samurai sword. A forceful return whizzed back, hit Inari square on her rubberized Justin Roper boot, and caused her to trip. She fell straight forward and hit the ground hard, knocked unconscious.

With the speed of a jack rabbit, Sonia ran to her side, perspiration running down her face in rivers. I gasped where I stood; I could see the fear on Sonia's face. Everyone in the stands stood up, looking anxious, as Inari lay still on the hot pavement.

Like a buttermilk pancake on a skillet, Sonia flipped Inari over. Sprinkles of cool water from a drenched rag finally woke Inari from her dazed spell. Sun rays beamed behind Sonia's head, causing a halo glow.

"An angel! Are you an angel?" Inari breathlessly asked.

"No, Inari. It's me! Sonia!" she said frantically, thinking Inari had suffered a concussion.

"Oh! Sonia! You look like an angel. Has anyone ever told you that?"

Flattered, Sonia sighed, "No, Inari. No one has ever told me that except you."

Inari chirped, "I think you're an angel. Yes! An angel!"

Hugging Inari around the neck, Sonia laughed, "That's about the nicest thing anyone has ever said to me! Thank you." In tandem, they pulled each other up from the ground, and the crowd began to applaud! Barbie Doll pompoms waved in the air, and red solo cups collided together in cheers of gratitude that Inari was not hurt badly. With resolve as strong as a railroad spike, waving to the crowd, Inari anteloped across the court, grabbed her racquet, and prepared herself for the next point.

Unfortunately, the remainder of the third set ended in a loss for Sonia and Inari, but the girls were satisfied that they gave it their best. They joined Della, BR, and the rest of the invited teams in the bleachers. By this time, BR's husband had arrived in her "Doggy Style" pet grooming van, filled with more libations and food. Sonia's three rowdy sons were there, along with Mavolyn's husband and two children. The only spouse not present was Della's.

The third set for Norma and Starr had also finished in a rather regrettable way. Both women had lost focus, and in sports, when you lose your edge, you lose the game. Norma kept glancing at her husband and Pearletta, wondering why they were there. Starr was peering at the stands too, watching the uniformed men and thinking about the handcuffs that were waiting for her there. During the final set and match point, she was looking that way, standing near the net and waiting for a volley, when the ball whizzed over and whacked her directly on her pink chewy—a bull's eye shot! It is a fact that on the rec level, some mean-spirited players will target their opponents, like a carnival duck shooting game, trying to injure them with a precision shot. The ball hit Starr's

Winnebago and ricocheted, bouncing off like a trampoline, and plopped over the net. Despite the fact that the ball made it across the net to the C4 side, the point was lost. According to USTA rules, nothing besides a racquet can touch the ball. The Alley Cats won the point, and the game was over.

Starr was unmistakably upset. The defeat of the match was clearly worse than the ball's impact. Shoulders hunched, her disappointment and guilt were clear. Normally when she would lose a match, a couple vodka tonics would take the edge off the loss. But this time was different. As they made their way to the bleachers, one hundred and sixty cheerleaders swarmed them with conciliatory hugs, kisses, and "better luck next time(s)." Starr went straight to the comfort of her husband's arms and cried desperately on his chest.

"Well, little lady," the Attorney General huffed, interrupting her blubbering. "We ought to get goin' to the Travis County precinct. I got a camera crew waiting on me to make a big announcement." Pausing a moment, wiping off BBQ sauce from his face with the back of his hand, the AG pointed with a meaty rib to the officers sitting on the bleachers. "But the boys and I wanna watch the rest of this game to see if your team wins this big shooting match." Smacking his lips, he went on, "Besides the barbecue and wine are tremendous!" As though Starr's arrest was a small secondary issue, he sat and turned to face Mavolyn and me on the court, where we waited for our third set to begin.

Breaking away from her husband, Starr turned around and gave the Attorney General a bone-crushing hug. "Oh, thank you! Thank you so much. It would be such a treat to watch the end of this match. Thank you!"

And with that, Starr and her husband, along with the Honorable AG and his law officers, settled in with the rest of the rowdy—and by this time drunk—women in the benches. Waving Barbie Dolls, eating barbecue, slamming down some liquid loveliness—the scene was becoming more of a carnival atmosphere than a usual tennis match.

The pressure was on! To recap: with the only decisive win, Della and BR made five points. The other pairs—Sonia and Inari, Starr and Norma—only earned one point each because they split third sets. Consequently, the final outcome of the whole season rested on our shoulders. It was imperative that we win our third set, which would put us ahead of the Alley Cats by one point!

Back on our court, we were in the midst of a game that is still talked about in tennis clubs around Austin.

Back and forth, back and forth, the exchanges were being hit with force and strength. The slutsters accompanied their strikes with grunts and moans; it was like playing in a XXX movie house. Mavolyn, with her lady-like politeness, asked Sindy to stop the rude noises.

Of course, that made Sindy and Stilts grunt even louder—tennisgasms—another distraction tactic. It wasn't working on us, but it certainly had the attention of the guys on the other courts. The queen of voyeurism, Sindy knows nothing quite gets a rise out of a man's winger-wanger than grunting, sweaty women. Of course, most of the spectators were women, so I thought she'd misjudged her audience. I had noticed something else, too. You see, watching an opponent's face from the other side of the net is important.

Subtle expressions sometimes indicate the advantage of the game is turning, and I had seen that Sindy's typically porcelain complexion was taking on a more greenish, peaked appearance. The rising heat index combined with Inari's *e.coli* rolls were beginning to take effect.

I could almost taste the searing autumn wind, and the sun was turning my skin a dark, ruddy color. I glanced at the large thermometer mounted outside the club's pro shop. It read 96 degrees! I thought I must be hallucinating, and wished for winter for the first time that season.

The score was 40-30, our ad, final set point. The competitive tension was as tight as a newly strung tennis racquet. Six exchanges went back and forth, accompanied by Sindy's climactic groans. In the stands, bystanders pivoted like bobble heads, watching with alert fascination. Then on the seventh exchange, Sindy called the ball out.

"What the heck!" I screamed. "That ball was clearly in. You realize, Sindy, when a ball touches the white line, it is considered in bounds."

"Well, it was out," Sindy retorted. "Wasn't it, Stilts?" Not waiting for an answer, she turned her back, walked to the service line, and took the obligatory *ready position* to receive the next serve.

"Listen here, little Miss Wimbledon Wannabe. That ball was clearly in. And you damn well know it," Mavolyn piped up, pulling off her sunglasses with unmistakable seriousness in her eyes.

"She said the ball was OUT!" A husky gargle emerged from Stilts's mouth. It was the first time anyone had heard her speak. "OUT!" she repeated. Under that sledge hammer voice, Mavolyn and I decided to move on. Why get in a brawl over Sindy's bad line call, especially when her partner had the physique and stance of a street thug? We didn't want to tangle with her.

"Sorry," Sindy purred insincerely, "But you know, according to USTA rules, when the ball is on my side, I get to call them IN or OUT." Sindy loved getting her way.

Sindy's alpha-cat was taking over, employing any means and method to win…including CHEATING! Some women truly believe their identities are wrapped up in winning, I realized. It defines them.

I stood back near the baseline and reminded myself: tennis is for fun and exercise. I just needed to try my very best. After all, we were not struggling to win a national title and big grand prize. But wait a minute! The heat was beginning to distort my judgment. This game was about "kicking vagina" and earning $32,000!

It was 40-40. I was serving and opened up with a double barrel, 12-gauge shoot into the net. And then another! I had double faulted. A gust of sighs, heavy with vintage Bordeaux, whooshed over from the bleachers. Sindy was jumping up and down like a teenybopper, completely unconcerned about looking unsportsmanlike. It was now their advantage—one point from winning the whole enchilada.

I looked over at Mavolyn. Four months of playing under the scorching sun had tanned her face and neck to the color of toast. Only when she took off her cap and sunglasses could I see the old her. Right at the hairline a band of cream-colored skin marked the boundary between Mavolyn, the wife, mother of two and NOW a Texas state senator, and Mavolyn, my tennis partner and best friend. There was no need for words. We knew what was needed—gird up our loins and win this thing. We gave each other a knowing smile across the court and got to work.

Despite the score I could sense we were winning. I knew it deep down in my inner-tennis czarina soul. I could smell victory along with Sindy's musky perfume—mingled with exhaustion and anxiety—drifting over the net. It's a feeling that grows from investing years of sweat equity on the court. Lord knows, we had a lot capital wrapped up in this particular slab of green asphalt, and I wasn't about to let Sindy steal it from us.

"30-40!" I shouted across the court to Sindy and Stilts. Tossing the ball into the air, I hit it into the middle of the T and served up an ace! The bleachers exploded with excitement.

Sindy stood at the service line spewing vile threats.

The score was back to deuce.

I could hear Sonia rousing the fans in the stands. Something had snapped inside her, and her puritanical demeanor had been overwhelmed by pure competitive rage. She later insisted it had been a hallucinatory, quasi-spiritual rapture by the devil himself causing her to profanely speak in tongues. (Whatever! It sounded like one of her son's excuses.)

With megaphone volume, Sonia began leading a twisted cheer: "Gallo, puta madre, comer una bolsa de miedra. Ducha bolsa, puta, chupa la teta madre. Somos el major equipo y a todos los otros aspiran IT'S A BALL rah, rah fornicar!"[5]

It was absolutely staggering, even bordering on sacrilegious, coming from Sonia's evangelistic mouth. She had gone completely bonkers. Counter to her ordinary Christly conduct, not only was she yelling obscenities in public, she was doing it in front of her three boys. Of course, they and the rest of the crowd just thought it was hilarious.

Sindy harrumphed with distain, but she couldn't really complain. She had used the same words, in different combinations, during this very match. I call it "Tennis Tourettes"—trash talk and swear words strung together in a disjointed pattern. Some would think a ship of sailors have the foulest language, but those folks have never been on a tennis court with a group of competitive women.

I have found that stress can at times be a character builder—no pressure, no diamonds, right? Boy howdy, in this match I was working on a twenty-carat rock! The match teetered back and forth, ad-in and then ad-out, until finally the advantage was ours at 40-30.[6] The upcoming final point was probably most stressful point I have ever played in a

◇◇◇◇◇◇◇◇◇◇◇◇◇◇◇◇◇

5 I know, I said in the legal disclaimer of my book that there would be no cussing, but what can I say? As unladylike as it is, the true translation is as follows: "Cock sucker, mother fucker, eat a bag of shit. Douche bag, whore dog, suck your mother's tit. We're the best team and all the others suck. IT'S A BALL rah, rah fuck!"

6 As my grandmother would say, "It was hotter than a goat's butt in a pepper patch." After the thirteenth ad-in, ad-out interchange, we allowed Sindy a small break. Unfortunate for Sindy, she was looking like that goat Grandmother was talking about. Sick as can be—stuff coming out at both ends, in my mind, a cosmic payback for stealing Inari's armadillo rolls. She hurled an acid tidal wave of green chunks at the net post, a strategic location, whereby we had to walk around her puddle of barf during changeovers. At the time I thought it was one of her premeditated stunts.

match. Sindy and her little bag of nasty tricks made for an even more nerve-wracking combination.

This time Mavolyn was serving. As she tossed the ball, Sindy's bedazzled racquet reflected the bright sun. The rays blinded Mavolyn, causing her to slice the serve. The spinning ball veered to the inside of the service box, catching Sindy by surprise. Returning the serve, she haphazardly smacked at the ball, causing it to fly out of bounds. However, it hit the scoring tower attached to the net post and deflected back onto our side of the court, where it thudded down.

Sindy jumped up and high-fived Stilts, thinking she had won the point.

"Now you just wait a minute here, little missy!" a voice boomed from the spectator's stand. "That ball is considered OUT!"

"Well, just who in the HELL do you think you are? Some kind of judge?" Sindy retorted.

"As a matter of fact, I am." The Attorney General stood up from the bleachers. "I also played tennis at Trinity University in the late sixties, so I do know a thing or two about the rules and regulations."

By this time Mavolyn was rummaging through her bag for the USTA handbook like a resourceful Girl Scout, always prepared for any emergency. It never failed; every match had some kind of conflict that needed to be mediated and Mavolyn's fastidious nature dictated that her smudged, curled copy was always in her bag to adjudicate disputes.

"That ball hit the score tower and obviously bounced on their side of the court. That is a 'permanent fixture' and is a part of the court. The rules are plain," Sindy defensively sniffed, with an air of expertise. "Of course, you were just sitting in the stands and probably couldn't see the ball very clearly. So I suggest you sit back down with the rest of the *dried fruits* (glancing at the Hot Flashes) and shut up."

"Oh, I saw the ball clear enough," the AG countered. "But that still doesn't preclude the fact that the ball was OUT."

It was beginning to look like a battle of wills. Sindy was not used to having her authority questioned. It infuriated her.

"Look here, old man! Back in the day, your team was probably playing with wooden sticks and rocks. I'm sure the rules have changed since then. I say, that ball was IN. It was fair play!"

The Attorney General was starting to look perturbed. He had nonchalantly walked to the side fence and rested his elbow on a chest-high gate. It was the only thing separating him from Sindy.

He said, "Mavolyn, have you found that rules book yet?"

Sindy, surprised that the old man knew Mavolyn's name, raised an eyebrow and surveyed Mavolyn like she was seeing her for the first time.

"Yes, sir! I just found it!" Mavolyn raised the battered book in the air.

"Would you please turn to page seven and read out loud rule thirteen-point-two?" Clearly, the Judge aimed to end this little spat right here and now.

The bleachers went silent; the spectators had drawn to their feet and were standing with statue-like stillness. You could feel the anticipation in the blistering air. It was about time for someone to put Sindy in her place.

"I don't give a rat's ass what you say, that ball was IN!" Sindy squawked.

"You know, you're a real piece of work," the AG said matter-of-factly.

"And do you know, I don't really care what you think about me," Sindy hissed arrogantly, crossing her arms over her Rubbermaid chest.

"Here it is! Page seven," Mavolyn called. She cleared her throat. "If the ball in play touches a permanent fixture after it has hit the correct court, the player who hit the ball wins the point."

"You see, I win the point!" Sindy crowed, looking extraordinarily pleased with herself. "You can just kiss my go-to-hell," pointing to her curvaceous ass.

"However!" Mavolyn continued reading, "If the ball in play touches a permanent fixture BEFORE it hits the ground, the player who hit the ball loses the point."

"Ya see, little missy. That ball was OUT!"

Jubilant screams erupted, and Barbie Doll pompoms were thrown in the air. The spectator stand thundered with wild abandon. It was finally over. Not just the match, but the whole season. The final score was Alley Cats 164, It's a Ball 165!

"Well, for crying out loud!" Sindy whirled around, hands over her mouth, eyes flashing with disgust. Sputtering a multitude of four letter words, she stormed off the court, leaving Stilts standing by herself.

Like a herd of horses, our teammates stampeded onto the court. We linked arms, overwhelmed that we actually won. Because it was the last match, the last time to be together for the season, no one wanted to let go. To leave the warmth of each other's embrace would mean accepting the ending. A circle of love and dysfunction. These were my girls! My soul sisters, eight wonderful friends, my "Racq Pacq." There was really nothing more to say, but it was sweet just to stand there, being together. It was almost sad, but the kind tinged with happiness. I tried hard to brand the picture in my mind—the smiling faces of my teammates, the clear blue sky, the sultry breeze, that exuberant feeling. I'm glad I did. I often return to the memory of eight fun-loving women celebrating our triumph on that autumn day.

In the midst of all the hoopla, we overheard the Attorney General having a little chat with Sindy. He was calling her "the most mean-spirited, ruthless bobcat" he had ever come across. Unbeknownst to her, his great grandfather founded Capitol City Country Club in 1899, and he was current chairman of the ethics committee. Because of her unsavory behavior at this match, he summarily stripped her of her membership. Sindy squealed like a stuck pig. Begging the Attorney General to reconsider, she shamelessly promised a multitude of sexual favors. But it made no difference. Cindy with an "S" was outta there!

We made our goodbyes to the other teams that had come to cheer us on, hugging and high-fiving them for their support. While we were picking up the tailgate party rubbish and packing the barbecue trailer, we giggled at all of the conflicts and strife leading up to this day, the calamities and preposterous mishaps that would otherwise never have happened to normal housewives and mothers.

I had a moment of clarity, an "aha" moment, recognizing that it was the challenges of the last four months that had brought evolutionary change and unexpected blessings to all eight of us. Mavolyn and I had begun it all by starting up a new tennis team. I reflected on the courage, and at times the sheer audacity, that I had witnessed each of my teammates demonstrate in overcoming these crises, and how they supported one another through difficult moments. As a result, they had all outperformed their own wildest expectations. For me, it was a life lesson, similar to the timeless wisdom Bernice had shared with me five tennis seasons ago. Her advice had cut through the nonsense on the court at the same moment it had singed my pink truffle with a forceful tug. It was that kind of collective inner strength that enabled us to leapfrog over all of those daunting problems and helped us to win.

The AG gave Starr's honey-baked hams an affectionate swat, and said with a hint of melancholy, "Well, Miss Daughter of the Confederacy, I had one humdinger of a time here, but it's time for you to go to jail." His voice carried new respect, which could only come from watching someone play tennis well. He escorted her to the waiting police car in the parking lot, without the humiliation of being handcuffed in front of her friends. Her husband walked by her side, hand-in-hand. In spite of the daunting months ahead, Starr's attitude rebounded and reflected a more positive outlook; however, her husband was much more solemn.

Before she got into the squad car, Starr turned to us, giving the team one final glance, and said, "I had a great time playing tennis with y'all this season." Choking back her emotion, she continued, "Even though I won't be seeing everybody for a while, I hope I can be on the team when I come back."

"There will always be a spot on the team for you Starr," I insisted, trying to dam my own tears.

Heavy-hearted, Starr crawled uncomfortably into the back seat of the car. She was trying to keep a brave demeanor, but could not hide the strain of this painful goodbye etched on her face. Through the open window, she said, "I love y'all. Goodbye." The car began to drive off, when halfway through the parking lot, she poked her head out of the window and yelled, "And congratulations, Senator!" Waving with both hands, "Remember what we won!"

We waved back and watched the CCCC gates close behind them. Though seven of us still stood together, it felt lonely without Starr. A deep, shared sigh broke the spell. Grinning at one another, we did indeed remember what we had won.

The Alley Cats had finally been knocked off their thrones and new Tennis Queens would reign. Now it was our turn to wear the crowns!

Game. Set. Match.

Out!

Afterward

I love scenes at the end of movies. You know the ones. Brief descriptions of how the characters have evolved after the story ends. With this in mind, here is what happened to the It's a Ball team after our winning season:

Unbeknownst to us at the time, Starr's illegal online *sportsbook* earned her an extra $5,000 (and an extra month in prison), which was oddly not seized by the Feds. She added the windfall profits to our $32,000 proceeds, netting us a big chunk of change. After Starr was released from the state pokey, we organized a humdinger of a Girls' Weekend to New York City and attended the US Open with box seats and backstage passes. We saw some of our favorite professionals play tennis and got to rub elbows with a few legendary players. It was another one of those unforgettable ventures, especially when we looked up in the nosebleed section and waved to Sindy and the other C4s. Sweet revenge!

Della

Della's personal strength grew during the season, and she wasn't afraid of the future anymore. After five failed marriages, she let go of the idea of needing a husband to care for her children and herself. Coming to the realization that some people aren't meant to be married, she filed for divorce the day after the match.

I've come to think of Della as a piece of sea glass. A once sharp shard, the waves of time have shaped her into something beautiful. She moved to Fort Worth to take a job as tennis coach at her alma mater, TCU— a job to which she is happily married.

Mavolyn

The first female to occupy the office of Texas State Senator of the 24th District, we were all invited to her official "swearing in." Inari had been practicing her profanity for weeks in anticipation of the event and was very disappointed to learn she could use none of it. The Attorney General afterwards had the whole team over to his office for a little get together, where he awarded us with honorary *social* memberships to the Capitol City Country Club, all expenses paid! As *social* members we have access to the restaurant, bar, and pool, but we can't play tennis or golf. That's okay with us. We prefer playing at Cedarway. But we do enjoy our new highfaluting privileges. Every Friday we have a few martinis at the C4 bar and poke fun at the dethroned Alley Cats.

Norma

At the end of our final match, Norma's husband explained that his recent trip to Mexico had been to start the legal process to adopt Pearletta—they were finally getting the family they had wanted and needed. After the adoption, the whole family moved to New York when Norma's husband became head wine curator for Sotheby's. We truly miss Norma's twinkling presence on the tennis court...and even her non-stop babbling.

BR

Recently featured on the front cover of Forbes magazine, BR was named one of the ten most innovative persons in the United States. Several of her inventions are now patented and produced; some were the newfangled thingamabobs I saw in her garage. BR now has a second home and new warehouse in California, where she manufactures integrated high-tech clothes for the military.

Inari

Working part time as a comedian at a local comedy club and engaged with a new job as a Japanese translator at a large tech firm in Austin, Inari is happier than ever. She still scoops up dead animals along highways and random county roads. Her collection now goes well beyond armadillos to include a vast array of preserved buzzards, squirrels, and possums—all shelved on a wall in her dining room as a personal reminder never to make sushi from roadkill.

Sonia

Like most families with three kiddos, Sonia is on the go all the time. Despite weekly treks to the principal's office and police station, Sonia still finds time for her Bible study group and tennis league. But something happened that day at the match, and since her little cheerleading routine, she habitually drops F bombs like a World War II fighter pilot. Built-up years of verbal restraint finally unleashed have now made her one of the foulest-mouthed women in the tennis league. But since her little cheer, Sonia's demeanor has been more tranquil and less uptight. Perhaps screaming four letter words is cathartic. Go figure!

Starr Noel

After her three-month stint in jail, Starr found her calling as a DJ for weddings. She specializes in 70's and 80's oldies and now has an excuse to listen to crappy music by Abba, the Captain and Tennille, Neil Sedaka, and Tony Orlando and Dawn. Her favorite diva mash-up is a Cher montage: "Gypsies, Tramps and Thieves"; "Half-Breed"; and "Dark Lady." Kinda fitting for a gal like Starr.

She still farts like a mule and talks about her constant bouts with butt-fire bowel movements, usually at our lady lunches. But she has quit drinking—a decision made while sitting behind bars with dozens of other women there thanks to the same influence: alcohol.

Me

After the exuberance of celebration had abated, I looked across the parking lot and saw my precious husband walking towards me with a huge smile. His congratulatory hug lifted me from the ground, but I could sense his relief that the tennis season had finally ended. For months he had been my "bitching backboard" and heard the same zany and ridiculous stories I have subjected you to in this book.

Without my knowledge, he had purchased a new RV and loaded it with provisions, as well as Sheila the kangaroo, and my black dachshund, Fred. We were off! It was time for a travel adventure…and a new book.[1]

1 You can contact me on the road at funnytennislady@gmail.com!

The Queen's English

A

ABC Sex – *[noun]* an acronym for sex only on anniversaries, birthdays, and Christmas.

Alcoholery – *[noun]* a restaurant or bar in which the casual, overindulgent consumption of alcohol is performed.

B

BAMF – *[noun]* an acronym for Bad, Ass, Mother, F*cker

Beauty Parlor – *[noun]* a hair salon.

Bitchitos – *[noun]* a Spanglish word for rebel rousing bitches. Most women of this type are members of motorcycle gangs, street gangsters, and the Junior League.

Blabber Infection – *[noun]* a noninfectious disease of the mouth producing annoying, non-stop talking.

Blondtourage – *[noun]* a group of bleach blond bimbos.

C

Camel Toe – *[noun]* a woman's tight fitting pants displaying the outline of her labia. This phenomena has the appearance of a camel's foot, a cloven hoof.

Caraoke – *[verb]* the act of singing karaoke in the car.

Crotch mop – *[noun]* feminine maxi-pad.

Cuntacious – *[adjective]* cunt-like behavior. (Sorry, I hate that word.)

Cuntacho – *[noun]* a Spanish slang word for cunt. (Again, I apologize. I really do hate that word!)

D

Drunkiggle – *[adjective]* tipsy.

E

Eyeolate – *[verb]* to stare at a guy (or girl) so strongly that it can violate the person's personal space.

F

Finger Fishing Trip – *[noun]* Similar to finger fishing for catfish in the bayous of Louisiana, but this type of expedition catches a specific kind of female fish…I think you can figure it out!

FUPA – *[noun]* an acronym for Fat Upper Pussy Area.

Farticles – *[noun]* particles of air contaminated by gas expelled through the anus.

G

Girlstache – *[noun]* a mustache on a woman.

Gossiprazzi – *[noun]* a group of people, mostly women, who spread gossip and/or rumors around town.

Gunning – *[verb]* - a jailhouse term for masturbating.

H

Howitzers – *[noun]* the BIG guns (i.e., tennis racquets) that hit hard balls.

I

Immaculate congestion – *[noun]* when traffic is congested on the highway for no apparent cause.

K

Kitty cage – [noun] – a vagina, pink taco, jewel box, easy bake oven, tinker bell, glory hole, bone polisher, meat counter, bait box, honey pot, pud pocket ...you get the idea!

L

Lotus Position – *[noun]* contemplatively sitting on the toilet.

Lunch Lady Arms – *[noun]* the flabby tissue under the arms once called triceps on ALL women over the age of forty.

M

Meatslapper – *[noun]* a slut.

Meow Down – *[noun]* a verbal confrontation between two or more women.

Mud Duck – *[noun]* a high-pitched sound accompanied by industrial prSoniane odor originating from a human rectum.

O

Oyster – *[noun]* a man's scrotum.

P

Pink chewy – *[noun]* - a woman's nipple.

Pink saloon doors – *[noun]* labia.

Pink truffle – *[noun]* labia.

Planet K – *[noun]* a local chain of "head shops"

Pornament – *[noun]* a pornographic tournament.

R

Religipoo – *[noun]* A person who is fanatically passionate about religions beliefs.

Roach Coach – *[noun]* a mobile food trailer.

S

Saggy Knee Syndrome – *[noun]* the condition of wrinkly skin developing above a woman's knee caps that causes them to look like an old man's penis.

Sausage Fest – *[noun]* a group of men with few women present. Sometimes refers to a gathering of gay men.

Scissoring – *[verb]* a sex act between two women.

Sexchange – *[verb]* swinging in the sexual sense, spouse swapping.

Shitster – *[noun]* a person who talks BS for the purpose to bamboozle other people out of their money or other things.

Slutrons – *[noun]* a group of slutty women that are mechanized lookalikes.

Slutsters – *[noun]* sisters or a group of close girl friends that are sluts. Example: certain sorority sisters on campuses at Northwest Texas and SMU are slutsters.

Spankasm – *[noun]* an orgasm achieved by spanking.

T

Tennisgasm – *[noun]* a loud orgasmic grunt after a tennis ball has been forcefully hit.

W

WTA – *[noun]* an acronym for <u>W</u>omen's <u>T</u>ennis <u>A</u>ssociation.

Waller – *[verb]* to roll around.

Y

Y'all've – a Southern double contraction for "you all have."

Numbers

4/20 – There are many theories regarding the origin of the term. Some consider it code for "Let's go get high." Others say April 20 is National Pot Smoking Day. And others believe it is Willie Nelson's birthday.

Acknowledgements

This book is for everyone living life to the fullest and doing the things you love with the people you love.

Karen – the finest "lady friend" and tennis partner in the world. Huggles!

Linda, Kristin, Olivia, Stel, Miwa, Natalie, Dale, April, Eilleen, Carmen, Kane, Pat, Mary Jo, Lana, Terrie, Gail, Laura, Claireve, Anne Marie P., and Anne Marie G. – the best teammates EVER!

A big high five and kisses to my other teammates across the river, especially Dr. Jacque.

Ivi – the prettiest tennis pro in the United States.

Barb – funniest woman in the world.

Terry – kick-ass Pilates instructor and all round nice gal. Thank you for teaching me the 'Downward Dog'. (My husband thanks you too!)

A special thank you to: Carolyn – my editor and literary sage, you are brilliant!

Heather at Austin Vivid Photography – the best photographer in Texas. Thanks for making me look 10 years younger and airbrushing those dimples off my ass!

Tamara – A big hug to the best girlfriend a woman could ever have.

Wendy, Lindsey, Karen (again), Lisa, and Betty – my moral support team and great friends that have held my hand through this whole book writing process.

My mother, Fran – let's kick Martha Stewart's butt for stealing all your decorating ideas. Lorie Lee – my favorite sister…okay, she is my only sister. But she still is my favorite!

Jamie and Grady – my wonderful children. You are the best kids ever and I'm so proud of each of you. I love y'all more than you'll ever know.

And my deepest thank you of all to Jimmy Bill – my precious husband. I could have NEVER written this book without your support. I love you so dearly.